GOLD FOIL

GOLD FOIL

Rupert Pennant-Rea

THE BODLEY HEAD
LONDON SYDNEY
TORONTO

For my parents

British Library Cataloguing
in Publication Data
Pennant-Rea, Rupert
Gold foil.
I. Title
823'.9'1F   PR6066.E/

ISBN 0–370–30126–9

© Rupert Pennant-Rea 1978
Printed in Great Britain for
The Bodley Head Ltd
9 Bow Street London WC2E 7AL
by Redwood Burn Ltd
Trowbridge & Esher
Set by Gloucester Typesetting Co Ltd
in Monotype Baskerville
First published 1978

CONTENTS

I
LONDON
October 15th

The London papers at first gave very little space to the strikes in South Africa. It was October, and there was plenty of news —the football season was full of excitement, a new parliamentary session was about to begin, and a gossip column favourite was going through the divorce courts for the third time. Besides, there was no longer anything novel about black workers going on strike in South Africa. The first rash of strikes had really been news—but that was back in 1973. Now they seemed as commonplace as strikes in Britain, with the important difference that they did not stop Fleet Street's readers from getting to work or keeping warm. So when the textile factories near Durban were surrounded by picket lines, and the car plants at Port Elizabeth went silent, news editors yawned and gave the stories a dozen inches on an inside page.

In the financial columns the treatment was only slightly better. The anonymous writer of the *Daily Telegraph*'s investment column offered his readers a thousand words of reassurance. This sort of thing had happened before. Remember South African shares after Sharpeville? They halved in the space of a week, but two months later they had completely recovered. Remember Soweto in June 1976, when more than 170 people were killed in the black townships of the Rand? That had shaken investor confidence, but only for a few months. The gold sales by the International Monetary Fund had been a far more important influence on the price of gold shares. Remember the strikes on the Rand in 1980, when migrant mine workers had demanded the right to live with their wives and families? Certainly the mining shares fell fifteen per cent in ten days. But that was only a hiccup, and didn't they reach an all-time high less than a year later? This time investors needn't bother to worry. Nor did they, for they were preoccupied with a market rumour that restrictions on London dealing in gold shares would soon be relaxed by the Treasury. The *Financial Times* gold share index rose by ten points.

Confident bastards, thought Caroline Manning, as she glanced quickly through the financial pages. At the beginning of the week she had needed a story; now it was Thursday and still nothing. She had thought her luck was in on Tuesday when a friend had telephoned to say that some pension funds were buying into commodities—copper and cocoa he had mentioned. About five years ago pension funds had been warned off investing in commodities. Apparently the Department of Trade had even got to the point of drafting legislation prohibiting such investment. The threat had worked then, but Caroline was prepared to believe they were up to their old tricks again. It would have been a story she could have made something of—speculators playing roulette with the man in the street's savings. If they lost, his retirement would suffer; if they won, the developing countries would be the losers. Either way, the pension fund managers would still go off to their large lunches. The only trouble was that she couldn't find any evidence to confirm her friend's tip-off. An hour on the telephone had been met with the sort of brush-off the City does so well—polite, very smooth, mildly offended that anyone would dream of doing such a thing.

'Of course, Miss Manning, there are a few bad apples, but we haven't heard about it, and naturally we wouldn't be a party to any imprudent investments—ours is strictly a blue chip fund, as you know.'

Yes, she knew that, and she wasn't for a moment suggesting they might be involved directly: she had only rung because of their unrivalled knowledge of the markets. A bit more mutual back-patting, and then she'd rung off. She couldn't afford to antagonise any of her contacts, though she sometimes choked on her own saccharine. Still, if any of these

8

people were involved in anything dubious, then the gloves were off and hang her contacts.

She smiled slightly, recalling the scoop which had made her name in Fleet Street and the City. It was two years ago now, but the memory was still very sweet. On the back of a lucky stake in a North Sea concession, a small British company had grown into what the popular press invariably described as an 'empire'. The man who got all the credit was in fact no more than a shrewd share-spotter, but which share-spotter ever got into the headlines? For that, he needed to set up his own show, which he adorned with the impressive title of the British Investment Bank. When they were being charitable, respectable men in respectable City institutions called him a con; normally they were less restrained. But to the average person, he was someone with the world at his feet.

The respectable men were right. It is always possible to make a lot of handsome balance-sheet gains when money is plentiful, interest rates are falling, and the stock market is bullish. The test comes when interest rates turn, asset values fall, and stony-faced bankers are suddenly unrecognisable as the cheerful chaps you flew up to Scotland in your private plane for a day on the Dee. The more sycophantic financial journalists were still extolling the brilliance of the British Investment Bank and its founder when he was working long hours to avoid the attention of the Fraud Squad.

He might have succeeded too, had it not been for Caroline Manning. She had never been taken in by the BIB's success, though she had attended her quota of journalists' lunches with the BIB board. Usually she was the only woman there, and a combination of contrived innocence and a delicious giggle had them falling over themselves to impress her. She never quite convinced them that she wanted to be informed, not seduced. Nor did she try very hard, for she had learnt at an early age that money and sex make fools of intelligent men. At BIB they were after both, which made them very stupid indeed. So she fluttered her eyelashes and listened, gradually piecing together the details of a real scandal. At the time

BIB was trying to reschedule all its debts against the shaky collateral of empty office blocks which had halved in value, Caroline Manning was being shown into the Editor's office at the *Guardian*.

Less than two weeks later, her story was on the front page. Misrepresentation of accounts, misleading the public, seventy-four separate breaches of exchange control regulations, incorrect tax returns—they were all there, chronicled in lip-smacking detail. Caroline had to share the by-line with a *Guardian* staff man, but that was only to keep the NUJ happy. Everyone in Fleet Street who mattered knew it was her story. Financial journalists on every paper were carpeted by their editors, wanting to know why they hadn't been on to any of this. Last month's articles, stacked with superlatives, were quoted back with relish at their authors. One unfortunate, who only four days earlier had coined what he thought was a splendid phrase—'the Midas Magicians'—in a particularly cloying piece on BIB, was told to write about local authority debt in future. The story ran a further three days, though by the end Caroline had run out of revelations. Fortunately the Home Secretary then announced that the Director of Public Prosecutions would be instituting legal proceedings against the BIB board, and the matter could decently be left to the courts.

With some difficulty, Caroline pushed these memories to the back of her mind. Memories don't pay the rent of this flat, she reminded herself, as she walked across to the window. From the sixth floor of the Barbican she had a fine view over the City. It had always amused her that the two most prominent buildings on the skyline were St Paul's and the Stock Exchange. God and Mammon. She couldn't quite remember the biblical quote about not being able to serve both at the same time, but she had little doubt which the tiny, scurrying figures on the pavement below had chosen.

'Bastards,' she said aloud, still thinking of the South African strikes. 'Parasites on society.' She found it very easy to slip into the quasi-Marxist jargon of her student days. But then, wasn't she a leech as well? The thought troubled her: after all, in a way she lived off the City, absorbing its gossip and then regurgitating it in a readable way; capitalising on its ignorance of economics by writing slick articles which showed off her Harvard education. Didn't she earn as much from these dubious activities as the average stockbroker?

No time for moralising, she told herself, as she folded the papers into a neat pile. She had promised her friends that when the self-doubts began, she would quit this brash life and do something worthwhile. But what did that mean? Go back to the States perhaps, and get an academic appointment? Appalling prospect. Say yes to Charles, the attentive, charming Englishman who was always asking her to marry him? He was only going to stay in the City another two years—'Just one more bull market' was the way he put it—and then he would go to Suffolk to breed pigs. He loved the way she always called them hogs, and said she would make a splendid farmer's wife, and everyone in Suffolk would adore her. Well, perhaps they would, she thought firmly, but they'd have to wait a bit. Writing, the City, independence—somehow these were like a drug, and she was still hooked enough not to let a bad week and a grey London day get her down. It was already eleven o'clock, and while she sat doing nothing, the sharp men in the City were at work. That was enough to break her introspection.

Caroline Manning was twenty-nine. Her friends said she looked exactly as she had done on the day she graduated *magna cum laude* from Harvard. Less innocent, perhaps, but still with a freshness which came, she told herself, from successfully avoiding the hazards of 'settling down'. She had rich black hair swept back off her face, a style which owed much to the expensive attention of the Vidal Sassoon salon in Brook Street. Her face and body needed little artificial adornment: hardly any make-up, well-cut simple clothes, one ring on the little finger of her right hand. She looked exactly what she was: a girl endowed with beauty and brains, who knew what she wanted and usually succeeded in getting it.

She had left Harvard with two ambitions—to remain a radical, and to make enough money to live very comfortably and very independently. The inconsistency between these twin goals did not bother her much, either then or later. She was more exercised by finding the kind of job which offered money and independence: the latter, she reasoned, was essential if she was to keep her radicalism intact. The summer after her graduation was spent in Europe, hiking around with a boyfriend. She wore the uniform of her kind, denim jeans and jacket, but also took the precaution of including in her luggage a very smart outfit bought at Saks Fifth Avenue. She had worn this to meet one of her father's business acquaintances in London, whose address she had been given. She arranged a lunch appointment with him, having first seen her boyfriend safely installed in the British Museum for the day. The Fifth Avenue clothes stood her in excellent stead in the discreet surroundings of a City dining club. The man was a director of one of the best-known merchant banks in the City. Over lunch he had asked her about Harvard, and she mentioned that her dissertation had been on Western investment in Latin America. She diplomatically omitted the fact that her analysis had been Marxist and her conclusions revolutionary: somehow it would have spoilt the agreeable atmosphere. He replied that his bank had many South American connections, and he was sure its monthly economic review would welcome a piece drawing on her research. Nothing too long or complex, he had said. That afternoon she had sat down in the City Business Library and scribbled two thousand words. She left an untidy sheaf of papers with a typing agency, and the next day had mailed the article to the editor of the bank review. Then she forgot all about it, caught the train from Euston and crossed over to Ireland. A week there, drinking Guinness and looking vaguely and not very successfully for ancestors' graves, and then a Jumbo back to New York. Her future was still as uncertain as ever; indeed, the only decision she had made was to break with her boyfriend, who had been talking too enthusiastically of a Californian commune. She had been kicking her heels at her parents' home in New Jersey for a week when a letter arrived from London. The bank was going to publish her piece; a cheque for fifty pounds was enclosed; the editor encouraged her to submit further articles.

That was it. She paused long enough to persuade her father to contact everyone he knew involved in financial journalism, however peripherally. From them, she extracted a few promises to consider for publication anything she sent them. Then she flew to London. In the early days her parents' generosity kept her afloat; but gradually, by the judicious use of her body and mind, she had collected a circle of sources and publishers. Within a year she felt confident enough to put her name on the Barbican waiting list. She joined a few left-wing political groups—the Women's Movement, Americans Abroad for Progress, and the Latin America Solidarity Committee. She helped to write a pamphlet on Chile and did a fine hatchet job on the activities of International Telephone and Telegraph Co. there. It helped that her uncle was a senior Vice-President in ITT—a fact that she did not disclose to her co-author, an intense, black-bearded young man who wrote at length on the need for British working-class solidarity with the Chilean people. In the language of the day she was Radical Chic, and after her *Guardian* triumph she was delighted to find she could afford to be both more chic and more radical.

All this, though, was far from her mind as she hurried towards the Barbican tube station. It was nearly half-past eleven, and she was cross with herself for having taken an extra half-hour's indulgence in bed. It had cost her a lunch date with a solicitor from one of the main City partnerships. He always had the seeds of an interesting story, but he had made other lunch arrangements five minutes before she telephoned. They had agreed to meet for a quick drink at six o'clock. That meant she could not possibly follow up any leads and write a story before Friday afternoon, and the *Sunday Times* Business Editor usually insisted on his five o'clock deadline for free-lance contributions. Maybe she wouldn't cover her rent that week after all—the first time in nearly two years. She decided to fill in the time following up the South African strikes. She had nothing better to do, and anyway she had a hunch about this story. Perhaps it was no more than a wish to find something to wipe the smiles off the jowls of the investment analysts. A mixture of motives, she decided, as she surfaced in Trafalgar Square and walked towards the handsome portico of South Africa House. There was a small crowd of people outside, holding up banners— HANDS OFF BLACK WORKERS — BRITISH CAPITAL SUPPORTS APARTHEID — POLICE BRUTALITY = PROFITS. Right on, thought Caroline Manning, vaguely tempted to stand with them for a while. But the clicking photographers were not only from the *Guardian*, the *Morning Star* and *Anti-Apartheid News*, and she didn't wish her name to be added to the thousands of other 'subversives' on file in that very building. At least, not just now. If her hunch was right, she might be needing the co-operation of the South African Embassy.

As she walked through the main door, leaving the cold London morning behind her, she saw a poster inviting her to come on down to the beach at Durban. Now that, she thought, is not such a bad idea.

2

MOSCOW

October 15th

There was another story which should have been in the newspapers that day, but wasn't. Any Western journalist would have given his right hand to have reported on a meeting which took place in a large oak-panelled room in the Kremlin. Eleven men and one woman convened at 2.30. The chairman, who sat in a high-backed chair with arms, said very little. He asked each of those present to speak briefly on a memorandum which they had received the previous day. No one spoke longer than ten minutes. The chairman listened to what each had to say, but his eyes were continuously scanning the faces of the others. He could not detect any hint of impatience, doubt or disagreement over what was being said. That satisfied him. When the last person had stopped speaking, there was some fidgeting and shifting of chairs. In the silence that followed, the chairman looked round the table and then spoke softly. 'So, comrades, it is agreed. We shall proceed immediately with our plans.' He rose, and walked away from the table. The other ten men and one woman followed him out of the room and then dispersed, back to their various ministries. Long months of meticulous planning had come to a head, and each in his different way felt a sense of satisfaction. The great machinery of the Soviet state was about to go into action.

Each of them also knew—and none better than the chairman—something of great importance about the nature of the government of which they were members. Within each department, the orderliness of their preparations helped to create a feeling of stability. In turn, this confirmed the party functionaries, the bureaucrats and the armed forces in their sense of impregnability. Their confidence then filtered down through Russian society, so the entire population became convinced that a state which was run so smoothly was beyond challenge—indeed, did not need to be challenged. The chairman knew this façade was convincing, so long as people only knew of the administration of a single region, or government department, or factory. Anyone who saw the system in the round also saw its fragility. For this reason very few people were ever allowed to understand how the different compartments fitted together. A few top officials in the Ministry of Economic Planning understood well enough that the Five Year Plan output targets for the economy as a whole were not consistent with the sectoral plans, nor with con- sumption targets. But the thousands of intelligent men who worked on small sections of the Plan did not know this, though privately some might suspect it. People who wrote articles about the Soviet Union's support for liberation move- ments against oppressive regimes in Latin America did not know about the Defence Ministry's contract to supply the Brazilian Junta with armoured cars. Even men in very high positions in a ministry were ignorant of such inconsistencies.

But the chairman knew, as did all the other people in the meeting that afternoon. They had for nearly a year been privy to another set of uncomfortable facts. Taken individually, each one could have proved a minor embarrassment to the government. But when they were collected together, they posed the greatest threat to the security of the Soviet Union since Hitler's invasion in June 1941.

The key points which the chairman and his close circle had had on their minds since the middle of the last winter were as follows:

The grain harvest for the past seven years had only averaged 140 million tons annually. This compared with the 150 million tons estimated by authoritative Soviet scholars in the West's universities and foreign ministries, and with the 180 million tons regularly proclaimed at the annual congresses of the Communist Party.

Soviet stocks of grain were down to three million tons, most of which was anyway unfit for human consumption. Figures for Russian grain stocks are one of the most closely guarded secrets in the world. It had been some comfort to the Kremlin that Western estimates invariably overstated the size of the stocks by a factor of at least ten.

The regular purchases of grain from the United States under the long-term agreement signed in 1975 had barely bridged the gap between output and consumption. The recent breakdown of negotiations between the two countries on another grain agreement had been described by the Kremlin as 'regrettable, but not serious'. In fact, it was a catastrophe.

Last January a crowd of two hundred people had besieged the Communist Party Headquarters in Mirnyy, a small town in Yakutskaya. Men and women workers carried placards saying, 'We were promised more meat —we have got less bread.' The local army unit had stepped in quickly, dispersed the crowd and arrested the apparent ringleaders. Extra grain had been carried overnight by road into Mirnyy, as well as half a ton of tinned food. This had defused the tension; fortunately not a word about the incident had got out.

Since 1977, the Ministry of Mines had been reporting a rapid decline in recoverable gold reserves in the Soviet mines. Mining output had reached a peak of 14·2 million fine ounces in 1975. Since then it had declined steadily, and in 1980 had been a mere 6·4 million fine ounces. Ministry of Mine experts did not believe there was any way of reversing this decline; their pessimistic forecast suggested that Soviet gold mines would be effectively exhausted within ten years.

Stocks of gold held in the vaults of the Central Bank now totalled some 12·5 million fine ounces. This compared with 96·4 million in 1975, and with an estimate given in the *Financial Times* of 68·7 million by Consolidated Gold Fields, London.

Soviet influence in Africa was deteriorating at an alarming pace. In the past fifteen months, the Soviet ambassadors in Mozambique, Angola, Namibia and Zimbabwe had all been called to the foreign ministries there and privately warned that Russia's military and commercial presence should be scaled down quickly. Amongst the reasons given for African dissatisfaction were: inefficient Soviet aid (tractors arriving with no spares or maintenance equipment, trucks built to withstand the Russian winter which overheated in the African sun); in both Ethiopia and Angola, misbehaviour by Cuban troops, bored after more than five years away from home; and pressure being applied on African delegates at the UN, including one instance where the KGB were caught framing Zambia's ambassador in a call-girl scandal. African discontent was now taking more overt forms; a Soviet submarine had recently been refused berthing facilities in Lobito; a major contract to build a telecommunications network stretching from

Namibia to Mozambique had at the last minute been given to the Chinese. Even more significant, this new mood was affecting the attitudes of the South African liberation movements. At a solidarity meeting in Moscow in July, a senior member of the African National Congress had spoken of the 'new brand of European imperialism' in Africa.

This disparate information—which came variously from the Ministries of Finance, Agriculture, Foreign Affairs, Industry, Mines and Defence—had been succinctly summed up by the chairman of the Kremlin meeting in his memorandum. The outlook for domestic food supplies was very serious, and food riots within the next year were a real possibility. Buying grain from abroad was unavoidable; but the gold which had for so long financed these purchases was itself running out. The rich African prizes won during the past ten years were now endangered. If Russia were dislodged from them, she would certainly lose her special relationship with the South African revolutionaries.

As he had pondered these matters over the past fifteen months, the chairman had decided that decisive action was unavoidable. It was no good waiting till the South African plum was so ripe that it would drop of its own accord. At a stroke he would silence African criticism; effectively corner the world gold market; and help to satisfy the appetites of two hundred and thirty million Soviet citizens. For all the strategy's alluring simplicity, the chairman recognised the high stakes involved. If it should fail, there would be little hope for him. He would have to make quite sure he carried all the potential opposition with him. For nearly a year he had patiently tilled the ground. This afternoon, with the nods of agreement around the table, he had had his reward. The people who mattered were of one mind, in the way that all men who feel their options closing in on them will sink their differences in the cause of their own survival. Now they were ready to move.

3

BASLE

October 18th-20th

A long line of official black cars was pulling up outside a tall, bulbous building in the Centralbahnplatz. In the square, the stolid, prosperous citizens of Basle hurried past, showing no curiosity. It was, after all, a regular event—the monthly gathering of Western central bank Governors at the Bank for International Settlements. Occasionally, the average person in Europe or America could read about these meetings in his newspaper—a sentence like, 'Central bankers have decided on emergency measures to support the Italian lira.' Very occasionally, he might see on his television screen a thirty-second flash of middle-aged and elderly men in dark suits entering the building. With scant respect for geography or the English language, the reporter might even trot out the well-worn phrase about 'the gnomes of Zurich'. Neither the newspaper report nor the television film would mean very much to the general public. Nor, incidentally, did they mean much to the newspaper and television journalists who wired their stories from Basle. As a result of such ignorance, central banking's reputation as an obscure, complex and boring business remains intact.

Once inside the BIS building, however, the dark-suited men cease to be caricatures. The Governor of the Bank of England, arriving with a small group of advisers, certainly didn't feel like a gnome. Sir William Dent-Cooper was a tall distinguished-looking man, with thinning silver hair and even features. From a distance he appeared relaxed and confident, but closer up there were lines around his eyes and mouth which made him look haggard. Whenever possible, Sir William like to be photographed coming down the steps of an airliner, briefcase in hand. Now he fumbled irritably in his pocket for his identity pass. Security had been tightened up considerably when the BIS had moved to its new building in 1977. Passes had to be shown at virtually every door, and they were changed frequently. This time the Governor had a green pass sealed in plastic, with an appropriately sombre photograph. An impassive security guard checked the Bank party's passes and briefcases, and signalled them through. Sir William turned to John Bowstead, the Overseas Director, who nearly always accompanied him to Basle. 'John, I'm going straight to our suite. Couperin apparently wants a word with me. We shan't be more than five or ten minutes, and then perhaps you and the others would go through the agenda with me.'

'Splendid, that'll give us plenty of time,' Bowstead replied.

The Governor took the lift up to the second floor, walked along a beige-carpeted corridor and opened a door fifteen yards down on the right. The United Kingdom suite at the BIS was in some respects Sir William's own creation. He had taken an instant dislike to the way the BIS had chosen to furnish it, and after several months of complaining, had got the Head of Administration to agree to change the main reception room. Now he felt as though he was walking into his drawing-room in Belgrave Square. The furniture was mostly French eighteenth century, richly polished and in perfect proportion to the room. A low table was littered with English and American newspapers, and the latest copies of *The Economist*, the *Field* and *Country Life*. Impressionist paintings hung on the wall, and the sofa and chairs were covered with a soft yellow print. An enormous vase of chrysanthemums added a final touch of warmth and colour. The other rooms were more functional, with upright chairs set around leather-topped tables, the walls lined with filing cabinets and bookcases.

Sir William rang a bell and asked for coffee for two. Before this arrived, there was a knock on the door, and Pierre Couperin, the BIS General Manager, came in. '*Bounjor*,' he said, and then, with a hint of apology, 'Good morning, Sir William.' The Governor's French was a private joke amongst the BIS officials, though Sir William himself was quite proud of it. He saw nothing incongruous in the fact that he spoke only one foreign language—and that rather badly—whilst his fellow European Governors were all fluent in at least three. The temptation to entice Sir William into a conversation in French was usually too much for Couperin. But today he was after more than his own amusement.

'Sir William, we need to make room for another meeting, I'm afraid. Fortunately, the programme looks quite straightforward, so we should be able to cut it short. I suggest Monday, after lunch—does that seem convenient?' He paused while a tray of coffee was brought in.

'Yes, I suppose so.' The Governor did not sound very enthusiastic as he poured out two cups. 'What's it to be about?'

'Well, can I put it like this?' Couperin was evidently choosing his words with care. 'Richter is arriving from Washington this evening.' Wilhelm Richter was the Managing Director of the International Monetary Fund, and did not usually attend the monthly Basle meeting. 'He has asked for a meeting on Monday with the Group of Ten Governors, by themselves, with no advisers present. He has certain proposals to put to you all, but he would first like to canvass your opinions individually. This he will do between this evening and Monday. He would like the whole thing to be treated in complete confidence, which I have assured him will be done.'

'Of course.' Sir William's curiosity was only mildly stirred. This kind of behind-the-scenes negotiating was fairly common in Basle; the Governors of the ten richest countries—the Group of Ten or G10—often met by themselves. Strange about Richter coming, though.

Couperin finished his coffee and rose to leave. 'Officially Richter is here to sound out views about increasing Fund quotas.'

'All right,' Sir William grunted.

A few minutes later, John Bowstead and the three other members of the Bank team came into the suite. They talked easily amongst themselves, colleagues over many years, who shared the same assumptions, the same loyalties. They deferred naturally to Sir William, laughing at his jokes, listening intently to his views, answering his questions with polite professionalism. For a few minutes, they brought each other up to date with the gossip in the corridors. Then Sir William said, 'Right, John, we ought to make a start on this agenda. Perhaps we'll move next door.' He led the way through to a small meeting room, and sat down at the head of a highly polished table. Everyone put papers and files down in front of them, Sir William fumbled for his glasses, and Robert Bennion, an Adviser from the Overseas Department, lit a Gauloise.

'If we're ready,' said the Governor, looking round the table, 'could you, John, lead off?'

The rest of the weekend was fairly routine. For the Basle regulars the only unusual feature was the arrival of Wilhelm Richter from Washington. But his presence was explained quite conveniently. He would be seeing the Governors to hear their views about new IMF quotas. John Bowstead insisted on briefing Sir William about this: the Governor could hardly refuse without arousing suspicion, and it was actually a relief to be briefed on something he didn't need to know about—it meant he didn't have to listen at all. Richter moved discreetly around the building from one delegation to another, an imposing figure in steel-rimmed glasses and a beautifully cut dove-grey suit. By midday on Monday, he had spoken to each of the G10 Governors separately, and as far as he knew, they had acceded to his request not to discuss his visit amongst themselves.

As he walked into the board room at two o'clock, Richter considered he had good reason to feel quietly confident. Seven of the Governors were there already, helping themselves to coffee from a sideboard. The other three and Couperin arrived soon afterwards, and the buzz of conversation increased. They all met here once a month, and had occasion to see one another at other times as well. Most were comparatively new to their jobs: the Governor of the Bundesbank, Herr Schmitoff, was the longest serving of them, with five years in the post. Sir William Dent-Cooper had been Governor for nearly four years; the rest had been there for between one and three years. In spite of this, and their different nationalities and interests, they were getting on very well. Veteran IMF and BIS officials could not remember any previous set of G10 Governors with such harmonious working relations and common viewpoints.

When everyone had drunk their coffee, Richter cleared his throat and moved towards the top of the table. The Governors joined him, still talking amongst themselves. Richter was flanked by Herr Schmitoff and Sir William Dent-Cooper, and Couperin sat directly opposite him.

'Gentlemen,' Richter spoke in English, his accent owing more to his days as a graduate student and lecturer at the University of Chicago than to his native Bavaria. 'Thank you very much for coming to this meeting, and for making yourselves available to me over the weekend. You will all by now know the gist of what I am going to say, but it would be as well if I recapped on what you have already heard.' He paused, glancing around the table. He had their complete attention. Now he had to choose his words precisely; no one must be offended, but equally, his meaning must be quite clear.

'The points I have been discussing with you are not new in themselves, but in our meetings so far we have never joined them together. That I will try to do now, and I will start with a statement on which I believe there is complete agreement.' Richter smiled slightly, but his voice was flat, even chilly. 'Since the war, governments in the Western democracies have promised their electorates more than they could in fact deliver. This has been most marked in the case of full employment. This, I believe, explains why each economic cycle has been associated with higher and higher inflation rates, larger and larger fiscal deficits. The last recession—roughly speaking, the 1977–8 recession—was ended only by very expansionist monetary policies in all your countries.' Richter was tempted to look reprovingly at the French

23

and the British in particular, but thought better of it. 'For a period these policies predictably resulted in rapid economic growth and falling unemployment. Again predictably, they also caused the accelerating inflation of 1980–1. Both then and afterwards,' Richter's tone was solemn, 'we were agreed that that inflation produced social and economic pressures which were virtually intolerable.' The Japanese, Italian and British Governors nodded vigorously—with good reason, thought Richter, remembering street riots and factory occupations. 'So now,' he continued, 'we are back into recession that is even worse than it was in 1975. The historical pattern is, I think, clear to all of us. And even now,' he shook his head regretfully, 'governments are contemplating ways of ending this recession which would, in my opinion, cause another bout of inflation more severe than the last. I believe it possible, even probable, that this next artificially engineered boom will tip the Western world into hyperinflation.'

Richter shifted his elbows on the table, to give anyone who wished the opportunity to speak. No one did. 'So much for the past, for the central diagnosis,' he said briskly. 'The consequences of this cycle of boom and recession and ever faster inflation have of course been profound. As far as we are concerned today, the main one has been the damage done to international trade and our currency arrangements. The system of floating exchange rates has not performed as its advocates in the early 1970s had hoped it would—and here,' Richter shrugged, 'I should at one time have included myself. It seems that floating has allowed governments to pursue domestic policies which would have been incompatible with maintaining the external value of their currency. But exchange rates are now moving so widely and erratically that world trade has been disrupted. The forward exchange markets have virtually broken down everywhere except London and New York, and even these are now under severe pressure.' Neither Sir William Dent-Cooper nor Dale Kendall, the United States Federal Reserve Chairman, took any exception to this.

Richter had now been speaking for nearly five minutes,

and felt the time had come to unveil his conclusions. 'Gentlemen, on every count, the outlook for the Western economy is very grave. It seems our politicians have no remedies, no interest even, beyond the next election. But we are agreed that the essence of the problem is clear. The world needs a stable unit of account; but paper currencies have been abused by governments. In these circumstances,' his voice was firm and dignified, 'central bankers have an obligation to shoulder their historic responsibility. We should be the guardians of our currencies, not the pawns of irresponsible politicians. We must establish a currency which commands universal confidence, and which cannot be manipulated by governments. In theory there are a number of forms which such a currency could take. In practice,' he spoke slowly and with emphasis, 'I think all the arguments point in favour of gold.'

Sensing that Richter had reached the main point of his argument, several of the Governors shifted in their seats, looking for an opportunity to speak. But Richter hadn't quite finished.

'I hope no one will misunderstand me. I am not proposing that we embrace all the features of the pre-war gold standard —far from it. Nor have I got a detailed blueprint to offer you of what we might call a modified gold standard. These details will obviously need to be worked out in due course. But for the moment it is more important that we should concentrate on agreement on the central principle rather than get bogged down in fine print.' He glanced quickly round the table and then continued. 'I believe a modified gold standard would bring many benefits to the international system of payments and to the management of our domestic economies. We need a reserve asset which countries want to acquire through trade. At the moment, none of our currencies have a stable value, so trade has become a lottery. That is also what private citizens feel. As we all know, gold hoarding has increased tremendously over the last decade, because people sense gold will keep its value while paper money will not. If everyone knows that notes are backed by gold, their confidence will return.'

Richter's voice had risen, but now he leant forward and spoke quietly. 'Gentlemen, good money will drive out bad, if only we give it a chance. Perhaps I should finish by stating my own conviction that we do not have much time. I would expect that within a year,' he spread his hands, 'possibly even less, so-called reflationary measures will have been taken. Between now and then we have to show governments that there is this alternative.'

After he had finished speaking, Richter leant slowly back in his chair. For a moment there was silence, and then Herr Schmitoff, who as the elder statesman often acted as an unofficial chairman, cleared his throat.

'I think I speak for all my colleagues in thanking you, Wilhelm, for coming here and for what you have said and done. For myself, I must confess this weekend has been a revelation to me. For whatever reason—habit, mental inertia, political caution—I had ceased to think boldly about our economic predicament. All our lives, we have learned to think and act conventionally. Perhaps that is why,' he smiled gently, 'we have become central bank Governors. But today I have seen another way, and that is where my duty lies.'

At the end of the table, Richter breathed a sigh of relief. Now it would be all right. Paradoxically, and in spite of their shared nationality, Schmitoff had been the most sceptical when they had talked privately yesterday. The German economy had been a model since the War, and Schmitoff was at first reluctant to think anything very fundamental was needed. As far as he could see, other countries should follow the German example, and then all would be well. Social discipline, fiscal and monetary restraint—that was what was needed, not some high-flown new international system. His change of mind was therefore very significant.

Over the next fifteen minutes, all the other Governors spoke briefly, and each indicated his general support for what Richter had been saying. The Governor of the Banque de France, a dapper man with greying hair cut *en brosse* and slightly tinted glasses, was the most enthusiastic. He could not resist pointing out that this was precisely what France had been advocating for decades—what General de Gaulle had called '*la discipline d'or*'. He sounded as though he was preaching a sermon on the text of the lost sheep and the repentant sinner. The Canadian Governor, a man with a puckish sense of humour, solemnly raised his hand and made the sign of the cross when Monsieur Lafitte wasn't looking.

Then Sir William Dent-Cooper leant forward, showing an inch of immaculate white cuff at each wrist.

'Gentlemen, could I be the first to raise a question of detail, but of considerable practical importance as well?' He glanced at Richter, who nodded.

'As I understand it, if gold is to be returned to a major role in the monetary system, then all central banks, the IMF and the BIS, will need to increase their holdings substantially. Even more to the point, they will need to be assured of a steady increase in these holdings. Without a guaranteed supply, it seems to me the system would be gravely weakened.' There were nods all round the table: it was an elementary point, but it needed to be made, and Sir William did this sort of thing rather well. 'I feel we have got to prepare the ground most carefully,' he continued, 'yet in such a way that for the moment no one has any hint of our intentions. Presumably we would rely heavily on South African gold, but no one can pretend the political situation in South Africa is very stable at present.'

At this point Richter intervened, but so smoothly that even Sir William didn't feel he was being interrupted. 'If I may say so, I think the Governor has put his finger on some most important points. As he says, we will need to convert a large part of existing reserves into gold, and then obtain a guaranteed supply of newly-mined gold every year. Inevitably, South Africa will play a central role in all this. Before anything else, therefore, we need to be sure of South Africa's co-operation.'

'But which South Africa?' The remark came from the Dutch Governor, Van Horst, a taciturn individual who, surprisingly, wore bow ties. As no one answered his question, he elaborated. 'Is it not possible the white government will soon be overthrown, or at least dismissed in some way? Perhaps we ought to be paying as much attention to the black side, to those who could form a future black government.'

There was silence at this, and several Governors stirred uneasily. It was not, thought Richter, that they were un-used to making political judgements: but they might be feeling that what had started out as a technical, central banking question was suddenly taking on new and unexpected dimensions. He felt it was time to intervene again.

'Governor Van Horst is quite right. At the very least we need to know how the black South African leaders might react to an enhanced role for gold. Naturally we cannot expect anything firm from this, but it is a necessary insurance.' He felt the meeting would now respond gratefully to a lead. 'So I would like to suggest that our first task is to sound out the whites and blacks and see what they think is the right gold policy for their country.'

There was a general murmur of agreement; the Japanese Governor asked softly, 'I take it the real purpose of our interest would not be revealed until later?'

'Quite so,' Richter nodded. 'We would really need a two-stage exercise—Stage 1, to satisfy ourselves that, irrespective of its government, South Africa would mine and sell gold steadily if the price was right. Stage 2, to get a formal agreement with the authorities there on the sale of their stocks and new production. At some point, of course, our governments would be fully involved. It is my opinion that if we here are all satisfied with the preliminary enquiries—Stage 1—we should proceed as though the modified gold standard will become reality. Stage 2, the actual agreement, can wait until the type of government that will rule South Africa over the next five years or so has been resolved.'

Richter saw this last remark might cause some confusion, and he hastened to explain. 'I would expect that within three months, at the outside, the current disturbances will either have died down, as they have done so often in the past, or

28

they will have led to something approaching civil war. We can use that time to explore the introduction of a new system, and begin persuading our governments of its value. That way, we shall be ready to go farther when the political outlook in South Africa has become clearer.'

The meeting considered this for a moment, and the expressions round the table showed that they thought it made sense. It was Herr Schmitoff who asked the first question.

'What about the mining companies? Do they have an independent role in all this?'

'At one time they certainly would have done. But today, no. The South African Government has really got complete control over the companies now—and has had since the Mining Finance Act of 1981. It is now illegal for companies to sell to anybody other than the South African Reserve Bank. Their output, their stocks, their investments, even their exploration plans are now directly controlled by the Reserve Bank. If we can get co-operation with the Reserve Bank, everything else will follow from that.'

The next question came from the Belgian Governor, a practical man who was evidently bored by some of Richter's discourse.

'So how do we begin Stage 1? Someone will have to sound out the South Africans, I imagine.'

'Exactly, and I have taken the liberty of discussing one idea with the Governor of the Bank of England.' Richter turned slightly towards Sir William. 'It seemed to me we should make Stage 1 as unobtrusive as possible. Of all our countries, the United Kingdom has the closest links with South Africa—largely for historical reasons, but the commercial ties are still very strong today. Additionally, as we all know, London was the most important gold centre until the South Africans decided to locate the primary market in South Africa. Even now, London takes most of the business in the secondary market. Queries from the Bank of England about South Africa's gold policy would therefore not arouse any suspicions. Sir William agrees with this. The Bank's relations with the South African Reserve Bank are very good indeed; and while Sir William admits,' Richter allowed himself a mild joke, 'that he is not in close contact with black nationalist leaders, he feels this could be arranged.'

'Does that mean Sir William will be our emissary?'

Before Richter had a chance to speak, Sir William cut in —no mean feat, he thought afterwards. 'We didn't think that would be wise. Herr Richter has asked if I can depute one of my staff to this job—an official who would not, for example, be known to the press, and so would not attract attention. I hope you will find this satisfactory and leave it to me to arrange.'

Again the grey heads nodded, and Richter realised he could bring the discussion to an end. 'One final point, if I may, gentlemen. It is obviously of supreme importance that our discussions today should remain completely secret. Until the preliminary investigations have been made there is no point in telling our governments of the way our thoughts are turning. Apart from ourselves and a few officials in the Bank of England, I would hope at this stage we shall have absolute secrecy.' Richter turned to Sir William. 'The Governor seems to think the first enquiries can be completed within a week or ten days. At that point I will communicate with you all, and if necessary we may convene a further meeting. Otherwise, I hope by next month we will have made considerable progress, on the technicalities, at least. But you will appreciate, this is not something which can be rushed— another variable that is beyond our control.' He shrugged expressively, and a number of Governors smiled wryly. On that note the meeting began to break up. Central bankers commonly ended their meetings by bemoaning how many variables were beyond their control.

Richter had a few words with each of the Governors—a joke here, squeezing a hand there—like a man who was celebrating what everyone knew to be a victory, without anyone actually calling it that. He spent longer with Sir William Dent-Cooper, talking earnestly and counting points off on his fingers. The Englishman nodded from time to time, and then smiled. 'Don't worry, Wilhelm, everything is

under control. I'll speak to you just as soon as I have anything to report. Have a good flight back to Washington.'

With that, the two men parted, and Sir William was
swiftly buttonholed by Dale Kendall, the Chairman of the
US Federal Reserve Board. He was something of an unknown quantity still, having been in office less than a year.

'May we have a word please, Governor,' said Kendall
rather stiffly.

'Certainly, Dale.' Sir William reflected how strange it was
that the American continued to call him Governor, while
he—supposedly epitomising the reserved, formal Englishman—always made a point of calling all the other Governors
by their first names.

'Could I come to your office in ten minutes?'

'Er, yes, if you like.' Sir William was slightly taken aback.

'You know, of course, that my party is going back to
London soon, and I imagine you will want to leave as well.
It's not something we can talk about here . . .?'

'No, I'd prefer not,' said Kendall shortly, and walked
away.

The rest of the Bank team were sitting around talking idly
when Sir William returned to the United Kingdom suite.
The weekend's work was over: most of the records of meetings held had already been dictated, and officials never really
relaxed until this all-important job had been completed. Sir
William found it difficult to understand their mentality—to
him, records were a bore; necessary perhaps, but a bore.
What really mattered were decisions, personal contacts, and
action. Records—especially those written in the formal style
he mentally termed 'Bankese'—never captured any of this. It
surely wasn't coincidence that no one at Richter's meeting
had taken a note. But he couldn't, of course, tell any of the
Bank people what had happened there, and his answers to
John Bowstead's questions were non-committal. Robert
Bennion, who was responsible for all the Basle arrangements,
asked him what time they would be leaving.

'There is a flight in an hour, which we could just catch,
and then the next one is at 6.30.'

'Well, it'll have to be 6.30, I'm afraid,' the Governor replied. 'I'm going to have a few words with Kendall. But,' he added, seeing Bennion's face fall for a second, and remembering the man had a young family, 'there's no reason why the rest of you shouldn't go off now. Perhaps you, John, would stay and go back with me on the 6.30?'

'Of course.' Bowstead was always happy to stay away from home, where he was under the thumb of a nagging wife.

Briefcases were packed, filing cabinets locked, and the three officials left in a rush. They would all see each other again tomorrow for the Basle debriefing. John Bowstead said he would try and have a word with Couperin about the agenda for the next month's meeting. The Governor agreed and they arranged to meet in the foyer in half an hour. When Bowstead arrived, Sir William was already waiting, his overcoat on and a briefcase by his side.

'All well with Kendall?' John Bowstead asked cheerfully.

'Yes, I suppose so.' The Governor seemed distracted, but he didn't volunteer any further information and Bowstead knew better than to ask. On the flight back to London, they usually talked and drank whisky. On this occasion Sir William said he ought to catch up with his reading, opening a copy of *The Economist* and burying his head in it. When the aircraft taxied to a halt at Heathrow two hours later, John Bowstead was surprised to see that the newspaper was still open at the first article.

4

LONDON

October 22nd

Walking down Bishopsgate at 9.20 a.m., James Glendinning
looked forward with real pleasure to the day ahead of him.
In fact his spirits were so high that nothing—not even the
idiocy of Miss Barker, his temporary secretary—could dent
his mood. It was a perfect autumnal day, the time of year
when autumn and winter are just beginning to struggle with
each other to decide whether or not the British office worker
should wear his overcoat. James had left his behind today,
despite dire warnings from his wife, Sarah. Now, as he paused
to cross into Threadneedle Street, his cheeks were tingling
pleasantly. He sidestepped some giggling teenagers who
came rushing out of a coffee shop, and walked towards the
main entrance of the Bank of England.

James Glendinning was just under six feet tall, and walked
with the slight stoop of a man who spends too much time
bent over a desk. Thick glasses with serious, tortoiseshell
frames couldn't disguise the open pleasantness of his face.
His hair was brown and tended to flop down over his forehead. He was wearing an unremarkable dark suit, pale blue
shirt and an inoffensive tie. He could, and did, pass unnoticed in the crowd of commuters who streamed into the
City at this time of the morning.

As he walked through the large doors of the Bank he
acknowledged the respectful nods from the pink-coated door-
keepers. Occasionally, he wondered whether they really
knew who he was—perhaps they nodded like that to everyone. He passed through the massive front hall with its marble
pillars and intricately designed stone floors and turned left
along a corridor to the Chief Cashier's office. It was all so

familiar, and yet somehow just as imposing as on the day he arrived as a nervous undergraduate for his interview.

He walked past some more pink coats: in a film recently made about the Bank, they had been described as looking as safe as the Bank of England. James had found himself murmuring in agreement until the awfulness of the cliché had struck him. In the American Federal Reserve, he always told his visitors, the attendants wore guns on their hips; but in the Bank it was only pink coats. He found this very reassuring—the difference between civilisation and the jungle. Whenever the pound slipped lower against the dollar, the pink coats were a comfort.

His office was large, beautifully furnished with antique desk, table and bookcase, and very quiet. On the leather-topped oak desk his diary lay open: next to it a neatly folded copy of the *Financial Times*. He had *The Times* delivered to his home in Little Hadham, Hertfordshire, and would often sit up in bed with Sarah, sipping an early-morning cup of tea and doing the crossword. The pink pages of the *Financial Times* marked the change from Little Hadham to Threadneedle Street. He glanced down at his appointments for the day. A visitor from the Central Bank of Kuwait at 10.30, and then Books at 11.30. Books was a Bank tradition, the daily meeting when the senior management met to swap information and discuss common problems. After that nothing until lunch, then a meeting at the Treasury on interest rate strategy. Mentally he placed long odds against Miss Barker remembering to arrange for a car to take him round to the Treasury. He ought to remind her. For the umpteenth time, he offered a prayer for the speedy recovery of Miss Higginson, his stalwart and efficient secretary. Another Get Well card might help, but he'd sent her two already, and she'd only been away for ten days.

He spent a few minutes reading the *Financial Times*, and was just about to ask Miss Barker to come in and take some dictation when one of his telephones rang. It was the Governor's circuit, which linked about forty lines and was outside the Bank's main telephone system.

34

'James, David here.' David Reid, the Governor's Private Secretary, rang him about once a week, normally to check whether he wanted a particular document circulated to him.

'Good morning, David, what can I do for you?'

'Could you stand by to see the Governor this morning? He is not going to Books, wants to see you instead. He's cancelled his lunch engagement and wants you, the Deputy, the four Directors and the Chief to eat at his table.'

Trying to keep the curiosity out of his voice, James replied, 'Certainly I can manage that—any idea what it's all about?'

''Fraid I can't help, but the Old Man seems quite exercised about something.' David Reid was a model GPS, building up the Governor one moment and making him seem ordinarily human the next.

'Oh well. Thanks, David, I'll come along at 11.30.' As he replaced the receiver, James sat back in his chair and frowned at the ceiling. He saw the Governor quite frequently, but usually in meetings, with a dozen other people present. There had been one occasion about three months ago when the Chief Cashier was on a holiday, and he'd been called in to brief the Governor about the Bank's tactics in the gilt market. They had spent about half an hour together, talking in a dry, technical way. He felt sure his competence had been impressive, and had himself been agreeably surprised by the Governor's grasp. He knew too that he was a 'high-flier'—at thirty-eight the youngest Adviser in the Bank—and could expect to be increasingly drawn into the Governor's orbit. After all, he had the training. He had joined the Bank straight from PPE at Oxford, and had followed the classic Bank career path of those destined for the top—five years in the Economic Intelligence Department, three in Overseas, then secondment to the International Monetary Fund in Washington for two years as personal assistant to the Fund's Managing Director. Back in London, he was secretary to the Monopolies Commission before returning to the Bank. This time he went into the Chief Cashier's Office, and after a slightly dull start while his temperament was being tested, he was made responsible for bringing the British banking system into line with practices in the EEC. This had meant frequent trips to Brussels and hours of explaining to suspicious British bankers. When the legislation finally passed through the Commons, the Chancellor of the Exchequer took the credit, though he did remember to refer in passing to the assistance he had been afforded by the Governor of the Bank of England. When he read the speech in Hansard, James was only mildly piqued. That day he had heard he was to be promoted to Adviser in CCO. The Chancellor would probably be turned out of office at the next election anyway, so his unearned bouquets were fast running out.

Try as he might, though, James could not think why the Governor wanted to see him at such short notice, and for lunch as well. The Governor was notoriously touchy about his lunch companions. Sometimes he had no choice in the matter—Governors of other central banks, however obscure, were by tradition invited. But, given a free hand, he would ask only his old City cronies, and the occasional senior civil servant. The Bank's four executive Directors sat at the Governor's table when they were in the Bank; but it was rumoured that the Governor didn't really get on with one of them, who had taken to lunching at his club. Now, out of the blue, James was being invited to join a very select band. If Sarah had known, she would have insisted on him wearing a different suit. That idle thought made him sit up and pull himself together. He was half tempted to ring GPS again and see if he couldn't get some idea of what was going on. But Reid sounded as though he genuinely knew nothing. He buzzed for Miss Barker, and for twenty minutes worked on his correspondence.

When the man from the Kuwait Central Bank arrived, James was relieved to discover he spoke perfect English and was anxious to show it off. Sometimes his overseas visitors were apparently incapable of more than a few words of English, and didn't want to ask any questions, even in their own language. But on this occasion James was able to sit back and stare at his visitor's glinting gold teeth. The man was explaining at enormous length what his government's position would be at some forthcoming IMF talks. OPEC had disintegrated two years ago, and with it joint representation of the oil producers. It meant the price of oil had fallen, but, on the other hand, each Arab state now insisted on separate representation at conferences. James was not sure the world wouldn't be better off still paying more for its oil. However, the conversation today was easy. They drank coffee, James interjected the occasional question, and then, while the man replied, had time to speculate on his meeting with the Governor. Perhaps a bank was in trouble. Things like that blew up quickly, and for obvious reasons very few people at the Bank were told. As he got up to shake the Kuwaiti's hand and see him out of his office, he could think of no other reason why the Governor would want him at such short notice.

At 11.25 he made his way along more corridors, and through the polished doors into the parlours, where the Governor and the Directors had their offices. 'Will you walk into my parlour . . .'; the nursery poem sometimes flitted across his mind when he went through that door. It was a slightly uncomfortable thought. He walked along towards GPS. David Reid smiled as he came into the room.

'Ah, James, won't keep you a moment—the Governor's just having his photograph taken for some City glossy—a commemorative issue or something.' At that moment a young man with lank hair and a duffel coat backed out of the Governor's office, clutching a camera. He looked very out of place. Reid knocked on the door: 'Glendinning for you, sir.'

Sir William Dent-Cooper would have found the last five minutes distasteful, but he was smiling as he came forward from his desk. 'James, thank you for coming at such short notice. I hope I haven't disrupted your diary. Do sit down.' He had the rare knack of putting many different kinds of people at ease immediately. That was one of the reasons why he was Governor, and not many others who were technically better qualified. It also owed something to the fact that he and the Chancellor of the Exchequer in the last Conservative government had been mutual admirers.

James sat down, and tried to relax. That was never easy in the Governor's office: all the chairs were stiff-backed and angular, specifically requested by the Governor so that none of his visitors would be encouraged to think he had all the time in the world to see them.

'Tell me, James, what do you know about South Africa?' The question took James by surprise, but the Governor was fortunately not waiting for an answer. 'These strikes are serious: I'm told, more serious than they appear to be. If they build up, the Government might well find it difficult to cope.'

'You are due to have talks with some of the banks next week about credits to South African borrowers.'

The Governor waved his hand dismissively. 'No, James, I'm not talking about that kind of thing. I've called you in this morning because I want you to take on an assignment of much greater importance than bank loans to South Africa. I hope you'll agree to do as I ask. I will spend about an hour outlining my proposals, and I'd be grateful if you'd keep questions until I finish. We'll discuss your reactions until one o'clock and then break for lunch with the Directors and the Chief Cashier. They haven't heard anything of what I am about to tell you, but they'll have to know soon. Now,' he smiled reassuringly, 'perhaps I should begin in Basle.'

5

LONDON

October 22nd

When the Governor had finished speaking he stared at his hands for a few moments before looking up. Across his desk, James Glendinning was motionless; partly the paralysing effect of an hour in one of the Governor's chairs, but mostly because he was stunned by what he had heard. It all seemed so remote from the measured calm of the parlours. Then his training reasserted itself, and he smiled at the Governor.

'Well, James, any questions?' Sir William sounded rather mischievous, as though he was beginning to enjoy himself now that someone else in the Bank could share his secret.

James caught his mood. 'Why pick on me, sir?' He was thankful that his voice sounded quite relaxed.

'Thought you might be a litttle bored in CCO,' returned the Governor. 'No, seriously, because we need someone young, but with experience—someone who would not be too conspicuous. If I got involved, for example, the press would be on to it in no time. You can fly off to Basle and Washington, even South Africa, without attracting attention. If things go wrong we can always say you were young and impulsive and exceeded your brief.'

As he said this the Governor's eyes had hardened, but then he continued.

'The first thing you must do is to get ready for some travelling. I would like you to go to Pretoria on Thursday. After reporting back to me, you'll need to go to Washington and Basle. That should all take the best part of a week. Throughout, I want you to keep in close touch with me.'

'Who am I to see in Pretoria?'

'A man called le Roux in the South African Reserve Bank —I'm told that's where the power lies. They've got the production, the stocks and the marketing completely tied up.'

'I think I'm clear about my immediate tasks, but I don't really see what my final goal is, and I certainly don't see how to get there.'

The Governor shrugged. 'Most bridges will have to be crossed as we come to them. In the first place, we need to sound out the South Africans. Do the blacks and the whites think the gold policy will be maintained? Steady output from the mines; reasonable Reserve Bank stocks; gold sales conducted in Pretoria, as at present, but still leaving a residual role for London and Zurich—that kind of thing. By the time you've finished doing that, it'll be easier for the G10 meeting to judge what the next step is.'

Sir William stopped speaking for a moment, his eyes watching James closely. 'But there are a lot of questions which we'd like answers to. For instance, how big are South Africa's stocks now? I'm told they've been building them up while the price is low—but by how much? Are the blacks likely to fall for a bilateral deal with the Russians? For that matter, has the white government been selling gold to the Arabs? All these are possibilities: since they've decided to move the gold market to South Africa, they've been able to be a lot more secretive. Also, I'm told since Angola and Zimbabwe the whites have felt betrayed by the West, and this has made them difficult.'

The Governor got up and walked over to the fireplace before continuing. 'These are the kind of questions we need answered in Stage 1. You may not find out a great deal on the political side, and it'll be easier there when Whitehall is involved. But whatever you can do at this stage will be useful. Now, let me give you a chance to ask about details.'

'To begin with—before I go to South Africa—I shall need to make contact with some of the exiled black organisations. How do I go about that?'

The Governor had clearly been busy. 'I'm told the main liberation movement,' he paused slightly, as though surprised to find the phrase crossing his lips, 'has its European office in London, and the leading chap is here at the moment. Fellow by the name of Sisekwe, Robert Sisekwe. You'll be getting some briefing material on all this later today. But we need to fix an appointment for you to see Sisekwe as soon as possible. I'd prefer it if you didn't mention the Bank at this stage, though it may be necessary.'

'I think I've a better approach. I was at Oxford with someone who is now near the top of the BBC's African Service. He's almost certain to know Sisekwe and could probably arrange for me to see him quite quickly.'

'I'm not sure I like that. He might smell a rat and blow the whole thing open.'

'Knowing the man, I can trust him absolutely.'

The Governor thought for a moment and then relaxed. 'We might have to take bigger gambles than this in the next few weeks. All right, let's try it.'

'I think I'll telephone him immediately, if I may, sir. It'll probably take him a few hours to organise.'

The Governor waved his hand at the telephones on his desk. James buzzed one, and when a secretary answered, he asked for Timothy Travers at the BBC, Bush House. In a moment the light on the telephone was blinking, and he was put through.

'Tim, James Glendinning.'

'James, how good to hear from you.' They exchanged a few pleasantries, and James could sense the Governor stiffening in his chair.

'Tim, could I ask a great favour of you? I need an introduction to Robert Sisekwe; I want to see him in the next day or so. Can you manage it, and can I also ask you to keep this absolutely to yourself for the moment? I'll explain why in due course.' He tried to keep his voice as natural as possible.

'What a strange coincidence. I've been trying for a week to get him interviewed by one of my chaps. He's damned elusive and also rather snooty—likes to hold court for a favoured few. Anyway, he's finally agreed, on condition that I do the interviewing. So tomorrow I'm picking up my tape recorder and going round to see him—haven't done any real work like that for five years now. Should be rather fun. Why don't you join me, and I'll see if we can fix a meeting there and then?'

James kept his tone matter of fact. 'That sounds a good plan, Tim, thank you very much. Where and when?'

'11 Sheffield Terrace, just off Kensington Church Street. I'll be outside in a Beeb van at ten o'clock.'

'Fine, see you then, Tim.' James turned to the Governor, feeling rather pleased with himself. He was not at all sure how he was going to tackle Sisekwe, but at least he was going to see him.

'Well, that's a good start.' The Governor smiled, looking at his watch. 'Now, what about some lunch?'

That day they were eating in a small dining-room on the first floor of the Bank. By the time Sir William and James had made their way there, the Deputy Governor, the Chief Cashier and the four Directors were chatting and helping themselves to drinks from a sideboard.

'Good day,' Sir William greeted them affably. 'I imagine you all know James Glendinning. Any of them strangers to you, James?'

'No, I don't think so.' James smiled at each in turn, and then walked over to the Chief Cashier. But the Governor was clearly in no mood to dally.

'I've arranged for us not to be disturbed,' he said. 'Food is on the sideboard, and I suggest we start by helping ourselves to some paté. Derek, would you mind dealing with the wine?' Derek Hayter's responsibility was the domestic economy, and all things considered he carried his cares lightly. He was also very knowledgeable about wine. The seven men worked their way through paté, Dover sole with potatoes and broad beans, and four bottles of chilled hock before the Governor thought he could claim their whole attention. The cheese board was passed around, coffee cups filled, and two large cigars were wafting smoke across the table when he spoke.

'No doubt you're wondering why I've called you all together. I'm sorry about the short notice, but it was important we met immediately. I should say that what I am now going to tell you must remain absolutely secret, within the Bank and outside.' Chairs were shifted slightly, and then the room was quiet as the Governor recounted for the second time that day what had happened in Basle over the weekend.

When he had finished speaking, there was a short silence. Then the Chief Cashier chuckled. 'Well, the Bank has been involved in some funny business over the years, but there are more cloaks and daggers in what you've just told us than . . .' His voice trailed away.

The Governor looked quickly round the table, and decided he wouldn't get much more reaction from any of them for a while. 'I've called you together,' he said, 'to ask you to give this absolute priority when James or I need any assistance. It should be possible to ask departments for selective help without giving away too much. I don't want anything put down on paper—it might reveal the whole picture. Yes, I know it's unconventional, Charles,' he said quickly, cutting off Charles Renton, the Deputy Governor, who looked as though he was about to speak. 'But these are not normal times.' The Deputy was a stickler for convention. He had been in the Bank all his working life and thought the Governor, with his merchant banking background, was inclined to be reckless. But Sir William was in no mood to listen to the Deputy today.

'Well, gentlemen,' he was smiling as he stubbed out his cigar, 'it looks as though we are in for an entertaining time. We might need another of these lunches next week, when James is back from South Africa and before he goes to Washington and Basle. In the meantime, I know he can count on you for every assistance. I'm sure we all wish him well.'

With murmurs of assent the lunch broke up. James walked back to the parlours with the Governor, his mind working quickly. First, he must get someone to replace him at this afternoon's Treasury meeting. In fact, he'd have to cancel all his appointments for the indefinite future. Just when he was beginning to steer some people in the Treasury round to his thinking on interest rates. Too bad. At least he'd have a perfect excuse for getting rid of Miss Barker.

When the Governor reached the door of his office he turned.

'You're to have unrestricted access to me, James. I'll tell David Reid. Any authorisation you may need for travel or expenses you can refer to the Chief or the Deputy. By the time you're ready to leave for Pretoria I hope facilities at our embassies will have been laid on. I can't think of anything else. Good luck.' The two men shook hands, each trying not to appear too theatrical. 'One final thing, be discreet, won't you, James?'

The central bankers' first commandment, thought James, as he came out of the parlours. After fifteen years in the Bank, discretion came as naturally to him as betting to a bookie. Even so unlikely a task as this would yield to the qualities that he had employed throughout his career, thoroughness, intelligence, anticipation, and of course discretion. The thought reassured him. For three hours, only the surroundings of the Bank and the faces at lunch had persuaded James that he had not been transported into some kind of film script. Now his mind was back on familiar rails and was running smoothly again.

That afternoon, he rang the Travel Section, and asked them to book him on a return flight to Johannesburg on Thursday. On the following Tuesday or Wednesday he would fly to Washington; on the Thursday he would go to Paris, and then on to Basle. Overnight in Basle, and then back to London early on Saturday week. He also asked them to book a single room with a bath at the Carlton Hotel in Johannesburg; the Mayflower in Washington; and the Schweitzerhof in Basle.

If Miss Higginson had not been ill, he would have left all these arrangements to her. But he could not trust Miss Barker to arrange a visit to the dentist, let alone a trip of 20,000 miles. He'd asked her to cancel all his appointments for the next two weeks, and suggested she might like some leave as well. Unfortunately she had not taken the hint.

By four o'clock he was starting to receive briefing material from different departments in the Bank. A note from Overseas provided details of the gold market in Pretoria, the South African Reserve Bank and its senior management, published data on its reserves and a recent newspaper interview with the South African Finance Minister on his gold policy. From the Economic Intelligence Department came details of total world gold reserves, their distribution by country, and recent significant transactions in the London and Zurich gold markets. In a long note, the Overseas Adviser on the IMF recounted the continuing saga of the IMF's attempts to write gold out of the world's monetary system in the 1970s. He concluded that the IMF had still not disentangled itself from the gold question, though he expected it would do so successfully in the near future. James chuckled, and made a mental note to quote this back at its author at some time in the future. There was also a page on the career of Wilhelm Richter, the Fund's Managing Director. At 5.30 a thick dossier on the BIS and its public and private views on gold came down, together with some material on South African politics.

James's confidence grew as the briefs piled up on his desk. He would spend the evening digesting them, and by tomorrow he would surely be prepared for anything. He emptied his briefcase of a pile of Treasury documents intended for that afternoon's meeting and refilled it with the files on his desk. He bade Miss Barker a surprisingly cheerful good night, but spoiled it by calling her Miss Higginson. Freudian, he mused, as he stepped out into the dimly lit bustle of Threadneedle Street.

He nearly missed the stop at Bishop's Stortford, so engrossed was he in his reading. Sarah was at the station with the car to meet him.

Their house was warm and welcoming, and they went into the kitchen, drank a glass of sherry and got some supper ready while she told him of her day at school. The twins had just started at Marlborough, leaving Sarah free to resume her teaching. While they had been growing up she had kept her hand in by giving private tuition at home. Now she was full-time at a large comprehensive three miles away, teaching French and English Literature. James reckoned she would be a headmistress within five years.

They sat down to lentil soup, quiche lorraine and salad, and some brie, and James told her what had happened that day. On the train journey he had pondered over how much he ought to reveal. Several years ago, a friend of his in the Ministry of Defence had admitted to him that he never told his wife anything about his work. He had been on the 'cod-desk' in the MOD, dealing with the fishing dispute with Iceland. James had thought it rather childish to be so secretive about what had become a stock joke. But now he remembered this man, and felt mildly guilty at telling Sarah the whole story.

'But it means, darling,' he finished, 'that I shall have to be away quite a bit. Will you manage all right?'

Characteristically, she was not overawed. 'Oh, I'll be fine. I'll ring Mother now and ask her to come and stay on Thursday, for the week you're jaunting around. But I promise she'll be gone by the time you get back.'

'Don't be silly, you know I'm very fond of your mother. But of course it's better she doesn't know what I'm up to. Tell her I've gone to Washington for a week.'

'Before I leave you to those files, James, will you promise me one thing?' Sarah's eyes were anxious as she put her arms round his neck. 'You won't be in any danger, will you?'

'Don't be silly. Since when has anyone in the Bank ever been in danger?'

6

WASHINGTON

October 22nd

The Secretary of State did not like being disturbed in meetings, particularly when he was doing the talking. He looked with irritation at a young man who was walking round the long table with an envelope in his hand and a worried expression on his face.

'Yes, what is it?' John Curzon snapped as the young man approached.

'I'm sorry to interrupt, Mr Secretary, but this is an urgent message for you.' The young man handed Curzon the envelope, and withdrew thankfully.

'My apologies, gentlemen.' Curzon smiled round the table at the other members of the President's Council of Security Advisers. He ripped open the envelope as a low hum of conversation developed. On a single white sheet, headed 'From the Secretary of the Treasury', there was a handwritten scrawl. 'Request an urgent meeting with you. Chairman Kendall and myself are waiting in your office.' It was signed Robert A. Fox. Curzon took a quick decision to keep them waiting a bit longer—what the hell was the Fed Chairman doing there anyway, he thought, as he brought the meeting back to order.

Curzon spent ten minutes describing progress on satellite surveillance of defence systems, and then he summed up briefly.

'Well, gentlemen, I didn't expect unanimity on this item, and I don't think we've achieved it. But we have made some progress. I suggest we return this paper to the Pentagon for revision in the light of our comments, and at the next meeting I would hope we could agree on proposals to put to the President. I think we can finish on that note.'

He pushed his chair firmly back from the table, to forestall any further objections from the Under Secretary at the Defence Department, who had haggled at virtually everything in the paper. Curzon was relieved to see the Under Secretary was taking off his glasses and gathering his papers together. But he had the look of an obstinate man, not a defeated one, and Curzon guessed he would regroup and return to the battle next week.

Once outside the conference room, Curzon quickened his pace, walking briskly along the blue-carpeted corridor to his offices. Security guards stood stiffly to attention outside the door, and his secretary and a young aide were in the first room to greet him.

'Secretary Fox and Chairman Kendall are inside waiting,' the aide informed him. 'I thought it best to reschedule your twelve o'clock meeting with Ambassador Richards, so you could carry on through to lunch.'

'Do you think that'll be necessary?' Curzon grimaced.

'I don't know—they won't say what they've come for.'

'Well, I won't find out by standing here and talking to you.' Curzon smiled amiably at the pair of them, and went through into his office.

The Treasury Secretary, Robert Fox, was a tall, heavily-built man with thick, visibly dyed, black hair, wearing an immaculately pressed dark blue suit. He looked what he was—senior partner in a leading Wall Street brokerage firm; chairman of the New York 'Republicans for Bennett' committee; and thence, to his own and other people's surprise, to the Treasury after his old friend George Bennett had won the Presidency by a whisker two years ago. He greeted John Curzon gravely; the two men got on quite well, and Curzon guessed that something serious must have brought him here this morning. Curzon turned and shook Kendall's hand. 'Good morning, Chairman.' They had only met twice before, and Curzon couldn't for a moment remember his first name. Kendall was also new to his job: he had come to Washington after spending his career at the St Louis Federal Reserve. His appointment had been applauded by the more conservative elements in the financial community: he had a reputation as a sound-money man, and the *Wall Street Journal* had opined that 'If anyone, at this late hour, can put a stop to the inflationary rot, then Dale Kendall is that man.'

'So, Bob,' Curzon indicated the chairs round a low coffee table, 'what brings you here?'

'We'll come straight to the point, John,' Robert Fox began. 'As you know, the regular meetings of the central bank Governors discuss a wide range of topics. Last weekend they were approached by Richter of the IMF and asked to think seriously about a return to some kind of reformed gold standard. A lot of the Governors have only recently taken up their jobs, so they were unknown quantities. Somewhat to our surprise, it turns out they have all been thinking on roughly similar lines. But until Richter brought it up, no one had actually dared to suggest what conventional wisdom had persuaded them was impossible and unnecessary. We won't bother you with the technical details.' Curzon nodded with relief—he still couldn't imagine what this had to do with foreign policy, but Fox was clearly in no mood to be rushed. 'But all the G10 Governors are agreed on the principle. They reckon they have about a year, two at the most, to persuade their governments to introduce some gold-backed monetary assets: even a declaration to this effect would do a lot to quell inflationary psychology. Now, as you know, I don't need to be persuaded, I have several times gone on record in favour of monetary discipline.'

Curzon decided to intervene. 'Sure, Bob, just like we all favour motherhood. But can you tell me how this involves me and the State Department?'

'I'm coming to that right now. Before taking such a momentous decision, everyone would need to be satisfied the gold supply was secure. It's true there are massive stocks, but the whole scheme would fail if anyone managed to corner the market in gold mines.' When he was excited, Fox still talked more like a Wall Street broker than the Treasury Secretary. 'Which of course brings us to South Africa, and so to the State Department and you.'

Curzon felt the two men's eyes on him. 'OK', but what exactly is it you want to know?'

'Specifically, whether we can be sure the government there will hold; what US plans are; what the Soviets might be planning.' As Curzon remained silent, Fox continued, 'Let me explain one further point. The Governors have decided to do a little preliminary exploring themselves. They've got an Englishman from the Bank of England going to check things out—try and get an indication that South African gold policy won't change. He's also going to speak to the black leadership—see what they're thinking. Dale here went along with this, because it seems to make everyone happy. But he agrees with me that this is an amateur exercise, and he's warned the Bank of England Governor that we reserve the right to act independently if need be. If we're going to get gold from South Africa, we must make sure it's stable. And no one knows better than you how goddam unstable it is with all those Russians and Cubans sitting on the borders.'

Fox's voice had risen sharply, and now he sat back in his chair, his face slightly flushed. Kendall blinked through his thick glasses, nodded vigorously, but said nothing. For a time there was silence in the room, as Curzon stared thoughtfully at his hands. Then he looked up and spoke briskly.

'It certainly does involve State—right up to the neck. How many others know about all this?'

Dale Kendall spoke for the first time, a deep Southern drawl. 'In the US, no one at all. Our Governors' meetings excluded all advisers, so only the Group of Ten Governors know, apart from some officials in the Bank of England, where this guy is involved.'

'Good. Can I ask you to keep it absolutely to yourselves for the time being? If we are going to take any initiative, I shall of course have to see the President and get his support. But the last thing we want is for Congress or the press to get wind of this. I'll come back to you, Bob, some time this afternoon, and perhaps the three of us may need another meeting. In the meantime could you, Dale, prepare a short briefing for the President—and me, for that matter—on the gold standard question. Not too technical, just the outlines. Mind you, I doubt the President will be hard to convince on this one.' Curzon got up and shook both men by the hand. 'It's about time we all had the courage to think the unthinkable,' he muttered, almost to himself, as he showed them to the door.

Curzon crossed over to his desk and buzzed through to the outer office. 'Bill, make sure I'm not disturbed again this morning.'

'Certainly, sir—so you won't be seeing Ambassador Richards?'

'No, I will not,' Curzon replied testily. Outside, the aide sighed at the secretary, a prim, grey-haired woman with forbidding spectacles. 'Sometimes I find it difficult to make the guy out. First he complains because those two have disrupted his morning, then he only has them in his room for ten minutes; but now he doesn't want his morning back like it was.'

Inside, Curzon was pacing slowly up and down his office. His mind was seething, and he was finding it difficult to absorb what he had heard and put his thoughts into some kind of order. Like most people who move in and out of Washington when the Presidency changes hands, John Curzon owed his present high office in part to luck. He would have been the first to admit that; the first, too, to point out that his diligence and shrewdness had been even more important. As a young man, he had learnt that the American way of doing things—he disliked the word 'system'—favoured those with money and connections more than those who worked and saved and lived out the Protestant ethic. John Curzon never had to worry about money: his father had made a substantial fortune manufacturing baby foods, and had conveniently died and left everything to his only son when John was twenty-eight. At the time John was on the Washington staff of a conservative Republican Senator from Illinois, and just beginning to make some valuable contacts for himself. He decided there and then what he would do with his money. (It had taken him exactly twenty-four hours to stop referring to it as his father's money.)

Two years later, the Curzon Center for the Study of International Affairs was opened in Maryland by the Chairman of the Senate Foreign Relations Committee. In his speech of welcome, Curzon had advocated a foreign policy which would be 'intolerant of intolerance, belligerent in the cause of peace'. It was the era of the Cold War, and what one commentator described as 'riddle-rhetoric' was enthusiastically applauded by the eminent people who attended the opening. For more than twenty years, the Curzon Center for the Study of International Affairs had prospered. At its twice-weekly seminars, visiting academics rubbed shoulders with foreign ambassadors, generals, international bankers and leading politicians from nearly every country in the world. And John Curzon rubbed shoulders with all of them. The Center published books, monographs, tracts, occasional papers and studies—and in each of them there was a foreword by John Curzon. Quite how much Curzon knew about foreign affairs was never very clear, but it hardly seemed to matter. He possessed just the right mixture of *gravitas* and wit—he put people at their ease, but they still listened to him with respect. Politically there was no doubt the Center stood to the right on the spectrum, but not so far to the right as to put it out of favour with successive Washington establishments. It was firmly anti-Communist, but never hysterically so; in favour of the Vietnam war at the beginning, but conveniently against it by the end.

Throughout the Seventies, John Curzon grew steadily more unhappy about the direction America was taking, both at home and abroad. This unease was reflected in the Center's publications, but only to a very slight degree. The truth was that John Curzon was bored with his role as host to the world's great and good. He felt Western leadership was weak and vacillating—'pygmies' he once described them contemptuously to a friend. He wasn't quite sure what policies they ought to be following, but he had grown convinced that, in their shoes, he could do better. When the

Cubans had intervened in Angola in 1975, Curzon's unease reached new peaks. Now he felt sure the Russians were bent on world domination, and détente was a mirage. He began to take an increasing interest in African affairs. He established a new Africa fellowship at the Center, and took to reading a variety of books and periodicals about Africa.

He persuaded two of the Center's research fellows to collaborate on a project which in the event was never published. Not because it wasn't up to standard—it was; or because John Curzon didn't approve of it—he did; but simply because it would have been too controversial. The study was entitled 'Soviet Subversion in South Africa—the American Response'. It ran to more than five hundred pages when maps, charts and tables were included. It described in enormous detail the various options open to the United States over South Africa. It concluded that the Soviet Union might decide to invade South Africa, in support of a black revolution there and using neighbouring black states as a springboard. But the exercise would present severe logistical difficulties, which the Soviets would probably underestimate. By limiting itself to a naval response, the United States could avoid that trap. A blockade of the main ports in Angola, Namibia and Mozambique would cut off Soviet supplies, and the USSR would have to decide just how committed it really was to 'liberating' South Africa. The study argued that this commitment did not run very deep. Faced with determined American resistance, the Russians would be unwilling to mount a full-scale invasion. The United States would not openly support the white government. A diplomatic initiative would portray the United States as defender of the right of the South African peoples to determine their own future.

When the study was presented to him, Curzon read it through twice. His enthusiasm for it had increased with every page, but so had his reluctance to publish it. It did not suit the tenor of the times. The Carter Administration had just unveiled the new American policy on Africa, begun to endorse liberation movements in Rhodesia, and was openly critical of the apartheid regime in South Africa. The Curzon

53

Center had never before gone so far out on a limb in opposing current US policy, and John Curzon was not going to start now. Accordingly, he suppressed publication of the report, though he offered the two research fellows $40,000 each in lieu of publication. This they gratefully accepted, and returned to their faculties in the Midwest. Curzon kept a copy of the study amongst his personal papers, and had reread it three times in the intervening years. When he moved into the State Department, it was one of the documents he had brought with him in a cabinet of papers to which no one except his secretary and aide had access.

Though he was a cautious man, by 1979 Curzon was determined to play a more active part in American politics. He invited each of the three leading Republican contenders for the Presidential nomination to the Center to speak on foreign affairs, and afterwards he dined with them alone. Without being too specific or appearing too pushing, he managed to convey to them that he might be persuaded to put his unrivalled experience, knowledge, and friendship with world figures at their service. At the end of this exercise, he calculated that one might offer him the Ambassadorship at the UN (which he would refuse); the second candidate might make him Ambassador at the Court of St James (which tempted him, but not enough); and the third, George Bennett, might make him Secretary of State. So when Bennett won the Republican nomination the following year, Curzon was naturally pleased. He was even more pleased when Bennett appointed him to head his panel of foreign policy experts during the election campaign. And he was positively overjoyed when Bennett scraped home in November and invited Curzon to become his Secretary of State.

But things had not gone well since then. Outwardly, the Bennett Administration continued the policy of détente with the Soviet Union: in his inaugural address, the President had used a phrase suggested to him by Curzon—'the new era'. It had been picked up by the newspapers, and two months later the Chairman of the Politburo had used it as well, which was a good sign. No one was quite sure what exactly 'the new era' consisted of, and Curzon had so far managed to avoid being too specific. The reason for this was simple. Both the President and the Secretary of State were privately determined that the American retreat before Russian expansionism would end. 'We need to give the Russian bear a bloody nose,' was the President's favourite way of expressing his ambitions to Curzon. But they never said anything of the kind publicly, since they reasoned that success would only be possible if they had surprise on their side. Moreover, Congress was unreliable, and might easily tie the hands of the White House if it got wind of any new foreign policy initiatives.

For nearly two years, the Secretary of State had been waiting for the right opportunity to show the Soviets the Administration's real mettle. He and the President were clear that they needed an occasion which would not carry risks of further escalation, and certainly not up to the nuclear threshold. It therefore had to be an issue on which the Russians did not feel their own security or prosperity was threatened. So far no suitable opening had presented itself. John Curzon had been largely instrumental in persuading the President and the Cabinet to stop grain sales to Russia. He had had high hopes that this would make the Russians more malleable in other fields, but if anything the reverse had happened. This convinced him that a brief show of American military strength was needed. He had happy memories of the day in 1964 when the marines had invaded the Dominican Republic. In a few hours, America had demonstrated her superiority and her will—and that, John Curzon was convinced, was more important than the particular issue which gave rise to it. Another example he was fond of quoting to the President was the *Mayaguez* incident in 1975, when an American ship was seized by Cambodian rebels. The air force had bombed the rebels, allowing the navy to slip in and rescue the *Mayaguez* and all its crew.

American foreign policy—or, more accurately, John Curzon's foreign policy—was increasingly coming to rely on the chance of another *Mayaguez*. In his mind, Curzon had planned this scenario (a word he used frequently) down to the last detail. The Americans would act decisively, preferably in the interests of world peace. Then they would immediately reassure the Russians that they were still wholly committed to 'the new era', which however depended crucially on mutual respect. This single act would restore the balance between the two countries, and raise America's standing throughout the world. It would also restore the morale of Americans at home. The world would thereafter be a tidier and a safer place.

As he paced the thick carpet in his office, John Curzon was more and more convinced that the opportunity he had been seeking had arrived. After listening to Fox and Kendall, it was clear that even more was at stake than his original plans. It all fitted in so beautifully: the financial necessities of a new monetary order provided the vital opportunity for his foreign policy. Curzon was a bit hazy about the gold standard idea: he had never really mastered economics, but Fox and Kendall were both brilliant men, and they could surely convince the President if he had any doubts on that score. Curzon stopped his pacing, and frowned down at his shoes. This was the one, he thought. All those years at the Center had at last led him to this. He had mingled with the men who held power, but until this moment he had found it eluding him. Now he could feel it in his hands, and the sensation was intoxicating. Almost against his will, he threw his head back and roared with laughter. It was fully a minute before he could stop, and even then the exhilaration still hadn't left him. He crossed over to a filing cabinet and twiddled the combination dial back and forth eight times. Then he slid the top drawer smoothly out, and selected a thick file before closing it and spinning the dial round to the right. He reached for a switch on his desk and buzzed the intercom.

'Yes, sir?' his aide answered promptly.

'Would you come in, please, Bill. There're a number of things I would like to get moving . . .'

7

LONDON

October 23rd

The BBC van was parked about twenty five yards from 11 Sheffield Terrace when James arrived at ten o'clock. It was a grey day, and Tim Travers was standing on the pavement muffled up in an overcoat and blowing into his hands. He was a stocky man—at Oxford he had been an enthusiastic scrum half who had just missed his Blue. He shouted a cheerful greeting as James walked up to him. 'Well met, James. I hope there won't be any delay from now on. By the way, who should I say you are?'

The question had been bothering James all the way in the train that morning. 'Could you just say I'm from Basle, here on an important mission, and think it would be greatly to his advantage to see me for about ten minutes? If you say it with enough conviction,' James added hastily, seeing Travers's disbelieving expression, 'it'll be enough for me to get my foot in the door. After that, I'll be able to handle it.'

He wasn't at all sure about that. He had been up till three o'clock that morning going through all his briefing material. One item, a study on the liberation movements in South Africa, had proved very helpful. From this, James had learnt there were two main black political parties in South Africa, the Pan Africanist Congress (PAC) and the African National Congress (ANC). It seemed clear the ANC commanded wider support than the PAC, and was better placed to organise and carry through a revolution. The leadership structure was very informal—years of clandestine activity within South Africa had taught the ANC the value of a hydra-headed organisation. But Sisekwe was one of a group of three men who directed ANC policy. At fifty he was also the youngest. He had had what was described as a classic career for an

57

exiled leader. Brought up in the Northern Transvaal, the son of a farm-worker; educated at a mission school; passed into Fort Hare University. Banned from the campus by the authorities for 'agitation', and went underground. Finally arrested, charged with plotting to overthrow the state, and sentenced to ten years' imprisonment on Robben Island. On release, escaped from South Africa, arriving in London to a hero's welcome from the liberal press, other South African exiles, and a group from the National Union of Students, who had 'adopted' him while he was in prison. The Home Secretary of the day had given him an entry visa and the right to indefinite residence in Britain—'An inadequate tribute to a man who has reminded us all of the true meaning of freedom,' he had said in the Commons.

This much James now knew. He still felt decidedly underbriefed, and turned to Tim Travers for some assistance. 'How come he's living in this street, Tim? I'd guess a house here must cost nearly two hundred thousand, wouldn't you? I always imagined political exiles lived in bed-sits in Notting Hill and cooked corned beef on a single gas ring.'

Travers's tone was slightly condescending: 'Now come on, James. All these guys have powerful, rich friends. Or perhaps I should say "friends" in quotes. This bloke may soon be President of the richest country in Africa, and all sorts of people need to curry favour with him. Invest now and get the pay-off later—surely that's the sort of language you understand well enough in the City. I'm told this house comes to Sisekwe courtesy of the Russian Embassy. They've also bought another in WC1 for the PAC chaps—not quite so smart, so they must be counting on the ANC coming out on top.'

James decided to try another tack where he hoped he wouldn't sound so ingenuous.

'How free is Sisekwe to travel?'

'Oh, completely. As I said, he's an elusive character. I know for sure he's been to New York, Addis Ababa, Moscow and Havana in the past six months. Rumour has it that he's also done an extensive tour through Southern Africa as

well: Tanzania, Zambia, Zimbabwe, Namibia, even Botswana. In fact there's only one country in the world he can't
go to, and that's his own.'

There was a hint of bitterness in Travers's voice, and James
moved on quickly to his next question. 'What sort of a man
is he?'

'Very able, energetic, and with a peculiar kind of power
about him. I suppose what we used to call charisma before
that word was prostituted out of existence.'

James had forgotten his friend had been editor of *Isis* and a
stalwart defender of the English language.

'Anyhow,' continued Travers, 'you'll find out soon enough.
The hour has arrived and we ought to be seeking an audi-
ence.'

He heaved a couple of large leather cases on to his shoulder,
had a word with the driver of the van, and together they
walked up to the door of Number 11. The bell was answered
by a young Indian with a beard who looked as though he
had just got out of bed. James hoped Travers wouldn't start
mentioning Basle until they saw Sisekwe himself. You
couldn't tell a made-up story too many times, particularly
one which relied so much on dramatic effect. Fortunately the
Indian didn't query James's presence, and showed them into
a smallish room on the first floor, with chairs placed round
the walls. It reminded James of a dentist's waiting-room
without the faded copies of *Punch*, and he began to feel
uneasy.

There were five other people in the room, two black men
whom James took to be diplomats from other African countries, and three whites who were probably journalists. One
was a strikingly attractive girl, with thick black hair and just
a trace of make-up round her eyes. She was sitting slightly
impatiently, smoking a cigarette and reading the *Guardian*.
After about ten minutes, a middle-aged African in baggy
grey flannels and down-at-heel shoes came into the room and
asked for all their names. The girl said she was Caroline
Manning from the *Guardian*. The man then looked at James,
but fortunately Travers chipped in. 'We're from the BBC—

59

I'm Tim Travers, and this is James Glendinning. I have an appointment to interview Mr Sisekwe at ten o'clock.'

'Ah yes, would you come this way.'

The man ushered Travers and James out of the room, and up another flight of stairs. James found he was sweating slightly; this wasn't quite the plan, but thank God for old Tim—he was pretty cool. I wonder how BBC people behave, he thought suddenly, but consoled himself that Sisekwe wouldn't know either. He decided not to reveal his identity for the moment. Their guide knocked on a door, and they walked into a large, airy room overlooking some gardens. The walls were covered with bright posters on which the words 'solidarity', 'liberation' and 'struggle' figured prominently. There were two desks in the room, piles of paper and some filing cabinets. A man rose from behind one of the desks, and held out his hand. 'Good morning, Mr Travers, I hope I haven't kept you waiting.'

'Not at all, it's a pleasure to see you again. May I introduce a colleague, James Glendinning—I hope you won't mind if he sits in on this interview.'

'Not at all. I hope several million people will be doing the same just as soon as the BBC can broadcast it.' Sisekwe's voice was deep and relaxed, and James had to admit there was something impressive about the man. He was tall and heavily bearded, with flecks of grey appearing in his hair. He was dressed in a dark suit, with a light pullover underneath. He turned to his companion, a young man wearing dark glasses. 'My assistant, Zola Nkambe.' The men all shook hands, but the young man said nothing and his expression was impassive. 'Now, Mr Travers.' Sisekwe returned to his chair. 'Can we get on with the interview? As you can imagine, I have a busy day ahead.'

James watched Sisekwe intently while he answered Travers's questions. He appeared very confident, though his hands played nervously with a pen throughout the twenty-minute interview. He described the strikes in vivid terms, going into detail on the kind of lives led by the black workers. Forty per cent earned wages below the poverty datum level;

they had been denied their own trade unions for decades; safety conditions in the factories and mines would not be tolerated in any other country in the world. James thought some of his claims sounded slightly extravagant, but could not be sure. Sisekwe's tone was even, persuasive. He ended with something of a flourish. 'But all the things I have been describing are not peculiar to the industries or the towns where the strikes are. Nor will they go away just because the management concedes higher wages. The exploitation which has provoked these strikes is endemic in apartheid. South Africans are now challenging the entire structure of apartheid society, because that is the only way they will ever obtain justice. Our aims *are* political—to throw out the rottenness of apartheid and replace it by democracy and freedom.'

As Travers switched off his tape recorder, Sisekwe leant back and relaxed.

'I hope that won't be jammed by the South Africans. I'm told it is now very difficult to pick up the BBC in South Africa. But then, of course,' he smiled at Travers, 'the BBC has always been a hotbed of Communist subversion, has it not?' All except the young man laughed at this, and Sisekwe came round his desk to show them out.

James realised it was time to act. 'I wonder, Mr Sisekwe, if I could speak to you for a moment on another matter?'

'Not another interview, I hope,' Sisekwe raised his eyebrows.

'No, strictly off the record.' James hoped his voice didn't sound as nervous as he felt. 'And I would prefer it if we could speak alone.' Sisekwe paused a moment, then shrugged his shoulders. 'If it is that important: Zola would you mind leaving us for a moment. Mr Travers, goodbye, I look forward to seeing you again. Perhaps you will come to South Africa to cover our independence celebrations, eh?'

As the door closed behind the two men, James took a deep breath and began. 'There are many people and governments in the rest of the world who have links with your country. You will appreciate they would like some assurance that these links will continue, irrespective of who governs

South Africa.' James hoped he wasn't speaking too quickly. He was about to continue when Sisekwe interrupted him.

'Mr Glendinning, let me assure you I have already received representations from all kinds of people on what ANC policy will be when we form a government. So far you have said nothing new. I gather you are not from the BBC at all, so I must ask on whose behalf you are speaking?'

'I have been asked by the central banking authorities to speak to you, to try to discover whether South African gold sales through established international channels would continue in the event of a change of government.'

'Do you mean established Western channels, Mr Glendinning?' Sisekwe's voice was hard.

'No, I do not. As you know, the primary market is in Pretoria, anyway. And as for the secondary markets, the country with the largest single involvement in London and Zurich is Russia. The fact that these markets are located in the West does not make them any less attractive to countries from all parts of the world.' He paused, pleased Sisekwe had so far only raised one rather elementary point. He felt he could now afford to be a bit more explicit. 'The alternative to these methods of selling gold is not to use other markets. It is to negotiate bilateral deals with individual countries, so the gold never actually appears in any market. Can you give me some indication as to whether the ANC favours bilateral deals or selling through the market?'

James sensed Sisekwe was becoming impatient. 'Mr Glendinning, you came here with Mr Travers, a man whom I think I can trust . . .'

James nodded. 'I can get a letter of introduction for you and bring it to another meeting.'

'That would be better,' Sisekwe replied. 'As you know, I have a number of important meetings today. I cannot cancel them. Nor can I possibly answer your question in a few minutes. In fact, if I can be quite candid with you, I would not know how to answer your question. You see, Mr Glendinning,' Sisekwe's face was set as he stared out of the window, 'the ANC and the African people have not had the time to consider in detail what will happen after our revolution. We are oppressed, and oppressed people can only really concentrate on one thing—how to get the oppressors' yoke off their backs. We have for years devoted all our energy to that; and even now, when our freedom is just round the corner, we cannot afford to think of details. But I will tell you this.' He turned back to James. 'The ANC is not interested in super-power politics. We will not exchange one kind of colonialism for another. We wish to establish friendly relations with all countries who wish us well. But those who have collaborated in our oppression in the past will pay a heavy price for their collaboration. That, of course, includes the mining companies. Indeed, there are some who feel we should close down the mines altogether, because they have only brought exploitation and death to the African people. But, as I say, I do not know what our policy will be. There is one point which may bring you some comfort. A friend of mine, an ANC member for many years, now lives in Dublin. He works for the central bank there, and I know he has given a lot of thought to this question. I think it would be wise to get him over here to talk to me. When he has cleared my mind, we might meet again, you and I. I give you no guarantees, of course.'

James had listened to Sisekwe with a mixture of exasperation and respect. How the hell could these people expect to govern a rich, powerful country if they didn't have any policies? And yet, in other ways, Sisekwe was not at all ingenuous. He had given nothing away, been courteous to James but obviously suspicious, and had cleverly bought some breathing space for himself.

'Well, that is all right by me, Mr Sisekwe. I shall be away from London for the next week, so can I call you when I come back?'

'Certainly. My assistant will give you a telephone number. Goodbye, Mr Glendinning.'

'Goodbye, Mr Sisekwe.' James paused. 'I wonder if I could ask you to keep this conversation confidential between us for the time being?'

'Mr Glendinning, until you show me that you are who you say you are, I would not bother to waste my colleagues' time telling them of your visit.' With a steely smile, Sisekwe politely closed the door.

8

JOHANNESBURG/PRETORIA

October 24th

As James emerged from the Customs area at Jan Smuts Airport a tall grizzled man in chauffeur's uniform stepped forward. 'Mr Glendinning?' he asked. 'I am from the Reserve Bank. Would you come this way, please.' He picked up James's suitcases and walked over to a large white Mercedes parked outside the main terminal. James followed him, thankful he had worn a light suit. In this heat, the London autumn seemed much more than seven hours away.

As the Mercedes purred towards Johannesburg, James tried some conversation. 'Magnificent plane, that Concorde.' The solid head nodded impassively. 'Rather like travelling to work every morning,' he continued. Another nod, and James decided not to try again. He looked out of the window, and soon concluded that in South Africa, too, the town planners' first commandment (the approach from airport to city centre must be made as ugly and depressing as modern methods permit) had been scrupulously obeyed.

They were coming into the city itself now, all bustle and noise and high glass buildings. James was already mentally calling it Jo'burg after hearing a couple on the plane using the word a dozen times. But they also called it Joeys, which he decided was altogether too familiar. In spite of the thick traffic, they were soon drawing up outside the Carlton Hotel. The chauffeur turned and spoke for the first time since the airport. 'Will you just register at your hotel and then I'll take you on straight to the Reserve Bank.'

'Fine. Give me about twenty minutes, and I'll have some sandwiches in my room.'

Inside, the hotel was blessedly cool. James's room on the second floor was quiet and bright. He unpacked most of his clothes, but filled a small case with some overnight things. When he had spoken to him on the telephone from London Dr le Roux, James's contact at the SARB, had suggested they might go away to his farm over the weekend if James had nothing else planned. Sarah had insisted he take a rather garish beach shirt bought for a holiday in Corsica. James looked at it with distaste—would it go down well in the South African bush? Sandwiches and a glass of beer arrived almost as soon as he had called room service, and he ate them while taking a shower. By three o'clock he was again sitting in the back of the Mercedes.

The Ben Schoeman Highway runs between Johannesburg and Pretoria, a wide, straight road which gave James a taste of Africa. Once they had cleared the Jo'burg suburbs the countryside began to open up—very flat and dry, for the rains were late that year—giving an impression of endless horizons. James relaxed in the back seat, and thought of what lay ahead. He could quote almost word for word from the brief given to him in the Bank on Dr Pieter le Roux. Fifty-three years old, married, five children. Father, now dead, was a prominent member of the Nationalist Party in the Transvaal. Educated Stellenbosch University, 1948–51; Rhodes Scholar, St Edmund Hall, Oxford, 1951–3 in PPE; back to Stellenbosch University in 1953–5, PhD in Economics. Thesis on 'The role of gold in South African external finance, 1933–47' (translation from the Afrikaans title). Joined SARB, 1956. Now Head of the Gold Department. Almost certain to be made Governor next year.

The brief went on to describe the SARB. Just as the Governor had said, the Reserve Bank had been given sweeping powers a few years ago to control the production and distribution of South Africa's gold. This had allowed it great scope to vary the level of stocks and so to influence the gold price. The brief also talked of the SARB's rigid internal structure—departments were very autonomous, and their heads had far more discretionary power than in the Bank of England.

Well, le Roux was obviously the right man to see, thought James. At least they had one thing in common—Oxford; which was not much to go on, he decided, as a sign by the side of the road told him he was entering Pretoria. There were a lot of police about, but not more than James had expected. Indeed, if anything, he had been surprised at how few signs of unrest he had seen so far. It seemed to confirm the generally relaxed view of events being taken by most people in the City. Then he remembered Sisekwe describing in his BBC interview how all the blacks lived in separate townships, and how the trouble spots were cordoned off so the world's press couldn't report what was happening. It was very difficult to judge.

The Mercedes came into Church Square and James jerked himself out of his day-dreaming. Church Square was filled on all four sides by heavy, impressive façades—not unlike the Bank, James thought. The Reserve Bank was on the north side, sandwiched between the Courts of Justice and the Old Mutual, which seemed to be the only commercial building in the square. The chauffeur opened James's door, and James thanked him and walked up the steps and into the Reserve Bank.

Inside it was very cool and, like most central banks, the atmosphere was heavy with serious purpose. James immediately felt back on familiar ground. A number of old men in beige uniforms hovered around, just like the messengers at the Bank. Even their guttural Afrikaans did not strike him as particularly foreign. It was going to be all right, he decided. After a short wait in a deep leather armchair, James was taken up in the lift by one of the messengers to the third floor. The corridors were thickly carpeted, and they walked in complete silence for nearly a minute. Then the messenger stopped, and knocked on an oak door. He half-entered the room and spoke softly, 'Mr Glendinning, *meneer*.' James walked into a solid, oak-panelled room as the door closed quietly behind him.

'Mr Glendinning, you are welcome.' The voice was stiff, formal, and the handshake was firm. Dr Pieter le Roux was a tall, powerfully built man with a handsome head—a rather leathery tan, dark, slightly curly hair going grey at the temples, and brown expressionless eyes.

'Dr le Roux, it is a pleasure. I am grateful to you for fitting in with my visit at such short notice.'

'Not at all. Did you have a good flight? I have myself been on the Concorde once; it is very cramped, isn't it?' The two men exchanged pleasantries for a few minutes, circling each other warily like dogs. Once James thought he had raised a hint of a smile round le Roux's mouth when he complained of the heat; but it might just as easily have been a condescending sneer. The man seemed as tight as a clam, and James gave up trying to make him unbend.

Evidently le Roux was also ready to cut out small talk, for he turned abruptly to James and asked, 'Mr Glendinning, perhaps you could tell me the purpose of your visit. As you know, we do have regular visitors here from the Bank of England, but I understand you are not one of them?'

'No, that is correct. I have come out here in an exploratory capacity, as it were.'

'To explore what?' Le Roux's tone was polite, but not friendly.

James tried to sound detached. 'You can imagine that the world, virtually every country in the world, is always interested in South Africa's attitude on gold sales.'

Le Roux spread his hands wide. 'But Mr Glendinning, our attitude is well known and has not changed for several years. We publish figures of production, sales and reserves every week.'

'Yes, Dr le Roux, but that is what has happened in the past. Now the interest lies in what your attitude will be in the future. As I am sure you appreciate, the political situation in South Africa has been causing some disquiet recently. In the event of any change in the political climate, is your government and the Reserve Bank likely to change its policies on gold? That is the sort of question people in London are concerned about.'

67

Le Roux swivelled his chair towards a window and did not speak for a few moments. His voice seemed rather distant when he eventually replied. 'There are so many dimensions to that question, *meneer*, and I am not sure which is the one that really interests you. The fact is,' he turned back towards James, 'I cannot see why you, as a central banker, should be particularly interested in our gold policy. In recent times we have had very few central bank enquiries about gold. Even the French have tended to lose interest. Our sales here attract private individuals, industrial users—but not the world's monetary authorities. They pretend gold does not matter, does not even exist. I think they are mistaken, but,' he shrugged his shoulders, 'that is their business. Then suddenly you come along, from the Bank of England, and ask about our policy. You link it to political developments here, but we have had similar minor disturbances before now, and no one from the Bank of England has expressed concern.'

Le Roux seemed to be thinking aloud, almost unaware of James's presence. James decided this was becoming uncomfortably like a Sherlock Holmes monologue and broke in. 'Oh, it's not as strange as all that. You know what the Bank's like—it's still inclined to regard the whole world as its province, and wants to know everything that's going on, even when it's not really relevant. We still haven't got used to the primary gold market being here in Pretoria, and not in London any more.'

Le Roux smiled briefly. 'Of course, Mr Glendinning: I apologise if I sounded suspicious. These are, you will appreciate, difficult times for my country—not because of what is going on here, but because events are so frequently misinterpreted by outsiders.' His manner was again courteous. 'Anyway, we shall have plenty of time to discuss all these matters during the weekend. I trust you will accept my family's hospitality at my farm.'

'It is most kind of you, I would like that.' James was glad to have broken the mood of the past few minutes.

'But before we go I expect you'd like me to show you

something of the Bank—at any rate, the part which is my concern.'

'Certainly, that would be most interesting.' James feigned enthusiasm, knowing from bitter experience at the Bank of England how meaningless these conducted tours were. 'Do you keep much of your gold reserves here, on the spot?' he asked as they walked out of le Roux's office.

'Oh, certainly.' Le Roux opened a door and ushered James through. 'We'll go down to the vaults and have a look, if you'd be interested.'

'Yes, I would—I'd like to see how they compare with the ones at the Bank of England.'

Gold vaults were a constant source of curiosity to outsiders: visitors who were visibly bored by the dealing rooms would brighten up immediately at the prospect of seeing the vaults. Although he had often seen the gold stocks in Threadneedle Street, James still felt a slight tingle of anticipation as the lift doors opened to let them out into a brightly lit corridor. Security was very strict, as he had expected. On the other side of a heavily barred gate, a burly man with a large revolver hanging down from his belt greeted le Roux in Afrikaans. Le Roux produced an identification pass which the man scrutinised and then returned. Le Roux took a key out of his pocket and turned it in a lock. In reply the guard used a key of his own, and then swung the huge gate open.

On either side of a short passage there were solid steel doors. With another key in his hand, le Roux went up to one of the doors and opened a panel concealed in the centre. Underneath was a set of illuminated numbers, covered by glass. Le Roux produced a small metallic device and ran it over the surface of the glass; one at a time, as if by some magnetic force, the numbers whirred and then clicked into place. Satisfied, le Roux replaced the instrument in his pocket. He turned, 'After you.' In reply, James pressed the door with his little finger and it opened smoothly and noiselessly. The room was small, cool and dimly lit. Lining its walls, to a height of no more than eighteen inches, were gold bars.

Against the white walls, they gleamed vividly, casting a curious glow which no picture, no photograph, and certainly no synthetic paint could ever quite reproduce.

For a moment the two men stood silent, and then James chuckled. 'I see you have the same trouble with the weight of the bars.'

'Indeed,' le Roux replied, 'we could put one more layer on top of this lot, but after that I'm told the floor would begin to buckle. It seems difficult to believe.'

'And how many rooms are there like this?' James asked casually.

Le Roux sidestepped the question easily. 'It depends how many we need, and that of course varies according to how large our stocks are at any one time.'

James resigned himself to not finding out anything solid on this vital point for the moment. A pity; it would be quite a coup to arrive at the IMF with a reliable estimate of the country's reserves.

'I'm most impressed by the security arrangements,' he said, as he watched le Roux go through the complicated procedure once again.

'Thank you. I take a particular pride in it—security is one of my main responsibilities. When I became head of the department I reviewed our entire security system and decided I would assume personal control of it. Before that,' he turned a key in the central panel, 'it had been left to a separate section within the bank, and they were very complacent. I have had an entirely new system installed recently, and as you might have guessed, certain parts of it cannot be operated without me.'

'Isn't that a bit risky?'

'Not as great as the risks which lie on the other side,' le Roux said firmly, nodding to the security guard as they passed through the iron gate. 'I believe our national wealth should be guarded as closely as possible. I also believe,' he glanced at James, 'that the less room there is for human error and human frailty the better.'

'Yes, I suppose so.' James was taken aback by the man's

70

sudden intensity, and they did not speak as they went up in the lift.

For the next fifteen minutes, James was shown round various offices and introduced to a number of people in le Roux's department. They were all stiffly correct, and after one attempt at a joke, James found himself behaving in the same way. It was a relief when le Roux said it was time to go, and they walked out of the sombre building into the brightness of Church Square. Le Roux pointed at an enormous statue in the middle of the square.

'Paul Kruger—a great leader of my country, but not a favourite of the British.' The remark could have been funny —James knew that Kruger had led the Transvaal Republic against the British in the Boer War. But le Roux's face betrayed no hint of humour, and he decided there was a certain similarity between his companion and the towering, granite figure in the comic top hat.

Le Roux got into the driving seat of the white Mercedes, explaining that he preferred not to be chauffeured around at weekends. Then he asked, 'Have you ever been to Pretoria before?' James shook his head.

'In that case,' said le Roux firmly, starting the engine, 'we must do a little detour. No one should come to South Africa without seeing Table Mountain and the Voortrekker Monument. There is no way to get you to the Cape just now, but the Monument is a few minutes' drive from here.'

'That would be splendid.' James tried to sound enthusiastic. He had a hazy recollection the Voortrekker Monument commemorated something important to the Afrikaner —was it the Great Trek, or perhaps the Boer War? Anyway, they felt deeply about it—like the English were supposed to feel about the Tower of London, but didn't. Only foreigners visited the Tower of London, but Afrikaners actually went out of their way to see the Voortrekker Monument. So be suitably impressed, he told himself.

The car was climbing steeply out of Pretoria, going southwest. The sky was hazy, a combination of heat and dust, but looking back there was a fine view of Pretoria. It seemed to

71

James small and vulnerable from up there, but he said nothing. Le Roux seemed slightly less stiff than he had been in the office, but was not inclined to talk much. They came round a corner and he pulled the car into a parking area.

At that time of the evening there was no one else about, and their feet crunched loudly in the gravel as they crossed the car park. James was grateful for a light breeze which cooled his body and ruffled his hair. He was thinking back on the day, and so was quite unprepared when le Roux stopped, waved his hand, and said with unconcealed pride, 'So, what do you think of it?'

The saying about beauty being in the eye of the beholder might well have been coined with the Voortrekker Monument in mind. To the Boer, it is beautiful: to most outsiders, it is not, though its ugliness is so impressively brazen that it takes the breath away. It is a massive, squat edifice with a confusing architectural pedigree. It owes its inspiration in part to the mausoleum of Halicarnassus, in part to the early civilisation of Zimbabwe, in part to Italy. Yet the sum of these diverse parts is wholly Afrikaner, the embodiment of Boer mythology, a national shrine. As if to underline this point, the Monument is surrounded by stone ox wagons, symbolically recalling the *laager* which protected the Voortrekkers against attack from hostile tribesmen.

Confronted by this massive challenge to his senses, James could think of nothing to say. Fortunately, le Roux was already striding ahead to the entrance. He ushered James inside enthusiastically and began to talk. It was soon obvious that he had done this often before, because he talked as though he was reading straight from a guidebook. 'The Voortrekker Monument was built in 1936 to mark the centenary of the Great Trek . . .'

James could feel his eyes glazing over, an irresistible reaction to sightseeing and guided tours which had stayed with him ever since he had acted as a guide to American tourists one summer term in Oxford.

'How interesting,' he murmured politely as le Roux's voice droned on. He decided the Voortrekker Monument reminded him of a gasworks which he saw every day from the window of the Bishop's Stortford train. It didn't look like a gasworks, of course, but it had the same lack of charm which comes when sheer size is divorced from gracefulness.

This irreverent thought was cut short when le Roux stopped dramatically in front of one panel, depicting a scene in a Boer camp. In their poke bonnets, women sat demurely round a table, while the men folk stood tall and protective around them, holding ancient muskets or cattle whips in their hands. 'Some of those,' said le Roux, 'are my ancestors.' He pointed at several of the figures with evident pride.

'Oh, really?' James was glad of the chance to escape the impersonal and seemingly impenetrable details of the Great Trek for a moment. 'They were on the Trek as well?'

'*Ja*. My great-great-great-grandfather and his family were part of the column led by Sarel Cilliers—a famous name in our history. They crossed the Orange River in the spring of 1836, and so went outside the British colonial boundaries. Then they moved on to the High Veld, towards the Vaal— the Vaal River.'

'How interesting.' James hoped le Roux wouldn't notice how many times he was using that phrase. But the Afrikaner was oblivious of such trifles.

'They had a number of battles with hostile natives on the way. But each time the *laager* saved them—you know about the *laager*, I expect?'

'Yes, a most ingenious idea, I always thought.'

'It certainly was,' said le Roux dourly, and led the way down some steps, continuing his detailed account of the Great Trek.

In the basement, the two men stood before a tomb with a perpetual flame burning on it. 'Same sort of thing as the grave of the unknown warrior, is it?' said James, conscious that le Roux had suddenly lapsed into silence.

'*Ja.*' The vault was silent again, until le Roux leant towards the tomb. 'You see that inscription—once a year, the sun comes through a narrow vent in the roof and shines directly on it.'

James came closer to read where le Roux's finger was pointing.

'What does it mean?' he asked.

'*Ons vir jou, Suid-Afrika*.' Le Roux's voice was low. 'We for thee, South Africa.'

9
EASTERN TRANSVAAL
October 25th

It was ten o'clock, and although the sun still had a long way to climb, it was already causing James's clothes to stick to his body. He was standing on a rock, about ten yards away from what he now knew was called a *koppie*—enormous granite rocks piled on top of one another, rather like an abstract painting. This particular *koppie*, James decided, looked like a pantomime horse—a long, horizontal section, which met a huge boulder at about 120 degrees. Smallish trees grew around and amongst the rocks, casting an inadequate shade against the shimmering heat.

James's throat was dry with dust, which also covered his face with a light film and promised to turn muddy if he sweated any more. He was carrying a shotgun in the crook of his left arm, and spent cartridges covered the rock on which he was standing. Le Roux had casually mentioned the possibility of some shooting as they drove east from Pretoria the previous evening. James had expressed enthusiasm, his mind full of big-game hunting. A lion, perhaps, or even a buffalo. About twice a year James shot pheasant on the farm of a friend in Gloucestershire. He had become competent enough not to make a fool of himself, and enjoyed the cold air, the crisp ground, the sight of the dogs in the undergrowth. But he had not bargained for this.

'This' had turned out to be a baboon shoot. When they had arrived last night, le Roux's farm manager, a man called

Jacobus Swart, had come in to tell them there had been a lot of trouble with baboons—'*babbejaans*' he had called them. Maize, grown specially to feed the farm labourers, was in danger of being wrecked by baboon raids, having just survived the worst effects of the drought. Swart had accordingly arranged a shoot first thing in the morning and was glad to see James—another gun would make it easier for them to surround the *koppie*.

Le Roux had provided James with a shotgun—a handsome enough Spanish gun, though le Roux himself had a pair of Holland and Holland, which he showed to James with considerable pride. He had then produced some clothes for James to wear, since James had balked at the thought of his beach-shirt on a baboon shoot. He wasn't much shorter than le Roux, but the Afrikaner was a heavily built man. A khaki shirt, with a belt and pockets like a Norfolk jacket, hung limp on James's frame. His arms, sticking out of the short sleeves, were exposed tot he sun. He had scratched one forearm ploughing his way through some thorny undergrowth on the way up to the *koppie*; it was still bleeding slightly, and this had attracted the attention of some irritating flies. A pair of khaki trousers, which stayed up only with the aid of a belt, flapped around his legs when he walked. He was getting blisters on his feet from a pair of thick leather boots which were too big for him, and his face and neck were beginning to burn in the sun.

No option but grin and bear it, thought James ruefully. He wondered whether he dare descend the rock and seek out some shade, but the action was about to begin again. They had cornered an enormous troop of baboons in this *koppie*. During the night a hundred Africans from the farm *kraal* had surrounded the *koppie* and lit fires to keep the baboons inside. As the sun came up, le Roux's party had arrived in two Land-Rovers, and spaced themselves around the *koppie* at a range of about thirty yards. In much the same way as beaters on a pheasant shoot in England, the Africans had then set up a racket to scare the baboons out—beating tin cans, throwing stones and shaking trees. Every so often, a grey furry shape would be glimpsed, and the Africans would let out a roar of excitement, their eyes switching to the nearest white man. To begin with it had been a massacre—baboons emerging from cracks in the rocks were immediately blasted off the rock face. Sometimes they were only wounded, and lay on the ground, screaming like a child. At first, James had been sickened by the spectacle; but some part of his brain told him to carry on. He was apparently doing what was expected of him as a white man. The Africans were delighted—their crops would be safe; perhaps they might even make something out of the baboons' flesh and fur. With these reassuring thoughts, he stayed on, the gun roaring in his ear and pumping against his shoulder. Once he had peppered a baboon with shot; it had fallen to the ground, and literally started tearing its own stomach out before he killed it with his second barrel. Jacobus Swart, the farm manager, had laughed loudly and called over to him, 'They always do that, *meneer*—trying to find the pellets.'

After an hour of frenzied activity, they had accounted for about sixty baboons. The rest—the villagers reckoned there might be another fifty—had grown understandably cautious and were holed up in the *koppie*. The next stage was to light a fire and smoke them out. While this was being prepared, the four white men stopped for some breakfast. James had hoped they might cook something, but in the event they ate from a thermos flask—hot sausages and bacon, washed down with coffee. The food temporarily restored James's spirits, but soon they were taking up positions again, their stocks of cartridges replenished.

To James, the next hour was even more brutal than the first. The fires were lit at the base of the *koppie*, and then the flames were covered with green leaves. A thick, pungent smoke was soon rising up through the rocks, and before long baboons came coughing and spluttering into the open, their eyes temporarily blinded by the smoke. Just as quickly as they emerged they were cut down by the guns. They were impossible to miss, and all were killed cleanly. That, for James, was the only saving grace. But now, as he wiped the sweat off his forehead once again, he was praying no more baboons would come out within his range. They were going to light another fire, but on the far side of the *koppie* this time. With luck, he would have to put up with nothing more trying than the sun in his eyes.

'Hey, James,' a booming voice broke into his thoughts. 'Come on over and give us a hand with this last lot.' It was le Roux, coming round the corner of the *koppie* about eighty yards to his left. He was smiling broadly—a different man again from the severe, unbending central banker in the oak-panelled office, and the theatrical figure at the Voortrekker Monument. James raised his hand in reluctant acknowledgement, picked up a bag of cartridges and walked over to le Roux.

'How much hotter is it likely to get?' he asked, trying to sound as jocular as possible.

'Hardly started yet.' Le Roux's smile widened. 'At this time of year it can go up to 110 degrees without difficulty. Then the rain comes, and we all cool off. I don't think that'll happen today, somehow.'

Their boots kicked up small clouds of dust as they walked through the scrub and round to the other side of the *koppie*. Swart was standing there smoking a cigarette. He was a large man with a very brown skin. He was wearing shorts, his legs bare from the top of his heavy boots. He and le Roux spoke in Afrikaans, and Swart's attitude was reserved, deferential almost. He had said very little to James, and now seemed to ignore him completely. Le Roux's son—Jannie or Jan—was standing fifty yards away. He couldn't have been any older than his own twins, James thought, but he was physically much more developed, and his attitude seemed grave and thoughtful. James suddenly felt exasperated with them all—so damned stolid and dour, slaughtering these wretched baboons without turning a hair.

They spread out again as an African signalled the fire was ready for smoking. The final stage didn't last more than fifteen minutes, and between them they shot another ten baboons. James felt intensely relieved as he took two unused cartridges out of the breech and snapped the gun shut. The Africans were descending on them from all sides—smiling black faces, chattering loudly, and oohing and aahing at the mound of grey bodies. Their thin, mangy dogs milled around excitedly. One picked up a baboon in its mouth, and was rewarded with a savage kick from le Roux's son. Close up, the baboons were surprisingly large and solid, with evil-looking yellow teeth. There were also a dozen or more babies, frail and defenceless, their bodies mangled by pellets. The sight of them was the last straw for James; he had to turn away, and unconvincingly pretended to be admiring a very ordinary thorn bush.

After a twenty-minute walk back to the Land-Rovers, they drove in silence to the house. It was clear that the farm was le Roux's pride and joy. From their conversation the previous evening, James had gathered le Roux had inherited it from his father about eight years ago. The farm was called Klips Nek. It lay in the Eastern Transvaal, near a town called Ermelo, about 120 miles from Pretoria. By British standards it sounded enormous—8,000 acres—but James had grunted noncommittally when le Roux had told him this, thinking it was probably average for South Africa. The countryside was surprisingly hilly, and they had passed a number of massive *koppies* silhouetted by the twilight against the sky. Fields on either side of the road were cultivated, but there was also a good deal of bush—thinly-leaved trees standing close together, the ground covered with scrub, thorn bushes and thick weeds.

Last night, le Roux had talked eloquently of the Afrikaner's hunger for land, born more than a century ago and nurtured through long years of survival in a hostile world. The instinct was never far below the surface, and James could see it in le Roux, a man who could easily be taken for a sophisticated, urbane city dweller. To get it into a perspective which he could understand, James thought it was like the French or Irish, with their strong attachment to the land, no matter how small or unproductive their little patches might be.

The Land-Rovers were bumping their way up a dust track leading back to the farmhouse. Le Roux broke the silence, his face animated as he spoke. 'You haven't properly seen the house yet, James—not in the daylight anyway. Well, what do you think?' His voice was full of pride. Understandably so, thought James, as he looked ahead of him. The sweeping lawns were a startling green after the dry bush, and bordered by banks of shrubs and flowers. For all its careful manicuring, the garden was distinctively African, blending into the rocky background and dominated by a massive fig tree. The house, whitewashed and thatched, with leaded windows, looked pleasantly cool and inviting.

James raised his hands expressively. 'What can I say?' Le Roux seemed satisfied, and James guessed he had been seeking some reassurance that it was indeed as beautiful as he thought it to be. They parked the Land Rovers, and walked across the grass and into the house.

'I was thinking we might cool down with a quick swim,' le Roux suggested.

'That sounds splendid, but again, I'll have to ask you to lend me some trunks.'

'Easy. Jannie, go and see if your mother and the other kids will join us in the pool.' As the boy left the room, le Roux continued, 'Then we'll have a chance to discuss business before lunch. This afternoon I'd like to show you more of the farm. This evening we are having a small party here—a *braaivleis*, if the weather holds.' Seeing James's quizzical expression, he apologised. 'I mean a barbecue—*braaivleis* is the Afrikaans word.'

In his room, James pulled off his sweaty, dusty clothes, and dabbed some Dettol on the scratches on his arm. When he washed the dirt off his face and neck he could see the sharp line between red and white skin where his shirt had protected him from the sun. He tried to put the memory of the shoot out of his mind, as he took a towel off the rail and walked down the passage. After all, Africa was a wild place, and it was unfair to judge it by Home Counties' squeamishness. The whole le Roux family was waiting in front of the

79

house, ready to swim. Five children, the youngest only about six years old, shouting loudly in Afrikaans and trying to get le Roux to give them a piggyback. Mrs le Roux—Aletta— was a handsome woman of about forty, her dark hair pulled back into a fold at the nape of her neck. She chatted politely to James as le Roux led the children, the little ones squealing with delight, up a path behind the house. Far from being the Hollywood-type pool that James had expected, this was actually constructed out of a natural rock formation. Only the water, which was sparkling blue, betrayed the fact that it was all man-made. Le Roux explained that the rivers and dams were—as in most parts of Africa—infected with bilharzia, an unpleasant disease which was carried by snails and could eventually kill humans. 'So we have to have all the workings of a normal pool, filtration system and so on.' He shrugged his shoulders.

The water was beautifully cool; James, floating on his back, his eyes closed against the sun, began to feel much more favourably disposed to life. Le Roux, playing with his children in the shallow end, was emerging as a more sympathetic figure than had seemed possible. Perhaps the world would be a better place if all business, all diplomacy, was conducted by businessmen and politicians at home amongst their families. It was really very difficult to maintain any pretensions with a six-year-old leaping up into your lap.

After an hour in and beside the pool, le Roux and James went off to change and get down to some work. They sat in deck chairs under the fig tree, with a tray of cold Lion beer beside them. James was now wearing his beach shirt, and could not resist a quiet chuckle to himself. If only the Governor, with his penchant for stiff collars and pin-striped suits, could see him—negotiating on behalf of the Western world in a short-sleeved blue, green and red shirt.

He had been debating how best to approach le Roux. The man was prickly, no doubt of that. But, today at least, he had shown himself to be human. The swim, the sun and now the beer in the shade had engendered a sense of well-being and security in James. He wanted to get on with le

Roux and he would go out of his way to do so. For five hours before and after lunch, the two men talked, first under the fig tree, and then as they drove and walked round the farm. Throughout, le Roux's manner was grave, correct; he asked a lot of questions, but never showed any surprise at the answers. He seemed content with the reasons James gave for the Bank's interest. Several times he said he couldn't answer for the SARB—the Governor alone could do that, and then only after consulting with the Government. James understood this perfectly—in fact, both men repeatedly told each other that they understood something perfectly.

To begin with, this sweet reasonableness was a relief after yesterday's stiffness; but gradually it began to depress James. The entire business seemed more and more unreal. At the time, it seemed le Roux was doing as much talking as he was. Only later did he realise that his host had given nothing away. He had been asking a lot of probing questions, and answering very few.

It had not all been business, however. They walked through fields, crossed rivers, and inspected barns. They spent an hour watching cattle being dipped—a strangely pathetic sight, with the beasts struggling frantically through a deep trough of disinfectant, their eyes rolling in alarm. An old, grizzled African was standing at one end of the dip thumping the cattle on their haunches till they emerged, wet and bedraggled. Le Roux spent a long time talking to the old man. They were clearly on the best of terms, and the old man laughed frequently, revealing a few stumps of teeth. James was remined of one of le Roux's remarks the previous evening: 'The Afrikaner has an historic destiny in South Africa, to civilise the natives and to educate them.' Here was le Roux acting out this role—looking and sounding every inch the wise teacher, tolerant of his pupil's foibles, yet firm. The old Shangaan was almost old enough to be le Roux's father, yet he appeared as the perfect foil to le Roux's paternalism. James recalled Sisekwe's words about the imminence of revolution, and wondered what he would say about this very unrevolutionary scene.

At length the two men returned to the Land-Rover. Le Roux leant on its bonnet and wiped his face with a handkerchief before speaking. 'Well, James, we have talked a great deal, and I must now think over all that you have said. First thing on Monday I shall talk to the Governor, make certain suggestions to him and get his views. I shall then telephone you in Johannesburg, and if there is time perhaps we can meet again before you leave the country. Naturally I cannot give you any assurances now, but I hope we shall have something to say which will have made your journey worthwhile.'

'That sounds very good to me, though of course I appreciate your position—as you do mine. The hierarchy of central banks seems to be universal.' James smiled and le Roux smiled back.

'Good. Now let us forget business. Tonight I hope you will enjoy the *braaivleis*. It is a great South African tradition—plenty of meat, drink, the fire and talking. We have one old man coming tonight—from the next-door farm—who swears he can remember the Boer War. I am not sure he is quite that old, but if he is in the mood he can tell a fine story.'

10

HAMPSHIRE

October 26th

The log fire burning in the grate crackled softly. An old and rather portly golden labrador snored gently in front of it. These were the only sounds to disturb Sir William Dent-Cooper's peace. It was Sunday afternoon, and he was sitting in the study of his beloved Broadwood. From this room he could look out through the leaded windows to a side lawn. Sir William was justifiably proud of the garden at Broadwood. 'Of course I seldom have time to do any work in it myself,' he would explain to admiring friends, 'but Camilla and I did plan it all. We both love pottering about—cutting off dead roses, that sort of thing.'

In fact he and his wife had just come in from an extended potter. Muffled up in scarves and old coats, they had walked arm in arm around the flower beds, arguing over whether they should plant a new line of rhododendrons or try something more exotic. Sir William had favoured the rhododendrons—after all, they would be certain to be a success because the soil round there suited them. Camilla had teased him for being so cautious. She wanted some flowering shrub with a long Latin name which Sir William had never heard of. They had not resolved the question, because there was no urgency about it.

'But I do like the rhododendrons,' Sir William said out loud, as though to convince himself. He was sitting back in a deep armchair, his stockinged feet stretched out towards the fire. Camilla scolded him like a naughty child whenever he forgot to take his wellingtons off. By his side was a large black briefcase filled with Bank papers. It seemed to be staring accusingly at him: if he didn't begin soon, he'd have to stay up late when they got back to London.

The door burst open and a small girl rushed into the room and bounced onto Sir William's lap.

'Grandpa, Grandpa,' she screamed, 'we've just seen a fox —all ginger fur, with an enormous tail.' Her eyes were wide with excitement.

'Well, well, Sophie, and did he eat you up?' Sophie squealed delightedly as he tickled her under her arms. For nearly twenty years, Sir William had successfully kept his study as a private preserve from his family. Then the grandchildren arrived. He may have been Governor of the Bank of England, but to his grandchildren he was an old man who played games with them and read them stories. If he was prone to grow conceited as Governor, the grandchildren soon put him in his place.

At that point, Camilla came into the room with a tea tray. She was a tall, well-preserved woman with grey hair, glasses and a slightly quizzical expression. She came of an Army family, and Sir William had often reflected that this background enabled her to put up with the endless round of receptions and official functions which they had to attend. She bore them all with stoical good humour, understanding very little of what was involved but not in any way feeling inadequate in her ignorance. To her, the really important things in life were not exchange rates or political events, but friendship and laughter. In the most unpromising circumstances, she was able to create a feeling of warmth and interest. She smiled at Sophie sitting on her husband's lap: 'Have you told Grandpa about the fox?'

'Indeed she has.' Sir William's voice was gruff. 'And disturbed the peace in doing so.' He could not keep up the pretence, and smiled indulgently at Sophie.

Other members of the household came in for tea: Richard Dent-Cooper and his wife Venetia, young William who was two years older than Sophie, and an elderly cousin. Camilla produced a gardening book with a triumphant flourish. 'Now, William, you can't pretend your rhododendrons are a patch on these. *Eukianthus Campanulatus*—with a name like that, they're bound to be beautiful.'

Sir William looked at the colour print and grunted, unconvinced. Camilla turned to the others for support, and for the next ten minutes they talked about the garden, drinking tea and passing round a plate of crumpets.

Sir William was in his element. Too often he had to bring business acquaintances down to Broadwood, and then they usually had to talk shop. In the 1970s there had been a number of Arab sheikhs, and Mrs Dawson from the village had got in a terrible lather over what to cook. Camilla had kept the whole thing on an even keel and the sheikhs had departed with fulsome praise. One had even bought a crumbling Georgian manor house and park nearby, so impressed had he been by English country life. But when it was just the family at Broadwood, Sir William relaxed completely, and had to be sternly ordered back to London by Camilla on Sunday evening.

The telephone on the desk shrilled loudly, and the mood was broken.

'I think that's an important call I'm expecting.' Sir William got up from his chair, and the family took their cue and left.

As his wife closed the door, Sir William picked up the telephone. 'Dent-Cooper.'

'Is that Alton 243?'

'Yes.'

'A call for you from Johannesburg.' There was a click and then James Glendinning's voice, surprisingly clear.

'Is that you, sir?'

'Yes, James. Tell me how everything's been, at least as much as you can.' The line was open, and they would have to be careful what they said.

'Well, sir, I'm now back at my hotel after spending most of the weekend with our friend. He seems quite confident there will be no serious developments out here. I've talked a lot to him, though without going into detail of course.'

'What was his reaction?' Sir William was reassured by Glendinning's matter-of-fact tone.

'Naturally enough, he couldn't commit himself to anything until he has gone further up the line. But he seemed broadly to understand our position: he's adamant that things will continue as normal—claims it's always been in their interests to deal straight, and always will be. I think they now feel in need of our support, and wouldn't risk offending us.'

'What are the chances of getting something in writing?'

'I've mentioned that in passing, but didn't want to make too much of it.'

'Yes, I suppose that's right—but it would help to have something concrete.'

'Yes, I can understand that, sir—I'll see what I can do.'

'James be sure to telephone me tomorrow just as soon as you've heard more. Is everything OK in other ways?'

'Fine. Except that I'm terribly sunburned.'

The Governor chuckled and put down the telephone. Outside it was nearly dark, and he turned on the lamp on his desk.

'Sunburned, by God,' he muttered. The old labrador stirred in front of the fire, and Sir William regarded her with affection. 'Well, old girl, it'll soon be time for me to go back

85

to London, but you can stay here and sniff around the garden. Lucky devil.'

Sir William stared at the briefcase for a few seconds, and then reached into the bottom drawer of his desk and took out a thick buff folder. The Bank's papers could wait a little longer; there was some personal business to attend to before he left Broadwood. The folder contained the details of Sir William's financial position, and it invariably depressed him. In simple terms, Sir William was a victim of the squeeze of the middle classes. Ten years ago, the Governor's salary had been nearly £25,000 a year. Since then, there had been four years of incomes policies which had either prohibited increases to people on high salaries or given them a few hundred pounds. In the years when there had been no incomes policy, the rate of inflation had been anywhere between fifteen per cent and thirty per cent; for the Governor of the Bank of England to have got a corresponding pay increase would have meant £5,000, sometimes more—and predictable headlines in the press. The Government discreetly let it be known this could not happen, and the men in top jobs had waived their pay rises on four separate occasions. When they had met in their clubs, these men ruefully observed that their sacrifices did not receive quite the same press attention as their increases would have done.

Now, as Sir William sifted through his papers, he could see the effects of this treatment all too clearly. Over the last ten years, prices had risen by roughly two hundred per cent and average earnings rather more. But the Governor's salary from the Bank had gone up by only fifty per cent. And all that was pre-tax, he reminded himself grimly. Tax rates had risen over those ten years, and allowances had not been adjusted to take full account of inflation. As a result, the Governor's post-tax salary had gone up by little more than a third.

Sir William had often heard his City friends complain of how their real incomes were being cut—it was a constant theme in their Budget representations to the Bank and the Treasury. But he had been too long in the City himself to shed many tears for them. He knew full well that rich men in the City had never looked to their salaries for their holidays in Sardinia and their children's school fees. They had to pay seventy-five per cent or more on each extra pound they received as income; but if that pound was a capital gain, the taxman only took thirty per cent, and it was up to two years before he asked for it. Within the square mile of the City of London there were more opportunities for maximising capital gains and minimising tax liabilities than anywhere else in the world.

Unless, that is, you were Governor of the Bank of England. All financial scandals are potentially embarrassing to a government, but none more so than those involving senior members of what in the 1960s was called the Establishment.

Just before Sir William's appointment, one such scandal had threatened. There were rumours—which started in *Private Eye* and quickly spread—that a Cabinet Minister had bought shares in an obscure ship-repairing firm which the Government had unexpectedly decided to include in its nationalisation plans. Fortunately for the Government, the Minister put an end to the rumours in the most conclusive possible way—by dying, in his bed, apparently of natural causes.

The experience had shaken the Government, however. With the minimum of fuss and no publicity whatever, the Prime Minister himself had let it be known that for eighty-five men and women in sensitive jobs, no conflicts of interest would arise in future. It was all done very politely. Just as soldiers on parade can choose whether or not to volunteer for training, so these eighty-five people were able to choose whether or not to accept the Prime Minister's offer to join the most exclusive investment trust in Britain. When the scheme was unveiled, even those least familiar with investment trusts could see that its most striking, indeed its only, merit was simplicity. Members were to deposit all their liquid assets in a Government account for the period they held office. They were to be paid the same interest as the ten million investors in National Savings Bonds, and nothing could be more democratic than that.

As Governor of the Bank of England, Sir William was one of the chosen. Last week he had received the quarterly statement of his account, and he was now surveying this with a baleful eye. To rub salt in his wounds, he had the *Sunday Times* Business News open at a page where the City Editor was gloating over how much his 'Supercharge Portfolio' had appreciated in the last eighteen months. Sir William compared the two, and groaned loudly. It simply wasn't worth it. As he had done on several occasions before, he began mentally to compose his letter of resignation.

Sir William hadn't gone beyond the second sentence before he had to admit he wasn't being serious. He wouldn't leave yet. Not because he still cared much for the job, but because, like every man in high office, he desperately wanted to be remembered. If you are famous, or even just well known in life, the experience becomes addictive; until eventually, as you approach retirement, you hanker after a permanent fix that will succour you even in the grave. Sir William had reached that stage, and was increasingly preoccupied with how and for what he would be remembered. Not just for good stewardship of the Bank, though that of course was important. No, he needed some real achievement, uniquely associated with his name. When he had time to be candid with himself, Sir William knew he had done nothing like that yet. Even worse, he knew he might not have much time. His fibrositis was very poor this winter, and his doctor had been pestering him to cut down on trips abroad.

There might only be one more year, two at the outside, he thought moodily. Now, the gold thing . . . if that were to come off, he would retire a contented man. He could feel his blood stirring at the thought: it would be a landmark in the twentieth century, and he personally would have played a considerable part in bringing it about. That was why he didn't want too many people in on it just yet. If only he could present the Chancellor with a fully worked-out plan. One which owed nothing to those Treasury people, who were always sticking their noses in, trespassing on what should be the Bank's territory. That really would be something. Then he could retire to applause from all sides, take his money out of that blasted account and begin to repair some of the damage it had done.

Sir William straightened up in his chair. If this was really the opportunity he was looking for, then he'd have to keep tabs on everything. He'd heard from Glendinning, and that seemed to be going along quite nicely. But he wasn't so happy about the Americans. Dale Kendall had talked of 'an independent initiative', but what did that mean? Well, there was only one way to find out—he had Kendall's weekend telephone number, and he would ring him up. After that, he really would get down to the files in his briefcase.

I I

LONDON

October 26th

'British Airways announce the departure of flight BA 2081 to Rome, Nairobi and Johannesburg. Would all passengers on this flight kindly proceed to Gate No 4.' The loudspeaker stirred Caroline Manning out of her daydream. In the last half-hour, she had bought *The Economist* and some duty-free cigarettes, and then passed the time sitting in the departure lounge, glancing idly at her fellow passengers and making up life histories for them. It was a game she had learnt years ago, and she played it whenever her brain was too fidgety to concentrate on anything important. For the past three days she had only just managed to stifle her impatience; now at last she was on her way, and the impatience was giving way to nervousness.

The jumbo took a long time to fill, and she began to wish she had booked on Concorde. But the expense was prohibitive, and she would have regretted it later. She buckled her seat belt, winced at the anodyne music that some overpaid consultant psychiatrist had doubtless prescribed as soothing, and let her mind run back over the events of the past week. She had spent four hours in the reading room at South Africa House, poring over every English-language newspaper from the past fortnight. Then she had read the translated summaries of the Afrikaans press provided by the Embassy staff. Finally she had spent ten minutes with a Mr Potgieter from the Press Office, a thickset man with a pock-marked face who had promised to arrange an itinerary for her if she wanted to visit South Africa, and had dismissed the labour troubles with a wave of his hand. 'Hell, it's nothing compared with what happens in this country every week.' This observation was accompanied by an aggressive glare, as though Caroline was personally responsible for all the shortcomings of British industrial relations. She had reminded him rather acidly that she was an American citizen, and a number of interviews had duly been arranged.

Those hours in the Embassy had confirmed her hunch about the strikes. She had been impressed by the accounts of factory closures and picketing, which made it clear the labour unrest was not confined to a few centres. She also learnt all police leave had been cancelled and army reserves placed on stand-by alert, a fact which had subsequently been reported in the British newspapers. But there were two small news items which had not found their way into the British press which really intrigued her.

The first was the postponement of a three-day conference being staged in Cape Town by Partners in Progress, an organisation only recently set up to promote better industrial relations at home and a favourable image to investors abroad. Earlier publicity for the conference had listed a number of black speakers; a Cabinet Minister; two promi-nent white businessmen; the West German Ambassador; and a very rich American named Cornelius J. Arbruck, who had made one fortune in Texas extracting oil from shale and another from South African mining. When Caroline learned from a friend who lectured at the School of Oriental and African Studies that the finance for Partners in Progress was rumoured to come from the CIA, her suspicions were further aroused. Why should a body like that postpone a carefully planned conference? Surely this would have been the ideal opportunity to show the world it was business as usual in South Africa, and play down the importance of the strikes?

The second thing which caught her attention was a small piece in the *Financial Mail*'s gossip column, which was called 'Fancy That . . .' It too referred to Cornelius J. Arbruck. Caroline gathered he had thirty racehorses in training near Durban, and sixty per cent of a conglomerate valued on the Johannesburg Stock Exchange at £50 million. Now, 'Fancy That . . .' informed her, he was reportedly negotiating to buy an enormous sugar estate on the Natal coast—20,000 acres of plantations, two sugar mills and a packing factory. Nor did there seem to be anything funny about the price: at 25 million rand, it was described as 'reviving happy memories of the boom days of the early 1970s'. As a rule nothing upsets foreign investors more than instability, so why was a Texan choosing this of all times to increase his stake in South Africa? Perhaps he really believed the Partners in Progress propaganda. Whatever the reason, Caroline wanted to find it out. She had taken another look at her bank account and the weather forecast and decided to go.

As the Jumbo turned at the head of Runway 1 and began to rev its engines, Caroline stared out of the window. Grey tarmac, grey clouds, grey rain. The turbulence of South Africa suddenly seemed very colourful and inviting, and her spirits lifted as the great plane lumbered into the sky. She rang the buzzer above her head and ordered a gin and tonic. This was going to be fun.

Over the Channel, Caroline ran through her plans. Even in her determinedly optimistic mood, she had to admit they were sketchy. The last four days in London had been spent ringing round the press to arrange commissions. She now had definite offers for an insider piece on the Johannesburg Stock Exchange, which would form part of a South Africa survey in the *Investor's Chronicle*; 2,500 words on the Rand for *International Currency Review*; and a feature for the *Sunday Times* on migrant labour in the gold mines. These three would just about pay for her air-fare. Beyond that, the *Guardian* had said they wanted a longish piece on political prisoners; and *The Economist* was prepared to consider anything, at least for its Foreign Report. She had promised the editor of *Spare Rib*, who was a friend of hers, something on black women. But *Spare Rib* only paid for copy if there was money in the bank, and at the moment there was very little. Assuming she had some luck, she might also get a story interesting enough to sell to the Press Association man in Johannesburg. Then there was Arbruck. A story on him would probably go down better in America than in Britain, so she had contacted the *Wall Street Journal* and been promised an answer by the time she arrived in Johannesburg. That commission would help a lot—for a start, it'd give her an ideal pretext to see Arbruck. Without knowing why, she felt it would be worth seeing him. Because he might give her an interesting lead? But to what? With no answers to these questions, she consoled herself with the thought of the sun. She had packed a bikini, and if she did nothing else in South Africa, she would at least revive her tan.

As they headed towards Rome, watches were put forward an hour, and lunch was served. Caroline had always been rather fond of airline food and ate it all. Sitting next to her was a middle-aged man; with one eye on his figure and the other on hers, he pretended not to want his strawberry ice cream, so she ate that too. He bought a bottle of wine, which they shared, then recounted an involved and seemingly endless saga about his wife's 'personality problems'. Caroline was very relieved when he got off at Rome. In the afternoon, there was a film, an excruciating Western. Westerns were enjoying yet another revival. Caroline unplugged the headphone and from her bag got out the itinerary which Mr Potgieter had prepared for her in London. She was to ring a Mr Loots at the Ministry of Information on her arrival. Interviews were being arranged by the press office of a large mining company, the Department of Mines, the Department of Labour, and a back-bench Nationalist MP who specialised in 'black affairs'. She might also be able to visit an African township near Jo'burg, and one of the black 'homelands'. Any other meetings she would have to organise herself—and these would be virtually impossible anyway. Journalists coming back from South Africa had told her they were prevented from entering the black townships; even talking to any prominent black was now very difficult.

When the jumbo taxied to a halt at Nairobi Airport, Caroline stepped from the cool of the cabin out onto the tarmac. Even though it was eight o'clock Kenyan time, it was still very warm. Black faces were everywhere, not just a small leavening as there was in New Jersey or London. The airport was bustling with activity; the tourist season was moving into top gear, with the pale rich from Europe and North America trying hard to extend their summers. Kenya was a country she viewed with mixed feelings. After Kenyatta had died, it looked for a time as though the corruption and inequalities might be swept away. But the new regime had found the Swiss bank accounts and the large tracts of land just as attractive as the old one had. It was all a long way from the African socialism which Caroline espoused so passionately from her Barbican flat. Yet she had never quite rid herself of a romantic fascination with the Kenya of Robert Ruark. At the airport she stared unashamedly at a bronzed young man with tousled hair and white teeth who was meeting a party from Detroit. They all had 'On Safari' labels plastered over their luggage, and one or two of the women were already clearly hoping the young man had a double sleeping bag.

Too quickly, they were being herded back onto the plane, and Caroline shook off her fantasies and tried to concentrate on what lay ahead. The last leg of the trip was uneventful. They turned their clocks back an hour, and arrived at Jan Smuts on schedule at eleven p.m. Caroline was surprised to find the airport guarded by police with ferocious-looking Alsatian dogs. Outside the main building there were three armoured cars, with small knots of soldiers in khaki-and-green combat gear standing by them. Her journalist's antennae were straining hard to gauge the atmosphere. But, beyond the obvious fact that it was different from London, her strongest instinct was to get to her hotel and soak in a hot bath with a glass of whisky.

When she travelled abroad, it was her usual practice to check into the best hotel for the first two nights, regardless of expense. If there were any newsworthy people about, they would be more likely to show up there than in some two-star suburban shabbiness. If she was lucky, she would pick up a story which would cover the extra expense several times over. If she was not, she left after two days, moved to somewhere less exciting, and wrote a sober piece about the country's balance of payments. Fortunately this hadn't happened often, and she was hopeful that it wouldn't now.

At the city terminus she picked up a taxi, and asked the driver to take her to the Carlton Hotel. It was part of the Carlton Centre, a large, modern complex on Main Street. Once inside, Caroline decided she might have been anywhere in the world; for a moment she wished she had looked for something more authentically African. But at least she could be sure they would have good bourbon, and the bath water would be hot. On both counts she was right. By one o'clock Caroline Manning was sleeping like a child.

She was woken at 7.30 by a knock on the door. At her sleepy reply, a black waiter in a smartly pressed white uniform glided into the room and put a tray of coffee and the *Rand Daily Mail* down on the table by the bed. Today, Caroline told herself, there would be no lying in. She drank some coffee, read the front page, the leading article, and the business pages of the *Rand Daily Mail*, and then got dressed.

She came out into the corridor, at the same time as a man from the next room. He looked very English in a dark suit and unfashionable black shoes, and he seemed uncomfortably sunburnt. While she fumbled with her keys, he glanced round as though to smile a standard good morning. Simultaneously they recognised each other, and their expressions made it impossible to pretend they didn't. Caroline spoke first. 'Good morning. I didn't think you found the BBC in a place like this any more. I thought you were always in a financial crisis.' She smiled at the man's puzzlement. 'In case you've forgotten my name, I'm Caroline Manning from the *Guardian*. We met at the ANC house in London last week. All I can remember is that you are called James.'

'Glendinning,' James replied rather gruffly.

'Of course,' Caroline continued brightly, 'I should have known. It would be most unfair of me to grill you for leads over breakfast, but could we meet for a drink this evening?'

James moved his head, rather gingerly because his neck was very painful, and Caroline quickly took this as agreement.

'Wonderful. Shall we make it 7.30 then? I noticed a bar downstairs called the Van Riebeck bar. I'm not sure I approve of Van Riebeck, but we can at least be grateful for the bar. See you there.'

With that, she turned and walked quickly down the corridor, swinging her bag over her shoulder and tossing her hair. Despite his annoyance, James had to admit the effect was agreeable. He wasn't sure he could be a convincing BBC man, even for half an hour, but she seemed pleasant, and after three days in South Africa, it would be good to talk to someone from London.

12

JOHANNESBURG

October 27th

The Van Riebeck bar was crowded when Caroline came down at 7.30. It had been a busy, hot day, but a long bath and some whisky had repaired the damage. She was wearing a long blue dress made from Indian silk, which clung to her in a way which several men at the bar obviously found interesting. A waiter came over, but she decided not to order a drink. This trip was already proving more expensive than she had expected, and with any luck her drinks would be paid for tonight.

95

She was looking forward to seeing Glendinning—their chance meeting was just the sort of break she needed at this stage. She was also very curious about him. She had spent two hours that morning ringing up various journalist contacts, picking up gossip and tips. To each of them she had casually mentioned that she had seen someone from the BBC by the name of James Glendinning. No one had heard of him. Of course, that didn't prove anything—visiting correspondents did not necessarily make themselves known to the resident journalists. But press people tend to congregate, usually in bars, and the grapevine might be expected to pick up the arrival of a BBC man. It was also odd he should be staying in the Carlton Hotel. When the Government had reorganised the BBC after the 1977 Annan Commission report, expenses had been one of the areas where drastic economies were made. Caroline had frequently heard BBC staff complaining, only half-jokingly, that they couldn't put a pub lunch on expenses without filling in a form in triplicate, and getting it signed by the Director General. Perhaps Glendinning was very senior: but then, that didn't square with him being at the ANC house in London, obviously accompanying the other man. She decided to suspend her judgement until she had talked to him.

She had found Jo'burg very claustrophobic, and was soon assigning it to the bottom end of her list of favourite cities, below Milan but just above Pittsburgh. From the little she had seen, it was hard to believe the country was verging on revolution. Certainly the blacks seemed sullen and rather menacing, the whites a bit shrill and aggressive, but friends in London had told her that had been true for many years. In the best journalistic tradition, she had started off with a taxi ride around the city, but the driver was bland and uncommunicative. In a rather seedy area she had seen walls freshly daubed with the words '*Amandla Ewithu*'. Workmen were already beginning to remove them, under the watchful gaze of six bull-necked policemen. When she enquired what they meant, the taxi driver had spat contemptuously, and then grudgingly informed her it was an ANC slogan meaning

'Power is ours'. This had cheered her: it was a reminder of heady days during her first year at Harvard, when the students had covered the town with anti-war graffiti. It would also make a good opening paragraph for her first article.

Her thoughts were interrupted by the arrival of James Glendinning, red-faced and uncomfortable in his dark suit. Her guess about the drinks was right—they were going on his bill. After two large gulps of gin and tonic, he appeared to relax.

'Well, how long have you been here? I hadn't noticed you till this morning.'

'No, I only arrived last night, so I haven't yet had a chance to catch the sun.' She grinned at his sunburnt face, and was surprised to see it could turn a deeper shade of scarlet. 'A real *rooinek*, eh?' she mimicked a thick Afrikaans accent, and then, seeing his puzzled expression, explained. 'That's Afrikaans for redneck, a term of abuse for the British.'

'You've been to South Africa before?'

'No, it's the only word I know, taught by a friend in London. But surely, this isn't your first visit?'

'Yes, it certainly is.' James spoke without thinking, and Caroline leapt at the chance.

'Do you mean to tell me the BBC has sent a complete stranger to cover a country on the brink of a revolution? I can't believe that.'

James mentally cursed his stupidity, and decided that he would have to change his story. 'Actually I don't work for the BBC at all. I'm not even a journalist. I'm a businessman, out here for a few days to see some clients.' That was better; on familiar territory it would be much easier to disguise the real purpose of his visit. In fact, with the air cleared, he might ask her to have dinner with him.

'But what were you doing in that house in London then? Didn't you see Sisekwe?' Caroline was persisting, but she was smoothing the sharp edge of her questions with a friendly smile which James found distracting.

'Oh, that.' He tried to sound lighthearted. 'Well, Mr

Sisekwe's going to be an important man. All sorts of people want to see him, and I was fortunate to have a friend in the BBC who was going to interview him. It helped me to get a foot in the door, so to speak.' He was relaxing now. The story sounded perfectly plausible, and he felt he could keep it up over dinner. 'I would offer you another drink, but I'm hungry. What are you doing for dinner?'

'Having it with you, by the sound of it.' Caroline hoped she had disguised the eagerness in her voice.

They walked across the foyer and into the Three Ships Restaurant, which was reputed to have some of the best food in Jo'burg. After the weekend's *boerwors*, James was relieved to see it specialised in French cooking. They had ratatouille, followed by lobster Thermidor, and drank a light chablis. James felt distinctly better. Caroline was charming, full of American-in-London stories, very knowledgeable about the City. She had decided not to question James at all over dinner, hoping he would let slip some clues on what he did and why he was here. With most men she had found she could get the information she wanted simply by allowing them into her bed. With James she was not so sure.

Just when she was beginning to wonder if there was anything worth finding out her luck returned. The head waiter, a swarthy Greek with a patent liking for after-shave lotion, came up to their table and said, 'Mr Glendinning, I have Dr Pieter le Roux on the telephone for you. He says it's urgent.'

James stood up, apologised and hurried out, leaving Caroline to sip her coffee. Now what's to be done? she thought. She couldn't be sure he had anything to tell her, but the dinner had been fun and it might just be worth persevering. Besides, underneath all that reserve and sunburn he was quite attractive and she had no other plans for the evening.

James returned. 'Sorry. That was some chap about an exchange control application I had made. Wanted to make sure I hadn't left.'

'Oh, are you going soon?'

'As soon as possible. I have to go to Pretoria first thing in the morning, so it looks like I'll be leaving sometime to-morrow. What about you?'

'I'll be here a few days, perhaps to the end of the week. I've got some stories to write, and I've also promised myself a day in the sun. I may even go down to the coast if I've finished my writing in good time.'

A vision of Caroline on the beach crossed James's mind and he did not find it easy to focus on the prospect of flying to London, Washington, Paris and Basle. Still, that was to-morrow. Tonight he could afford to relax: le Roux had sounded encouraging on the phone; at least, as encouraging as he was ever likely to be.

'What about some brandy, Caroline?' he heard himself saying.

'I'd prefer Grand Marnier, but only if you're having something.'

'Why not? We don't do this kind of thing very often—at least I don't.'

'No, quite.' Caroline took up the idea promptly. 'Whenever I'm away from home on a trip, I get this curious feeling that I've left me behind, and all my obligations and worries. The person who's in Jo'burg is someone else, playing a part, acting out her fantasies. Do you know what I mean?'

'I suppose I do.' James looked slightly unsettled for a moment.

'What part would the other Mr James Glendinning like to play?' Caroline's voice was lazy.

'Oh, I don't think I know.' James could feel the brandy spreading pleasantly through his veins. 'I'm a fairly straight-forward sort of chap, really.'

'Buttoned up, that's your problem.' Caroline laughed affectionately. 'Too much work, too many cares. Forget them for a while—there's nothing you can do about anything tonight.'

'True—except have some more brandy, I suppose.' James grinned at her. 'No, seriously, I have enjoyed this evening. After the last few days, you've been like a breath of fresh air.' He beckoned to a waiter for the bill.

Caroline saw her opening. 'James, you might be interested in an article I came across today. It's about the effects of sanctions on South Africa. Let me stand you a drink while you look at it. Oh, waiter, could you send another brandy and a Grand Marnier up to Room 215 please? That's what you want, isn't it?' she asked James, and was pleased to see him smile slightly at the ambiguity in her question.

They walked out of the restaurant and up the stairs, chatting idly about what they had seen that day. In her room, James sat in a chair, brandy in hand, trying to make sense of a complicated article which ran to at least forty pages in an academic journal. He was finding it increasingly difficult to concentrate. Caroline was leaning over his shoulder, pointing at various sections he ought to read. Her hand was resting lightly on his shoulder, and he could feel her hair against his cheek.

'It's heavy going at this time of night, Caroline.' He could hear his voice cracking. As he turned his face to look at her, she brought her mouth down on his. Her lips were very soft and warm, and her tongue played gently round his mouth. 'Relax, relax,' she murmured, 'this is the other James, remember?' He pulled her down onto the chair, and kissed her face and neck. The other James Glendinning was very susceptible to the blend of brandy and Caroline's scent. The Indian silk seemed to be sending off sparks under his touch. He reached round to unzip her dress, and felt her back, smooth and cool. She stood up and shrugged off the dress. James fumbled ineffectually with her bra strap. 'This one opens at the front,' she said softly, reaching to unclip the hook. Her breasts were round and firm, white against the outline of suntan. He bent to kiss their brown tips, and slipped her pants down.

'Your turn now,' Caroline said firmly. While he ran his hands over her body, she began undressing him. 'Not so buttoned up any more, James?' Her voice was soft, her eyes excited. 'Would the real Mr Glendinning please stand up . . . that looks real enough to me.'

Some time afterwards James said, 'That was marvellous. Tomorrow I may feel differently, but thanks anyway. I really ought to go now. I've got to see that blasted Reserve Bank man first thing.'

'There you go again.' Caroline snuggled up against him. 'Just relax. Besides you were much too good to get away with only one performance.' James winced as she ran her fingers along his arm. 'Wow, you really are hyped up, aren't you?'

'Nothing like that, I'm afraid.' James grinned in the darkness. 'It's only my blasted sunburn.'

'Oh, I am sorry.' Caroline moved her hand. 'Well, let's see if I can find somewhere that isn't so sunburnt ... better?'

'Much better.'

13

JOHANNESBURG

October 28th

It was after eight o'clock when Caroline woke up. She rang for some tea, and then lay in bed while her mind went back over the previous night. She was quietly pleased to have added James Glendinning to her list of lovers. Admittedly the brandy had helped, but once he had been pulled over the threshold, he had proved surprisingly enthusiastic. She'd done what she planned to do: but had she got any new information from it?

She showered and dressed, her face puckered in concentration. The only lead was the telephone call at dinner—Dr le Roux—an exchange control application—and then didn't James mention that 'blasted Reserve Bank man'? She took the telephone over to the dressing-table, and sat down at the improvised desk. She asked the switchboard to put her through to the Reserve Bank in Pretoria. There was a short delay and then she was connected.

'Hello, Reserve Bank.'

'Good morning, I wonder if I could speak to Dr Pieter le Roux in Exchange Control?'

'Certainly . . .' There was a pause. 'Did you say Exchange Control?'

'Yes.'

'But Dr le Roux is not in Exchange Control, there's no one called le Roux in Exchange Control.'

'Oh, I'm sorry, I must have made a mistake. Could you tell me which Department Dr le Roux works in then?'

'Dr le Roux is Head of the Gold Department.'

'No, that doesn't sound like the man I'm after. Sorry for wasting your time.'

Caroline put the telephone down, drew in her breath and whistled, softly at first, but getting louder and louder. Then she began to think clearly again. Glendinning had lied to her about le Roux: they weren't going to talk about exchange controls at all, but about gold. So who the hell is he? she thought impatiently. He was from the City, she was almost sure of that. If only she was back in London, she could have found out about him in half an hour. That provided the answer. She asked the operator for the dialling code for London, and then rang Charles. She contemplated ringing another journalist, but knew that would only arouse interest and she'd have to explain what she was doing. Charles, dear devoted Charles, wouldn't ask questions—except perhaps when she was going to marry him. The line crackled and squeaked, but they got through. Thank God, he was in the office, obviously thrilled to hear her, but she cut short his welcome.

'Listen, can you do me a favour, rather quickly. I want to know which City organisation a man called Glendinning, James Glendinning, works for. It could easily be one of the merchant banks which deals in gold; or a broking firm which specialises in gold. Or even,' her voice trailed away for a moment as the thought first occurred to her, 'or even the Bank of England.'

'What was that last one?' Charles shouted down the line.

'The Bank—the Old Lady.' Caroline's voice sounded very loud in the quiet of the hotel room.

'Roger. What's your number, I'll ring you back soon. Oh, Caroline, it is good to hear you. When are you coming back?'

'Soon, darling—even sooner if you get on and find out who Glendinning is.' She rang off before he had a chance to say any more.

The next half-hour went very slowly. Caroline rang two contacts, and then tried to start a piece for the *Sunday Times*. But she couldn't concentrate, and when the telephone finally rang she snatched at it with relief. Charles's voice was clearer this time. 'Elementary, my dear Manning. Can't you give me a real assignment—this journalism stuff's too cushy.'

'Come on, Charlie boy, tell me who he is.' Caroline could feel the impatience rising up in her.

'You were right, actually—he is from the Old Lady—an Adviser in the Chief Cashier's Office—something of a high flier, so my chum said. Are you still there, Caroline?'

'Yes, I'm here.' Her voice was pensive. 'Thank you very much, Charles—I'll give you a medal when I get back.'

'Keep the medals, darling—but I might reward you with a ring.' Caroline chuckled and hung up.

For twenty minutes she lay on her bed, thinking. Then, praying for a good line, she dialled the London code and afterwards 601–4444.

'Bank of England,' said a voice.

'Could I speak to Mr Glendinning in CCO, please.'

There was a click, and then, 'Mr Glendinning's secretary.'

'Could I speak to him, please?'

'I'm afraid he's not here at the moment. I'm Miss Barker, his temporary secretary, standing in for Miss Higginson—could I help in any way?'

Caroline decided Miss Barker sounded promising. 'Oh, that would be most kind. Could you tell me where I could contact him, either now or in the next few days?' Miss Barker rose to the fly quite beautifully.

'Well, he'll be in London tomorrow, but is then going off

to Washington, and isn't expected back in the Bank till next week.'

Caroline silently blessed Miss Barker, thanked her and put down the telephone. 'Curiouser and curiouser,' she said out loud to her reflection in the mirror, winked broadly and lay down on the bed again. Obviously a very lucky bed, which was now helping her to think straight.

For half an hour she stared up at the ornate ceiling. She was on to something, no doubt of that. But was it big enough —and saleable enough—to justify cancelling all her other commissions in South Africa, and flying off to Washington in pursuit of Glendinning? Be practical, she decided. Work hard here for a few days, write some stories, and then try to catch up with all this in London. She might miss Glendinning in Washington. He might not even be staying in a hotel there, and she didn't like it much anyway. The last time she'd been to Washington had been on one of the Vietnam demonstrations. They had camped on the pavements of Pennsylvania Avenue, and it had been terribly cold. No, she decided, she wouldn't go to Washington.

She spent the next hour on the telephone, arranging some interviews. Now that her plans had changed, she was going to concentrate on the most commercial stories. She intended to see the wife of a Nationalist leader who had been on Robben Island for ten years; an interview with a young woman MP from the Progressive Federal Party; and a man who had just retired as editor of the *Rand Daily Mail*. She would write her piece on the Stock Exchange for the *Investor's Chronicle*; two others, on the Rand and the balance of payments she could knock off back in London if necessary. With luck, she could get through all this by Wednesday evening.

That would leave her with a full day for Cornelius Arbruck. When she'd arrived in Jo'burg last night, there was a cable from the *Wall Street Journal* to say they'd like a piece on Arbruck. But would he see her? Caroline rang a man on the *Financial Mail*, whose name she had been given in London. Yes, he said, he knew Arbruck, who was always eager to talk to 'my friends of the press'. He was supposed to be in South Africa at the moment. She dialled the number he gave her and a simpering female voice replied, 'The Bar Four Stud.'

'Could I speak to Mr Arbruck, please?'

'I'm sorry, Mr Arbruck is not available just now. I'm his PA. Is there anything I can do?'

'Yes, my name is Caroline Manning, of the *Wall Street Journal*. I'd like to come and interview Mr Arbruck for a story we're planning to run on his empire.' Flattery often opened a lot of doors.

There was silence at the other end, and for a moment she thought the girl had put down the telephone. Then suddenly a Texan accent boomed down the line.

'This is Cornelius J. Arbruck, ma'am. What can I do for you?' Trying to make her voice as husky as possible, Caroline explained she would like to call in to see him on Thursday afternoon.

'Why sure.' Mr Arbruck had clearly fallen for the huskiness. 'But why don't you stay for dinner—why, you could even stay the night in one of my rondavels.' Mr Arbruck's imagination was now in top gear.

'That would be delightful.' The huskiness was becoming trying. 'Shall we say I'll arrive at 4.30?'

'Fine, fine. You can pick up a cab from Durban—it'll take about forty minutes from the centre.'

Caroline put down the telephone with relief. Cornelius Arbruck sounded very stupid. Now that she had picked up a promising lead through meeting Glendinning, her original ideas about Arbruck seemed a bit far-fetched. Still, it was done now, and at least she would save an hotel bill. As a precaution she put through a call to the *Wall Street Journal*, and told the Features Editor she would be sending him a piece on Arbruck's South African interests.

By now it was twelve o'clock, and Caroline made one further decision—to move out of the Carlton and check into somewhere cheaper. The best hotel in town had again served its purpose admirably. If she had been looking for some rich companion for the evening she might have stayed on—but now it was all going to be work. She called the reception desk, paid her bill and took a taxi out to the Atlantic Hotel in Hillbrow.

14

PRETORIA

October 28th

After his last experience with the taciturn SARB chauffeur, James knew better than to attempt friendly conversation. In the padded back seat of the Mercedes, he thought ruefully about Caroline. Take away all the trimmings, and you were left with the fact that she had seduced him. Very cleverly, and, he had to admit, most enjoyably.

He pulled himself together. This was the last lap of his mission in South Africa. After this morning he'd have found out as much as he was likely to of the views of the white South Africans—it was for others to judge the next move. On the telephone, le Roux had sounded cautious, which was typical of the man. But he had spoken to the right people, and would have something concrete to tell James.

It really had been very straightforward. True, le Roux had been prickly, but then who else did the whites have to turn to? They couldn't afford to alienate the West. Sitting there, James felt the same satisfaction that he sometimes got in the Bank, when a bank was carpeted for breaking the rules. No need to be crude or tough about these things. Politeness and power went together very well, when you thought about it.

The car pulled up in Church Square, already shimmering in the morning heat. James nodded a thank you to the driver and walked into the Reserve Bank. On this occasion he waited only a moment before being escorted up to le Roux's office.

'Ah, James, welcome again.' The Afrikaner stretched out his hand, a slight smile on his face.

'Thank you for arranging the car, Pieter.'

'No trouble.'

'And thank you for an excellent weekend. As you can see,' James rubbed his neck gingerly, 'I carry the scars of battle with me still.'

Le Roux chuckled. 'Yes, I should have warned you about our sun.'

'I have arranged for a small present to be sent to you and Aletta, here in Pretoria. It is only a token, but it comes with my thanks for making me such a welcome guest.' He had ordered a dozen bottles of Veuve Clicquot, to be delivered to le Roux's house.

'Very kind—you needn't have bothered. Now, James, I'm afraid I have a full diary today, so can we get on with business?'

'Absolutely.' James sat down in a deep chair and waited for le Roux to speak.

'I have had words with the Governor, as I said I would.' Le Roux's chair was swung to one side, so that he was facing the wall. 'For reasons which I think we all appreciate, we have not been completely straight with each other. Now,' he lifted a hand, as though he expected James to take issue with his last remark, 'that's not to say we don't understand one another. I think your intentions are plain, and if I may say so, prudent. All this the Governor understands. He was in fact very frank, and gave me permission to be frank as well. We in South Africa,' James was now accustomed to the way he ran the two words together, 'are determined to maintain our traditional policies. Politically we will weather this little outburst, as we have always done in the past. We deal straight, with the blacks in this country, and with others outside, whether they be businessmen or sovereign governments. We know we have friends in the West, and we do not forget our friends. From what I have just said,' le Roux turned his chair and leant forward, 'you can be quite certain we are not planning any changes in our gold policy. Naturally we respond to market conditions, as we have always done in the past. Sometimes we may withhold a little from the market, sometimes we may release a little from our stocks. But our basic operational targets are the same: a high and stable price in the free market. We remain opposed to bilateral deals in principle. That,' le Roux rocked back in his chair, 'is the essence of what the Governor said. He says it with the full authority of the Minister of Finance—he spoke to him on the telephone in my presence this morning. He was not keen to put anything in writing. He felt it unnecessary, and I agree. You can return to the Bank with as firm a commitment from us as anyone could expect—not so?'

James nodded agreement. 'Yes, indeed. I wouldn't expect that in writing, because your word and your Governor's are good enough for us. But, Pieter, there may in future be detailed points which we need to consult about. Can I leave it that you and I will keep each other informed about anything which might be relevant—changes in output, transport difficulties, anything like that?'

'Of course. In fact it is very important that we should be the contact points. The Governor specifically said he does not want to be involved personally from now on.' James nodded assent as le Roux went on. 'You can telephone me any time you like, and you know we would be very pleased to see you out here again.' He stood up and shook James's hand warmly. 'Are you going straight back to London?'

'Yes, indeed.'

'Well, have a good flight. I think we are clear, so if you'll excuse me . . .'

'Of course. Thank you once again for everything.'

After the door had clicked behind James, le Roux stood for a few moments, staring thoughtfully at his hands. Then he picked up a telephone and waited for his secretary to answer. Speaking in Afrikaans, he said softly, 'Would you please get me Mr du Plessis at the Bureau of State Security.'

BOSS—the Bureau of State Security—was founded in 1968. Its function in South Africa has never been clearly defined, but constitutional experts agree it is exempt from financial control—some would say, any kind of control—by parliament. Its first head, General Van den Bergh, enjoyed particularly close relations with the then Prime Minister, John Vorster—a friendship nurtured while the two men were interned during the Second World War for pro-Nazi activities. Ever since, its Head has reported directly to the Prime Minister.

In its comparatively short life, BOSS has attracted much adverse publicity. It is said to have been involved in the torturing of political prisoners, infiltration of subversive organisations (and BOSS has generous powers to define subversion), and spying on individuals it considers a threat to South Africa. What is less well known is the extent to which BOSS has become enmeshed in the whole fabric of South Africa's official institutions. Over the years it has taken responsibility for vetting applicants for posts in the civil service, the armed forces, and in private companies which perform 'sensitive' work for the state. It organises security arrangements at all official buildings and installations, both at home and abroad, which might be the target of an attack by insurgents. It provides the bodyguards for the President, the Prime Minister and other leading national figures. It has effectively become an estate of the land—an unsung estate, but then the Bureau has never been keen to court publicity, except on its own terms.

It therefore came as no surprise to Pieter le Roux that one of the first people to visit him on his appointment as Head of the SARB's Gold Department was Hendrik du Plessis, a senior official from BOSS's Domestic Security Division. He brought with him an officer from his Division, and le Roux was supported by the SARB's security adviser. The four men spent a morning discussing the security arrangements in force at the Reserve Bank. Du Plessis was very critical. He maintained they were designed exclusively to prevent robbery—which was an obvious temptation, given that twenty-five tons of gold passed through every week, and millions of rands' worth of notes and coins every day.

Naturally, du Plessis accepted that deterrence of would-be robbers was important. But, he went on to argue, the real threat came not from bank robbers, but from what he called 'politically motivated terrorists'. Attacks on government property in South Africa had become common during the 1970s, and only recently an electricity station near East London had been blown up, and a customs post on the border with Zimbabwe had suffered the same fate. Du Plessis insisted the Reserve Bank would make an ideal target for a terrorist attack. The publicity value alone would be enormous—'Bomb at apartheid's financial citadel'—le Roux could just imagine the headlines. The arguments for over-hauling the SARB's security plans were strong, he could see, and he quickly agreed to have further discussion with BOSS.

On that note, le Roux brought the meeting to an end. When the security adviser and du Plessis's assistant had left the room, le Roux turned to du Plessis with a broad smile on his face. 'So, Hendrik, here I am, eh?'

'*Ja*, Piet, and I would like to congratulate you again.' Du Plessis spoke as if to an old friend. 'It is a great day for the Bond.'

'Indeed. And now look at the pair of us. It doesn't seem so long ago that we were just joining the Bond, and today . . .'

Le Roux's voice trailed away and the two men lapsed into silence. They were both thinking back to an evening four years previously. It was the first occasion they had met; but even more important, they had been invited to attend their first Broederbond meeting. The Broederbond—literally, the Association of Brothers—is a secret organisation, the only one not to be banned in South Africa. To belong to it, you must be an Afrikaner, a Calvinist, and male; above all, you must occupy an important position in South African society. The membership is small—only about 8,000—and no one may apply to join. But likely candidates are watched closely by other Broeders, and then invitations are issued to those who have been chosen. The Broederbond's objects are simply stated: to advance the Afrikaner cause, its language, its politics and its culture.

Pieter le Roux and Hendrik du Plessis had become

Broeders in a ceremony which neither of them would ever talk about openly, but which neither would ever forget. Twelve men had been there, amongst them a Cabinet Minister, the Secretary of the Transvaal Teachers' Association, the senior partner in a well-known firm of attorneys, and two ministers of the Dutch Reformed Church. They met on a farm just outside Pretoria. In a barn lit by a single, guttering candle, le Roux and du Plessis heard why they had been chosen to follow in the footsteps of the great Boer leaders of the past. They were reminded of the immutable Afrikaner virtues—solidarity, stoicism, determination. The two men had sworn on a bible held by a solemn *predikant* to defend the Afrikaner *volk*, its heritage and religion. Their incantations were echoed by all the others, voices rising and falling in unison. Then le Roux and du Plessis stood before a table in the centre of the barn, on which there was a bowl, a sharp surgical knife and an old, rusty dagger. Le Roux was instructed to cut the middle finger of du Plessis's left hand with the knife. Du Plessis's blood dripped steadily into the bowl, and he in turn cut le Roux's finger. Eventually, the man presiding over this blood-letting was satisfied. He lifted the bowl, and swirled its contents round, ten times to the left and ten to the right. Then the two initiates put their right hands into the bowl and daubed each other's cheeks with their mingled blood. They swore to stand by one another and by all Broeders, and to work for the greater power and influence of the Broederbond. Then each in turn dipped the dagger into the bowl and turned to a straw effigy propped up in one corner. With a cry of 'Traitor!' they plunged the dagger into the effigy's left side, where the heart would be. This act was repeated by everyone present, and the effigy —of a man named de Klerk, who had given secrets to the British in the Boer War—was then burnt. Finally, the fourteen men stood in a circle and linked their hands above their heads with a loud cry '*Ons vir jou, Suid Afrika*'—'We for thee, South Africa.'

Pieter le Roux rose quickly in the Broederbond hierarchy. He became secretary of the cell in Pretoria to which he and du Plessis belonged; then the Transvaal's representative on the Broederbond executive, known as the 'Twelve Apostles'. Though clandestine, these regular meetings had nothing of the grisly drama of the initiation ceremony. Between ten and twenty soberly dressed, middle-aged men would gather for up to three hours to discuss matters which they considered relevant to the Broederbond. Political strategy for the Nationalist Party in the Transvaal; the likely effects of television on Afrikaner youth; new doctrinal developments in the Dutch Reformed Church; the growing influence of Afrikaner capital in the country's financial system—these and many other questions were raised, always with a view to ensuring that the people concerned were acceptable to the Broederbond. If not, plans would be laid to replace them with more sympathetic figures. Given the Broeders' influential role, these manoeuvrings were, more often than not, successful.

Pieter le Roux's elevation within the SARB was considered a notable advance for the Bond. The financial community had traditionally been dominated by English-speaking South Africans; although the last four SARB Governors had been Afrikaners, they had been essentially apolitical men who were not members of the Broederbond. Indeed the Bond had found it very difficult to influence the Reserve Bank, except through the Government, of course. But Pieter le Roux, with his family background in the Nationalist Party, was an obvious Broeder. Now he seemed destined for the top in the SARB, and the Bond's executive was well pleased. So pleased in fact, that they had chosen him as their Chairman.

Le Roux and du Plessis met regularly to discuss security at the SARB. Their Broederbond membership had given these meetings a special intimacy, and the two men gradually came to hold the same views on security. In his subconscious, le Roux had always regarded the gold reserves as more than entries in an arid balance sheet. Now he began to think of them as the nation's patrimony, with the Reserve Bank in the role of principal trustee. In his new job, he saw himself personally embodying that trust. To his colleagues in the Bank, he explained in a rational way the necessity for improving security, and they were persuaded that money should be spent as he suggested. One or two eyebrows might have been raised at le Roux's personal involvement in security matters, but then everyone knew he was a thorough man.

For le Roux, however, it had become more than a question of thoroughness. One night the previous year, he had had a dream, a dream so vivid that every detail was etched on his mind. He was sitting at his desk in the Bank working. From a distance he heard the muffled sound of drums, and voices chanting loudly. The voices came closer, and he realised they were chanting a war-cry. Now he could hear the drums pounding, pounding, pounding, and feet stamping. He ducked down below the window in his office and peered out cautiously. Below him, Church Square was filling up with hundreds of black bodies, clad in loin cloths and daubed with ochre. They were shuffling their feet, kicking up puffs of dust. Every so often, they would simultaneously leap into the air with a deep-throated roar. Suddenly, there was a rifle in his hand, and he was firing at the advancing black figures. And then he realised he was not wearing a dark suit at all, but a khaki shirt and trousers, stained with sweat and dust. He could feel the gun pumping against his shoulder, though he didn't appear to have hit anyone. The ground was hard beneath his knees, and he shifted his position, leaning on the wagon in front of him to ease the stiffness in his legs. The wagon gave him a curious sense of security, and he glanced quickly round at the circle which was formed by about twenty wagons. Women and children huddled safely in the middle, while their menfolk fired out through the gaps.

Pieter le Roux woke up at that point. His body was bathed in sweat, and his breath came in short gasps. By his side, his wife stirred slightly, and then lay still again. It took him some time to realise he was safe in his bed, and his first feeling was one of intense relief. But he did not go to sleep again for several hours. He lay on his back, staring into the darkness, his mind working furiously. The *laager*—that was the key to it. The tried and proven aid of the Boers down through the centuries, that had kept the marauders at bay. If the *laager* defences were breached—which admittedly had happened, though very rarely—then all inside the encampment were trapped. But then, wasn't it better to die together, defending the Boer inheritance, than to cut and run like so many jackals? Pieter le Roux finally drifted off into a fretful sleep.

The following morning, he felt a little foolish. After all, it had just been a dream. But he found he could not shake it off; he became increasingly convinced that the ox wagons of the last century held lessons for the Reserve Bank of the 1980s. The next time he met du Plessis, he outlined his conception of an ideal security system. Six months later, its installation was completed. With certain modifications and refinements, du Plessis had translated le Roux's ideas into reality. The most modern equipment had been bought from the United States, West Germany and Japan. No expense had been spared. A number of people were familiar with parts of the system—the manufacturers of the equipment for example, and the SARB security staff. But only du Plessis and le Roux understood how it all fitted together, and they knew they had turned the Reserve Bank into an impenetrable fortress. Inside that fortress there lay a sizeable proportion— on occasions, even a majority—of the world's official gold reserves. Access to those reserves was effectively in the hands of Pieter le Roux and Hendrik du Plessis. No one knew this. Some people knew—but wouldn't say—that le Roux was now Chairman of the Broederbond, and that he and du Plessis were bound to one another by a solemn oath.

15

DURBAN

October 30th

The sun was deliciously warm. The waves were rolling in rhythmically from the Indian Ocean, their white crests sparkling. Caroline Manning was stretched out on a rubber lilo about twenty yards from the edge of the sea. By her side was a large glass of something called Durban Delight, with ice and fruit floating on top. She had changed in a beach cabin, and was pleased to find enough remained of her Riviera tan to disguise the fact that she had just arrived. Two hours of toasting like this more than made up for the cost of her flight.

And all the writing. For the past forty-eight hours she had probably worked harder than she had ever done before, as a journalist anyway. A string of interviews, interspersed with scribbling into her notebook. Then back to a dingy hotel room, to sit up until three a.m. composing stories and swallowing cups of coffee and sandwiches. The finished products weren't too bad, considering how quickly they had been written. She had the journalist's knack of changing her style to suit the publication—deeply-felt outrage for the *Guardian* story, racy and fact-filled for the *Investor's Chronicle*, thorough and measured for the *Sunday Times*. By the time she had filed the last story at the UPI office in Jo'burg that morning, she had hammered out 12,000 words. The effort had temporarily exhausted her; but now, as she turned over to brown her back, her spirits were reviving. If anything came of the session with Arbruck, the *Wall Street Journal* fee alone would pay most of her travelling expenses. She could write that and two more pieces on the flight back to London, or even over the weekend if necessary.

She realised she was automatically assuming that her best

bet was to follow James Glendinning back to London, though she still had no solid reasons for thinking this. Sure, there was something going on which Glendinning wanted to hide from her—but that was as much as she knew. There were a hundred questions still to be answered, she decided, and it was no good bothering with any of them right now. Draining her glass, she ambled down to the sea and into the water. A bronzed youth with short hair whistled at her. Caroline took no notice, but as she kicked out into the ocean, she had to admit that the whistle was mildly flattering, even if it did come from a nasty little racialist.

Four hours later she was sitting in the back of a taxi as it drew up outside some huge wrought-iron gates, over which hung a sign, 'Bar Four Stud'. The gates were closed, and the taxi driver hooted impatiently. A stolid black man in a grey uniform with the Bar Four Stud crest—a leaping stallion—on the breast pocket emerged from a hut to see what they wanted. Caroline leant out of the window and shouted that she had an appointment with Mr Arbruck. The man consulted a board he was carrying, then pressed a switch on the gate post and the gates swung silently open. As the taxi crunched up the long gravel drive, Caroline was relieved to find she was thinking clearly again. The sun, the swimming, and two more Durban Delights had combined in a most agreeable way, so that she had been very loath to leave the beach at all. Fortunately, the lethargy had gone now. She was wearing a blue and white checked shirt and white jeans, both rather too tight. Her contact in Jo'burg had informed her that Arbruck, as well as breeding horses, was himself reputed to be 'an enthusiastic stud'. Certainly he should be easier to string along than James Glendinning, she reflected.

The car turned a corner round a long line of blue gums, and started down a gentle hill. The Bar Four Stud was spread out below her. The sight of it temporarily took her breath away. The main house was in mock-Spanish style, very large and very pink. White railings surrounded green fields, and lines of stables stretched out on either side of the house. In the early evening sun, the entire effect was like a stage set for a Hollywood extravaganza of the 1950s. The taxi drew up at the front of the house, and Caroline paid the driver off with a handful of notes and a cheerful wave. Then she picked up her bags and, hoping her apprehension was not too obvious, marched up to the front door. It was adorned with the words 'Welcome to the Bar Four Stud', with the rearing stallion motif underneath it. An impassive black face answered the bell, took her luggage and showed her into the hall. The furniture and pictures were doubtless the most expensive items to have passed through Sotheby's Johannesburg showrooms. But what artistic merit they possessed was overwhelmed by the walls and carpet, which were as pink as the outside of the house. Caroline stared round her in amazement.

'You must be Caroline Manning.' Caroline recognised the voice of Arbruck's secretary and turned round to greet her. 'Hi, I'm Madeleine Stewart, I hope you've had a good trip.' The girl and her surroundings were a perfect match. She was wearing a pink halter-necked top, and pink jeans. Her hair was as blonde as modern chemistry would allow, and piled high on top of a pert little face with a vacuous expression. Caroline guessed that her typing speeds would be negligible, but that she managed to make up for this deficiency in other ways.

'Let me show you out to a rondavel. Lazarus!' She screamed so loudly that Caroline jumped. The servant who had opened the front door scurried in. 'Take madam's cases out to the rondavels.' For someone so brainless, Madeleine Stewart was surprisingly adept at giving orders to blacks—just the way white Americans had behaved before the blacks started burning Whitey's cities, Caroline thought, as she followed the girl into the bright sunshine.

The rondavels were set about two hundred yards behind the main house, on the other side of a magnificent garden. A dozen sprinklers were watering the lawns and flower beds, the drops glistening in the sun. After the horror of the house, it was a colourful, harmonious scene, and Caroline ignored

Madeleine's chatter as she drank it all in. There were four rondavels, whitewashed and round with conical thatched roofs. They were set at each corner of a massive rectangular swimming pool. Madeleine led the way into one, and Lazarus put the luggage on the floor and retreated. It was beautifully cool inside, and Caroline noticed with relief that there was no pink in evidence. Apart from the leaping stallion on all the bedclothes and towels, the person who designed the rondavels had had some idea of how to use money to good effect.

'There's a shower and toilet in there.' Madeleine pointed at a door off the bedroom. 'And the fridge has got some cold beers and ice for the bourbon. Why don't you unpack while I go and tell Mr Arbruck you've arrived? He'll be in his study—the pink door to the left of the long flower bed.'

As she unpacked, Caroline's mind ranged angrily over what she'd seen. That stupid bitch, ordering the black servants around. They probably lived their lives in some squalid compound, while this luxury was saved for the occasional guest—who would be white, of course. And where the hell had Arbruck made his cash? A large part of it in South Africa, from the sweat and blood of the miners and the workers on his sugar plantations.

Steady now, she told herself, remember you're from the *Wall Street Journal*. She picked up a note pad and pen, pushed a pair of enormous dark glasses back into her hair, and wandered slowly towards the house. Nerving herself against the prospect of more horrific pink, she knocked loudly on the study door and walked in.

The study was indeed pink, but that was not the most striking thing about it. Caroline's contact in Jo'burg had not told her what Arbruck looked like, and as he rolled across the room to greet her, she was temporarily stopped in her tracks. Cornelius J. Arbruck was undoubtedly the largest man she had ever seen. He was dressed in a khaki safari suit, and knee-length cowboy boots, complete with gleaming silver spurs. Great patches of sweat stained his jacket, which was stretched tight across his massive blubbery form. His head was almost completely bald, and his neck had long since disappeared under mounds of flesh. Two piggy brown eyes and a slit of mouth broke up the swollen lump of flesh which passed for his face. But Mr Arbruck's appearance did not seem to inhibit him at all. 'Why, hello there,' he gurgled, 'and hasn't Wall Street come up with another winner here! Brains and beauty in a single portfolio,' and he clasped Caroline's shoulders with pudgy, sweaty hands. Somehow Caroline managed a smile, and put on her best New England accent. It sounded very strange against the Arbruck drawl.

'Mr Arbruck, it's a great pleasure to meet you. My editor asked me to convey his best wishes to you.' As she suspected, Mr Arbruck was a snob.

'Well, isn't that very courteous of him. But I'm still mighty glad he chose to send you out here rather than come himself.' He beamed at Caroline, displaying a set of gold fillings. 'Say, why don't you and me go down to the stables to look at the horses. We can talk about business on the way, and carry on our discussions this evening. You are going to be staying the night, aren't you?'

Caroline had recovered herself by now, and decided to play this one for all she was worth. She smiled pertly, ran her tongue round her lips, and cooed, 'That would be delightful, Mr Arbruck.'

'Why don't you call me Cornelius, honey,' said Mr Arbruck, apparently having some difficulty with his breathing. And with a loud chortle, he showed her out into the garden again, and clapped his hands loudly.

A few seconds later a black figure scurried round the side of the house.

'Bring me a big buggy, pronto,' Mr Arbruck roared, and the man darted away again. Mr Arbruck mopped his brow, lit an enormous cigar and put a Stetson on his head. A battery-powered golf car appeared around the corner, the black servant at the wheel. He hopped out, and Mr Arbruck unnecessarily helped Caroline in before wedging himself behind the wheel.

They only had about six hundred yards to go to the first

line of stables, but Mr Arbruck at once launched into the pedigrees of all the horses he had in training. He continued talking loudly as they walked from one stable door to another, patting the soft noses peering over the doors.

'This here is my real treasure,' he exclaimed, coming to a particularly handsome chestnut head. 'Here, boy,' he bellowed at a young African who was walking across the yard. 'You lead Black Magic out so that the lady can see him. Black Magic,' he turned to Caroline, 'won this year's Durban July—the biggest race in Africa, and the proudest moment in my life.' The horse edged reluctantly out of its stable, muscles quivering under the brilliant sheen. It snorted slightly and pricked its ears up. As a teenager Caroline had ridden a lot, and there was real admiration in her voice as she said, 'Well, that is a magnificent animal. What are you going to do with him now?'

'He's about to get his reward for all that hard work. There're mares all over the world wanting an evening with him.' Mr Arbruck winked hugely and shook with laughter. He was still chortling as they got back into the buggy and continued their sedate progress.

Caroline thought it was about time she steered the talk on to Mr Arbruck and his businesses. She was glad to hear he had a dossier in the house on his activities in South Africa —that would make writing a piece very much easier. 'And how do you see the future?' she asked casually, as the buggy headed back towards the house.

'Why, fine, fine. Plenty of opportunities here—just like there used to be in Texas before the goddam taxes went through the roof.'

'You're not worried about South Africa's security?' Caroline pressed the point a bit further, but it didn't seem to affect Mr Arbruck's good humour at all.

'No way, honey. People in this country are tough, and besides, they'll be safe with Uncle Sam. Well, here we are.' They had arrived back at the house before Caroline could pick up this remark. 'Say, honey, why don't you take a swim or something, and then come over to the house about 7.30?

We'll have drinks, a little supper, and then we can talk awhile.'

'That sounds lovely, but remember, Mr Arbruck— Cornelius—I've got to find time to get material for a story out of you.' She grinned naughtily.

'We'll fill a book, you and me.' Arbruck's piggy eyes leered back at her, and she was thankful she could turn and walk away.

Promptly at 7.30, Caroline returned to the main house. She had swum for twenty minutes in the pool, showered and helped herself to a Lowenbrau lager from the fridge. She had looked at the file of papers on Arbruck's business, put some of the most interesting figures into a table, and had begun to write her piece around that. It was a reliable technique: she would colour the story with descriptions of Arbruck, his horses, and South Africa, and the whole would make quite a reasonable article. Even if the *Wall Street Journal* decided not to publish it, she was sure she could sell it to another paper, perhaps in Texas. Now she needed Arbruck to elaborate on what he thought might happen in South Africa, and on his Partners in Progress activities. She was dressed to lead him on, at any rate, wearing a blue cotton print dress with a scooped neckline and a billowing skirt, which would keep him guessing whether she had anything else on underneath. She shuddered at the thought of his fat, moist frame, and determined to stop before the end if it were humanly possible.

Arbruck was squashed into a chair in another enormous pink room, and it was evident he had been drinking quite heavily. He erupted with a roar of delight as she came into the room. 'My, oh my, what a picture! What'll you have to drink, honey? I'd like you to meet my manager round here, Ray Scranton, and this is his wife, June.' A couple in their late thirties got up from a sofa and greeted Caroline in Texan accents. While Ray Scranton mixed her a cocktail, Arbruck explained how the Scrantons had been employed by him in Texas, and had come out to South Africa five years ago, to oversee Arbruck's businesses and his racing stables.

The Scrantons had little chance to shine over dinner: Arbruck dominated the table, ate hugely and drank twice as much as anyone else. When he had got half-way through his after-dinner cigar, Arbruck dismissed them.

'Well, we can't keep the *Wall Street Journal* waiting. Me and Miss Manning have still got a lot of business to get through.' They were lucky, thought Caroline moodily, as the Scrantons departed. She had already decided the evening was a complete washout, and Arbruck the most loathsome man she had ever met. She would keep up the act for half an hour to see if he would confide anything more than lecherous intent. If not, she would let rip, tell him exactly what she thought of him, and leave. Even if she could never write for the *Wall Street Journal* again, it would have been worth it. Arbruck returned to the sofa, another whisky in his hand. His bloodshot eyes ogled Caroline. 'Now then, honey, let's you and me get down to things,' and he lunged a hairy fat hand in the direction of her thigh. Caroline evaded this with relative ease, and said playfully, 'First things first, Cornelius. I've got an article on South Africa to write and I need your help. So tell me: you don't think Western investments are in any way threatened by political instability here?'

Arbruck threw his head back and belched loudly.

'No way. Take it from me: the West is too deeply involved in South Africa to allow any real instability. First signs of an insurrection, and Uncle Sam will be in here pronto.' Arbruck was slurring his words, but something about the changed expression in his eyes made Caroline take him seriously.

'You can't mean that literally?' she began, but Arbruck stopped her with a wave of his hand.

'Every goddam word. Listen, you ought to do your homework better. My kid brother is a four-star general—you didn't know, did you? Vietnam for three years, but now stuck behind a desk in the Pentagon. He also happens to be a big beneficiary of the Arbruck family trust, so he's mighty interested in the security of my investments. You've heard about my plans to buy a big sugar estate up the coast? Well, I got a bit windy over that, so I consulted my brother.' The Texan vowels were fading fast, but Arbruck continued to slosh whisky into his glass. Caroline thought it better not to say anything.

'I spoke to him this evening,' Arbruck continued, 'and he gave me the thumbs up. I don't reckon he'd do that unless he knew something. Reckon we might even have the marines landing at Durban, eh?' This idea obviously appealed to him, and once again he was convulsed by laughter.

Caroline decided to test him a little further. 'Of course, Cornelius, I will treat all that in complete confidence,' she said, her voice serious. 'I mean, you wouldn't want me to put anything of that kind in my article, I expect.'

'No, ma'am, I certainly would not.' With some effort, Arbruck straightened up and his red, sweating face seemed to compose itself for a moment. There was no doubt he was genuinely alarmed that he might have gone too far. He drank heavily, and slumped back on the sofa again.

Caroline's mind was reeling. The intellectual part of her dismissed all this as the rantings of a drunken fool, but the story appealed to the romantic side of her character. It fitted in with all her political beliefs: it would be the ultimate in US imperialism, stepping in to defend the bloated profits of apartheid. It would make fantastic copy as well: mentally, she was already composing the opening sentences of an article which she could claim as an exclusive, the greatest exclusive of all time. Such exaggerated thoughts brought her smartly back to reality. Like any good journalist, she would try to check out this story, but she had to admit there'd probably be nothing in it. Still, the evening might have been worth it, after all, she concluded, realising that Arbruck would now be after his pay-off. She steeled herself and turned to the figure on the sofa. Her relief was so great she found it difficult to stifle a giggle. Cornelius J. Arbruck, multi-millionaire and enthusiastic stud, was fast asleep beside her, his mouth open and snoring gently.

16

WASHINGTON

October 30th

James walked purposefully up to the main entrance of the International Monetary Fund Headquarters on 19th Street. The tiredness he had felt on the Concorde flight had now lifted: he was beginning to understand how politicians could keep going on so little sleep. As long as they were successful, that is; success built up its own momentum, but failure left them exhausted.

Definitely success today, thought James, as he pulled open the two sets of doors, and had a word with the guards inside. This was another reassuring groove. Ten years ago, virtually to the day, he had left this building after a stint as personal assistant to the then Managing Director of the IMF. Outwardly, very little had changed in the building. The same waterfalls in the centre courtyard; the same luxuriant tropical plants, carrying the quaintly American sign, 'Please do not water me, I'm looked after by the maintenance staff'. By a woman employed solely for that purpose. It seemed incongruous in an organisation usually so critical of excessive public spending. James had often wondered what the improvident governments which endured the IMF's strictures (and contributed to its budget) would think of the plant-waterer.

James passed through the foyer to some lifts on the right-hand side of the building. He was met at the top by Rodney Dowling, who had only recently been seconded from the Bank of England to be Richter's assistant.

'Hello Rodney, how are things?'

'Bearing up, thanks.'

'I must say you're looking very well. I was rushed off my feet when I was here, but then my master was perhaps less organised than yours.' They both chuckled: Wilhelm Richter's efficiency was something of a legend.

'I'll show you straight in. Kendall is already here, and it's just the three of you.' Rodney Dowling did not know why James was in Washington, but he was far too discreet to ask.

In an outer office, James gave his coat to one of the three secretaries. The other two did not look up from their typewriters as Rodney Dowling knocked on the main door. 'James Glendinning is here, sir.'

Wilhelm Richter strode across the room, his hand outstretched. 'Mr Glendinning, I'm very pleased to see you. Have you met Dr Kendall?'

'No, I don't think I have.' James shook hands with the two men, and they moved across to a sofa in one corner. Richter's office was enormous, with light wood panelling on the walls. Much of the space was taken up with bookcases, and memorabilia presented to Richter on his travels around the world. The view James had through the glass opposite him was dominated by the Watergate building.

'It might be best if you recap on what has been happening,' said Richter briskly. 'We've naturally been in close touch with your Governor, but we'd like to hear it again at first hand.'

'Certainly.' James's mind was clear. 'Very simply, I've now sounded out the Reserve Bank people. I've made less progress with the black side so far, but I gather you are helping to take care of that?'

Richter nodded. 'The Nigerian Finance Minister is in the building at the moment, and he's going to give you a letter of introduction to Sisekwe, so that you can talk to him again.'

'That's splendid—thank you. Anyway, as far as the Reserve Bank is concerned, their policy looks very encouraging. They want stability—they feel they've got more of that since moving the market to Pretoria, but I am fairly certain they would be happy with an alternative on the right terms.'

'So you think we could interest them in our plans?' Richter leaned forward.

'Yes, but my impression is that we'd do best to approach it indirectly.'

'By which, you mean . . .?'

James weighed his words carefully. 'The whites in South Africa are sensitive to world opinion, even though they pretend not to be. Sir William suggests that we might offer to conduct gold sales in London on their behalf. They would probably take this as recognition—support, even—from the West.'

There was a short silence before Richter spoke again. 'I think I see where this is leading. We could make out a very convincing case for a change without revealing our real motives. We could argue that we don't want political disruption in South Africa to cause any untoward movement in the gold price. That would only make our foreign exchange markets even more uncertain than they are already.'

James nodded. 'The Reserve Bank would understand that kind of line. If I may say so, I think it would be even more plausible if the Fund was directly involved.'

'How?'

'Well, we're really talking about the international effects of an erratic gold price. This would be a legitimate concern of the IMF—indeed, the South Africans would be surprised if only the Bank of England appeared to be involved.'

'True enough. Yes, I agree. I will prepare a memorandum which will propose that gold sales will be handled through London in future. I think it would be most persuasive.' Richter sounded very pleased—with an idea which, James reflected, had been his originally, but which Richter was well on the way to claiming for himself.

'What do you think, Dale?' Throughout this conversation, Dale Kendall had been silently staring out across the Jefferson Memorial, watching the aircraft flying in and out a National Airport. Now he straightened up in his chair and grunted. 'It seems the right approach. Better to have the Fund take it over. But, tell me,' he turned to James, 'how was it out there? Are the whites jumpy?'

'Hard to say. So many of the trouble spots have been cut

off, there's very little news. The people I spoke to were hardly a random sample, but they all seemed pretty solid.'

Kendall blinked behind his glasses, but said nothing.

'Well,' Richter took charge again, 'I'll inform all the G10 Governors that the Fund will draft a memorandum, and it'll be circulated early next week.'

'I've put one or two thoughts on paper, which might be helpful,' James ventured.

'Yes, thank you.' Richter was on his feet. 'Dale, many thanks for coming over. I'll keep in touch.'

Dale Kendall nodded a goodbye at both men, and walked out.

'A man of very few words, as you will have gathered.' Richter's mouth curled slightly. 'Anyway, let's see about this introduction to Sisekwe for you.'

While James was meeting the Nigerian Minister of Finance, Dale Kendall was at the State Department, talking to John Curzon. Kendall reported briefly on what he had just heard —so briefly that the two men spent only fifteen minutes together. The Secretary of State seemed satisfied with Kendall's account, and shook him warmly by the hand as he showed him out. Then he returned to his desk, picked up a red telephone and said, 'Get me the President, please.'

17

LONDON

November 1st

The tentacles of BOSS spread far beyond the borders of South Africa itself. During the 1970s, there were frequent revelations in the Western press of BOSS activities in Britain, France, West Germany and the United States. In London, Liberal and Labour MPs often asked questions in Parliament about these activities. The Government spokesman would express abhorrence of BOSS, but usually went on to say that there was no firm evidence on which to base a prosecution, or even a diplomatic protest. 'If my honourable friend would furnish me with the facts which lie behind his question, the Government would consider . . .' And the honourable friend would send him details of how a constituent's flat had been broken into and some documents stolen. The constituent was an exiled South African; it couldn't simply be coincidence. But neither was it proof, so the complement at the South African Embassy remained the same, and half a dozen attachés continued at their posts. Their working lives did not correspond to their job descriptions, but the Foreign Office chose not to point this out.

Johannes du Toit was a commercial attaché at the South African Embassy, and this morning he was at Terminal 1 at Heathrow Airport. He stood at a bookstand, idly flicking through a paperback bearing the ambiguously alluring title *Hot before Noon*. Du Toit was a man of limited intelligence, but his brain was quite capable of concentrating on several things at once. His main interest this morning was the arrival of BA 523 from Basle. The flight was overdue by fifteen minutes, but du Toit was not an impatient man. He glanced at his watch, and walked casually over to the arrivals area.

A man in a brown suit with a cap was leaning up against a pillar, looking very bored. Du Toit knew only that he was a chauffeur at the Bank of England, waiting to meet a man called Glendinning from Basle. Du Toit's orders were very simple: follow Glendinning from Heathrow, and then ring Mr Carlson for further instructions. With any luck he'd be taken off this assignment today, and then he'd have Sunday to doze in bed.

The doors from the arrivals area slid open and people began coming out. They were almost certainly on the flight from Basle, thought du Toit, mostly businessmen clutching a briefcase and a bag of duty-free liquor. The driver in the brown suit straightened up and then walked towards a tallish bespectacled man in a grey suit. Du Toit heard him say, 'Mr Glendinning? I'm Parsons, sir, with a car.'

'That's fine. I've got all my stuff here. Perhaps you'd be good enough to give me a hand.'

The two of them crossed the terminal floor, with du Toit following at a discreet distance. Outside there was a dark blue Ford, parked unnoticed on a double line. The driver loaded the cases into the boot, opened the back door for Glendinning and then got into the driver's seat. Du Toit had meanwhile signalled for a taxi, and said to the driver, 'Follow that blue car, please.' It always gave him a secret thrill to say that—it was just like the cheap American films he had seen as a boy at the Pietersburg bioscope.

The drive into London was uneventful. The blue car drove steadily along the M4, and the taxi had no difficulty in following it in the thin traffic. It turned left into Hammersmith Broadway, then up to Shepherd's Bush roundabout, and along Holland Park Avenue. The driver stopped the car in Campden Hill Road, and Glendinning got out, carrying a briefcase. Du Toit hastily paid off his taxi and followed. Glendinning walked along Sheffield Terrace, and rang a bell at Number 11. After a short pause, the door was opened by a man who du Toit thought looked like an Indian. The Afrikaner lit a cigarette and settled down on a nearby bench to wait.

About forty-five minutes later, the door reopened and Glendinning came out. He walked back to the blue car, and for a time du Toit thought he was bound to lose the trail. Eventually he found a taxi, and with some lucky breaks at traffic lights they had caught up with the blue car before it reached Marble Arch. After that it was simple: the Bank car drove east through London to Liverpool Street Station, where Glendinning got out with all his luggage. Du Toit saw him take the 12.15 to Broxbourne, Bishop's Stortford, Audley End, Whittlesford and Cambridge, which left on time from Platform 4. The Afrikaner went into a telephone booth, closed the door and dialled a number. When his call was answered, he spent three minutes describing in Afrikaans what had happened to an aunt of his, how she had stopped at 11 Sheffield Terrace, and eventually caught the Cambridge train. Then he replaced the telephone, and bought the *Evening Standard* to see if there were any good skin-flicks on at the cinema. He had completed his mission, and need not worry about Glendinning again.

In a flat just off the Embankment, John Carlson was listening to a tape recording of the conversation he had just had with du Toit. He made the occasional note as du Toit's voice droned on. When the tape clicked and went silent, Carlson turned it off. He went into the kitchen and prepared a plate of bread, cold beef and pickles, with a bottle of iced Lion lager from the fridge. The beer was issued to all members of the South African Embassy staff, and for Carlson it was one of the few perks that really mattered. He had never taken to the flat English bitter, and most of the imported lagers were too gassy and synthetic.

He ate and drank slowly and deliberately, listening to the one o'clock news on Radio 4. South Africa was mentioned only once, and that had nothing to do with strikes or riots. In what amounted to a minor diplomatic coup, the Springbok rugby team had arrived secretly in France for a short six-match tour. Originally the tour had been planned to begin at the end of November, but protests from the trade unions and opposition parties had caused the French Government to announce that the tour would be 'indefinitely postponed'. The opposition, their honour satisfied, had promptly lost interest. France's rugby authorities—assisted, some thought, by the connivance of the Government—had then sprung this alternative tour on an unsuspecting public. This afternoon, the first match of the tour was taking place, against the Central Provinces in Lyons. The opposition had obviously tried to regroup, for the polite BBC voice told Carlson that demonstrators were already gathering outside the ground, and riot police were standing by. Carlson listened impassively. Years of close acquaintance with the opponents of apartheid had taught him not to get agitated. His mind filled with confusion when he was angry, and in his job you couldn't afford to be confused.

He turned off the radio. Two hours to the kick-off. With

a bit of luck, he could wrap up this Glendinning business quickly, and then listen to a commentary on the match. He played du Toit's tape through once more, carefully checking his notes against it. 11 Sheffield Terrace—ANC headquarters; Sisekwe, the most senior man there. The 12.15 to Cambridge: almost certainly Glendinning on his way home—Bishop's Stortford, and then a drive to Little Hadham. It seemed very straightforward. He would go to the Embassy and telex this information through to du Plessis, personally. The latter was standing by ready to receive it. Most unusual to catch him working at weekends. For the life of him, Carlson couldn't understand why this simple exercise should mean so much to du Plessis. Still, that was none of his business, he reminded himself, putting on his hat and coat and double-locking the front door of his flat. Following the Glendinnings of this world, playing international rugby—they were part and parcel of the same fight, the fight to keep South Africa free. Carlson squared his shoulders and walked briskly downstairs.

18

LONDON

November 1st

Neither James Glendinning nor John Parsons, the Bank chauffeur, were aware they were being followed back into London from Heathrow. James was relaxed, chatting with Parsons about nothing in particular, and enjoying being back in England. Even more attractive was the prospect of being home for lunch with Sarah. He had rung her most evenings from wherever he had happened to be, but twice a combination of flying and different times had made this impossible. He had scribbled an air letter to her from South Africa, and sent an improbable postcard of lions in the Kruger National Park to the twins at Marlborough.

There was still one important thing to do before he could go home. He had to see Sisekwe, armed with his credentials from the Nigerian Finance Minister, and instructions from the Governor. Parsons had handed him a white envelope with the Governor's distinctive red ink and his sloping writing on the front: 'J. R. Glendinning—Personal—By Hand'. He unfolded a single sheet of expensive paper and read it through three times.

> 'JRG. Welcome back. As I told you when you were here on Thursday, you have an appointment with Sisekwe at eleven o'clock. You have already got the Nigerian introduction, and I understand word has independently been passed to Sisekwe that you expect something definite from him. As with the SARB, don't press for anything in writing (though that would be useful). I'm told Sisekwe is internally in a strong position and anything he says can be taken seriously. Reputedly, he is also an honourable man, who will not mislead. Good luck. Ring me at Broadwood on Saturday, about 7.30.'

James stared out of the window, his eyes not taking in the rush of traffic on the motorway. 'When did you get that letter from the Governor?' he asked Parsons, who was Sir William's chief chauffeur

'Last night, sir. I drove him down to Hampshire and he gave it to me personally. Never known him do a thing like that before.' Parsons chuckled. They did not speak again until they were driving along Holland Park Avenue, when James said, 'You know I want to go to Sheffield Terrace, but I think you should park the car a few streets away and wait for me there.'

'Very good, sir.'

It was a cold morning, and James walked briskly down Campden Hill and along Sheffield Terrace. After all the travel of the past five days, he felt tired. But as far as he could tell, his mind was clear, and he hoped for more success this time with Sisekwe. Certainly he was better prepared. On

Wednesday in Washington he had met the Nigerian Finance Minister, who had given him the letter of introduction. 'So you will be seeing Robert on Saturday?' The Nigerian had beamed through his thick spectacles. 'Ah, what a man! Please remember me to him with great affection.' They had chatted about Sisekwe for a few minutes, and James had gained an impression of a staunch opponent but an equally staunch friend. 'If Robert's on your side,' the Nigerian was adamant, 'you can be sure it's genuine. He is not a chameleon.' James remembered the straight, hard gaze of Sisekwe the last time they had met, and he did not doubt the Nigerian's judgement.

The door to 11 Sheffield Terrace was opened by the same sleepy-looking Indian, who appeared to recognise James and took him straight upstairs. This time there was no waiting around, and James was shown into Sisekwe's office at the top of the house. The young assistant in the dark glasses was nowhere to be seen, and Sisekwe walked across the empty room to meet James.

'Mr Glendinning, come in,' he said quietly, and shook James's hand.

'Thank you for agreeing to see me at such short notice. May I first give you a letter from a friend of yours—Mr Obugwe from Nigeria.' James took an envelope from his briefcase and put it on the desk in front of Sisekwe.

The African picked up a paper knife, slit open the envelope, and read quickly through the letter. 'Yes, I spoke with Obugwe on the telephone yesterday. He was not quite sure what you want to see me about, but he assured me you were OK. In fact,' Sisekwe flashed a smile, 'he said you were "the genuine article"—which I had suspected anyway. But you will understand I cannot be too careful.'

'Of course. I apologise if I put you in a difficult position the last time we met.'

'Not at all. Well now, Mr Glendinning, we can talk openly. Perhaps you would begin by expalining to me what you are looking for.'

James took a deep breath and began. 'For many years,

South African gold has been sold on the open market, most recently in Pretoria itself. Your country is the biggest gold producer, so its actions have the biggest effect on the market. Now, gold—as you said yourself last time—is no longer a major part of the world's monetary system. But it is still important—some central banks hold it in their reserves, individuals buy and sell it for coins, for jewellery and so on. So long as there is no great shift in anyone's policies, gold's new role seems to be working quite well. Your country earns a substantial amount of foreign exchange, and other countries and people get something they want. If this were to change in some way, there is a danger that the ripples from a disturbed gold market would spread. You will appreciate that those responsible for the international monetary system have to try and anticipate every kind of ripple. This is what I have come to talk to you about—to establish what your intentions might be, what ripples you might cause.'

While James was talking, Sisekwe had been listening intently, his head slightly to one side, resting on his hand. Now he got up from his chair, and walked over to the window. James stayed silent, waiting for his reaction. At length Sisekwe spoke. 'Mr Glendinning, I understand what you are saying—and let me say I think your concern is understandable, legitimate. Since we last met, I have spoken to a friend of mine—I think I told you about him. He works for the central bank in Ireland, and knows much more about these things than I do. It is important to distinguish between two aspects of the ANC policy on gold—such as it is.' He turned to James, and for a moment his expression was that of a tired man. 'First, the domestic question. It will be an absolute priority of a democratic government in South Africa to re-organise the gold mines. Wages will be raised, working and safety conditions improved, the migrant labour system will be abolished. Whether this is done by taking over the gold mines—nationalising them—or through the agency of the mining companies need not immediately concern us. The international question is separate: how will we dispose of the gold we have mined? On balance, I think, we will continue

134

to sell through the usual channels, to buyers throughout the world. This I imagine is what you want to know, and you will probably find that reassuring.'

James nodded, but Sisekwe continued. 'Let me tell you why our minds are working that way. Two reasons: first, we have never underestimated the capacity of white South Africa to exploit every situation to their advantage. If they have chosen to sell gold in a particular way, it is because it will be more to their benefit than any other way. We have the same general motive, though its operation will be quite different: we aim to ensure the maximum return for our country. Not so that return can go straight into the pockets of a privileged few, but so there will be as much as possible to spread around amongst all our people—in wages, yes, but also in hospitals and schools.' Sisekwe's voice was steady but James now sensed the passion building up in the man as he spoke.

'The second reason is this. We do not want to be shackled. We will not throw off our chains only to submit to another form of slavery, less obvious perhaps, but just as real. Deals with particular countries—bilateral deals—are, we think, the stuff of neo-colonialism. If we agree to sell all our gold to a single country or buyer—or even a group of them—we will be tying our hands. If the contract price is lower than the world price, the buyer is naturally not keen to change—and we lose out. If the contract price is higher, then in one sense we gain: but we would lose in another more important way. We would lose our independence—to criticise, if necessary— and we become beholden to the buyer. When all these factors are taken into account, we are inclined to take our chance with the world market. Now,' he raised a hand, as though to prevent Glendinning speaking, 'that does not mean we shall sell regardless of price. If we consider the price is too low, we can behave like workers in a trade union—they can with- draw their labour, we could withhold our gold. But that's not uncommon, is it? OPEC, CIPEC—they've all done it. The lesson we learn from OPEC is that they were too greedy, and in the long run buyers were able to do without their expensive oil. We would not fall into the same trap. I can assure you of that.'

Sisekwe had finished speaking, and for a time the two men sat in silence. It had been an impressive performance, James admitted to himself. No ranting, no ideology. Just a man with presence and a love for his country, who seemed to have his ideas worked out.

'You have made yourself plain, Mr Sisekwe, and I am most grateful. I don't think I can add much. I hope I am right to conclude that whatever gold's future, you think it will be determined by much the same influences as we have seen in the past. That will greatly assist me and many others concerned with the world's monetary system. Of course, I would not expect you to commit yourself any more than you have done already. The future is uncertain—'

'And more uncertain for me and my people than for you,' cut in Sisekwe, his voice suddenly harsh.

James realised his mistake: here he was, a smooth, well-fed central banker, secure in his world, talking to a man exiled from his country, who could just as likely be killed as end up as President. Who the hell was he to talk about an uncertain future? He hastened to correct himself. 'Of course. I know what your position is like, and if I may say so—' he hesitated —'I have sympathy with it. I was only saying that our meeting has cleared up some uncertainty for those I represent.'

Sisekwe's face lost its sternness, and his voice when he spoke was weary. 'Good. I wish I could say the same for me.' For a moment his eyes, brown and liquid and infinitely patient, held James, and then he straightened up and said briskly, 'Goodbye, Mr Glendinning. I hope we shall keep in touch. And one day I hope you will visit my country. But not, of course, until it is free.'

'I would like that very much,' said James, shaking Sisekwe's outstretched hand.

A moment later he was closing the door behind him, and hurrying down the stairs. Out in the street he walked slowly and thoughtfully back to the waiting car. He thought of Sisekwe's words—'But not, of course, until it is free'—and the look of suffering he had glimpsed in the man's eyes. For one of the few times in his well-ordered life, James Glendinning felt there was something really wrong with the world.

19

LONDON

November 2nd

Covent Garden could seldom have heard applause quite like it. Even after the curtain closed for the fifth and final time, the cheers and clapping went on unchecked. From her seat in the stalls, Caroline Manning frowned to herself. She was annoyed, mostly because she had not been concentrating for the last two and a half hours and so had missed a vintage *Tristan*. But the reason for her lack of attention was also irritating. Try as she might to relax, she could not get the business of South Africa out of her mind. She had run through every detail at least a dozen times, and still there was no real pattern. Tonight she really had to get some clue out of her brother.

The applause was dying away, people were getting up from their seats, and the aisles were beginning to fill. 'Wasn't that quite splendid?' Charles Trehearne said enthusiastically, taking Caroline's hand and squeezing it. 'I am glad you came back in time for this—there's no scoop in the world which would compensate for missing it.'

'Sure thing,' said Caroline, emphasising her American accent, which always drew a smile from Charles. She hoped he hadn't noticed how little she was taking in, and made an effort to appear carefree. 'It's given me quite an appetite, anyway. It's funny how just sitting there can make you hungry.'

'All the passion, that's what it is. "If music be the food of love" and all that.' They shuffled their way out of the theatre and into the street. It was a cold night, but dry, and they decided to walk the short distance to *L'Opera* restaurant in Great Queen Street, where Charles had booked a table.

The restaurant was warm and inviting, and they ate and drank slowly, talking easily about inconsequential things. By the time she had worked her way through a mound of mussels, Caroline had shed her earlier mood and forgotten South Africa. It was one of those evenings when she could easily weaken if Charles raised the question of marriage—as he almost certainly would. They were getting on perfectly, she felt happy and relaxed with him, and it hardly seemed to matter that he didn't hold the same political views. As a matter of fact, Charles refused to get exercised over politics at all—which, she reflected, might be preferable to a rampant right-winger or a soggy social democrat. Charles simply believed that politicians and political activists, like everyone else, were motivated by a mixture of self-interest and altruism. The only difference was that they had an overdeveloped sense of self-importance. This was true whether they were left- or right-wing; the actual policies they proposed, and in some cases implemented, had much less effect on people's lives than they liked to imagine. Caroline pretended to find this attitude outrageous, but privately she was prepared to admit there could be something in it.

They lingered over coffee, neither of them wishing to break the spell of the last hour. Charles asked if she would be coming back to his flat that night. Caroline was about to nod dreamily, when she remembered the call she had to make to her brother.

'Do you mind if we go to the Barbican instead? I've got to make a call to Washington, and tomorrow I'm on television, remember?' Charles's expression showed his displeasure, but he said nothing. 'Anyhow, you know you really prefer the view from my flat,' she teased.

'But your bed's not so comfortable,' he replied, smiling to concede defeat in the little game they had played so often. He beckoned to a waiter, paid the bill, and they walked out of the restaurant arm in arm.

Fifteen minutes later they were back in Caroline's flat.

138

'Why don't you go to bed, huh?' She kissed him gently. 'I'll be along just as soon as I've spoken to Paul.'

'OK.' Charles returned her kiss and walked slowly across the room.

'You can use my toothbrush,' she shouted at him, as he closed the door. For a few seconds she sat gathering her thoughts. Her mind, lulled by claret and undemanding conversation, began to focus again on South Africa. She picked up a note-pad and pen and went over to the telephone. She dialled a Washington number and was rewarded with a click and complete silence. 'Damn you,' she said aloud, not sure whether to curse the British or American telephone systems. At the third attempt she was rewarded, and imagined the bell ringing in her brother's Washington apartment. She glanced at her watch it would be seven p.m. there.

Paul Manning was two years older than Caroline. As children they had been very close, and the bond between them had survived Caroline coming to live in London. Paul was an academic—a Professor in the Law School at the University of Maryland. He was very clever, but possibly too self-effacing to be really successful. Top academics had to be just as competitive, even ruthless, as their counterparts in business. Caroline had rung Paul from Jo'burg yesterday, to ask if he could find out anything about American policy on South Africa. After what Arbruck had told her, she had hinted there might be some contingency planning in the Pentagon or the State Department. Did this have any status? Had there been any new developments? She knew Paul himself couldn't answer these questions, but she also knew he had a lot of friends from his college days who had gone into government service. Many had been radicals then: even if their radicalism had been watered down, Caroline felt confident they would at least believe in 'open government'. That, as far as newspapermen were concerned, meant being prepared to talk off the record about things which the public had a legitimate right to know. Paul had promised to see what he could dig up. Now she was going to discover whether this was another part of the jigsaw.

'Hello.' Thank God, the line was good. 'Paul, it's Caroline. How are things?'

'Fine—you caught me just in time—I was about to take a shower.'

'Paul, any news?' She was already impatient to know.

'Not a great deal.'

Damn him, he sounded almost casual about it.

'Or perhaps a lot—depends on how you look at it.'

'Paul, would you stop talking in riddles and tell me what you've found out.'

'OK, OK, keep your hair on and I'll tell you. I've been on to a number of friends in the State and elsewhere.' 'Elsewhere' was the term they used for the Pentagon: they had developed a simple code as students, when it was part of the mythology that everyone in the radical movement had their telephones tapped. It made them all feel as though they were living dangerously. Even now Caroline felt a quick thrill as they slipped back into the old language, making their voices sound as natural as possible.

'No one is saying much,' Paul continued. 'Of course, there always have been contingency plans for the South—that's nothing new. But apparently these have been dusted down in the last week, though no one's quite sure why. There seems to be a bit of a blanket over everything—probably scared of Mr Hill.' That was a reference to the Congress, with its buildings on Capitol Hill.

'Any idea what these contingencies involve?' Caroline's interest was aroused, but at the same time she could feel her disappointment growing. He wasn't really going to tell her much she hadn't already guessed.

'Well, a whole range of possibilities, from strike through to polite diplomatic gestures.'

'And which one is attracting most attention?'

'That's the interesting thing. I meet a blank wall on that. Either the guys genuinely don't know, or they do know but aren't telling.'

'But why shouldn't they tell?' Caroline demanded impatiently.

'Search me. My guess is there might be something big which we'll all know about pretty soon, so they reckon it's fair to keep quiet for a couple of days.'

'Paul, could you do one more thing for me? Could you find out exactly where all the fleets are at the moment, what they're doing, how many ships, people and so on. I'm only interested in the ones which could go down South.'

'Now, look here, Caroline . . .' Paul's voice tailed off, and she sat waiting, smiling at the thought of her brother debating with the lazy side of his nature. 'OK, OK. What's the best way of going about this?'

Caroline paused, thinking. 'I guess the front door. Call the State, or elsewhere, and ask them. If necessary, get one of the Hill family to ask. Do you think you could do that tomorrow?'

'Tomorrow! OK, I'll do it.'

He was still reluctant and she chipped in immediately, 'I knew you would. You're OK, Paul—you'll get your reward. I'll call you back around midday—your midday, right?'

'Right. There's one consolation anyway.'

'What's that?'

'You're paying for the calls. Good night.'

Caroline chuckled softly as she replaced the receiver. She had known she could rely on Paul, and he hadn't let her down. Still, when you analysed it, what had he said that she didn't already know? Very little. Sure, they were alerted in the State Department and the Pentagon—but that's what bureaucrats were paid for—to be ready for contingencies. And yet . . . somehow, her conviction that something big was afoot had been reinforced by what she had heard. From her student days, Caroline had been a firm believer in the conspiracy theory of politics. Everything always linked up—the real challenge was to find the links. The *Washington Post* had found them over Watergate. But Watergate hadn't signalled the end of conspiracies—merely made the conspirators more careful to cover their tracks, and so made her job more difficult. But Glendinning, gold, Arbruck, his brother, the State Department—these would link up, too. She was sure of that: her problem was to convince an editor, at least to the point where he was prepared to take a risk for the greatest scoop since Watergate . . .

Whoa, girl, she told herself, and got up from her chair. All that could wait until morning. Things always looked different in the morning. She switched off the lights in the flat, and quietly opened the bedroom door. A light from the bathroom shone dimly on to the bed, showing Charles stretched out and fast asleep. Caroline undressed, smiled down at the peaceful expression on his face, and shook him gently by the shoulder.

'Mean of me to wake you, Charlie Boy. But you know what they always say?' Charles grunted and turned his face into the pillow. 'You've got to be cruel to be kind.' She brushed her breasts against his shoulder.

Charles turned over and kissed her. 'Well, it was cruel. I was having a lovely dream. But now I appreciate your kindness—this is far better than any dream.' He ran his hands over the silky smoothness of her belly. 'Did you have any luck with Paul?'

'Too early to say. But I'm hopeful.'

'You're always hopeful, that's partly why I love you.'

He drew her down beside him. 'And if you succeed this time, will you be satisfied? Will you give it all up and marry me?'

'And be faithful to you and your farm, for evermore?'

'Yes, that's the idea.'

'One day, my darling,' Caroline held him very close, 'I'll probably come with you, but right now, unless you're quick, I'm going to come without you.'

20

NAMIBIA

November 2nd

In the afternoon heat, the flies seemed the only living creatures with enough energy to move. For the last hour they had been directing their attention at a rotund figure who lay dozing, slumped in a hammock which was precariously suspended between two trees. Captain Felipe Guardia was in charge of a small contingent of Cuban soldiers, stationed in Southern Namibia. Every day they left their camp to patrol within a radius of ten miles, which took them right up to the border with South Africa. Once a week they participated in joint exercises with other groups of Cuban soldiers, under the command of Russian advisers. The term 'advisers' was a standing joke amongst the Cubans; it seemed to imply some choice as to whether the advice would be taken or not.

Today, however, was Sunday. No joint exercises; no serious patrolling; above all, no Russians telling him what to do. If it hadn't been so hot, Guardia's contingent would probably have travelled the twenty miles or so to the next Cuban encampment to play football. But in this heat ... Felipe Guardia made a vain attempt to swat the flies swarming around his head, and thought longingly of home. They had been out here six months now, but it had all been playing at soldiers, without any action or excitement. Seven years ago, in Angola, it had been different. Then he had been involved in some real fighting; and right at the end he had conveniently been wounded in the leg, just badly enough to be sent back to Cuba. But this time there was no fighting and no prospect of going home. Though they had been promised their wives would be joining them, there was still no sign of it. It was all very well to be told you were doing a fine job advancing the revolution, but that was a poor substitute for a warm body to share your bed. No wonder some of his men had taken a shine to the local girls. But that hadn't gone down well with the Russian district commander, who had summoned Guardia to his office and talked humourlessly about the need for revolutionary discipline.

From a long way off, a new sound disturbed Guardia's repose. As it grew louder, he opened one eye and stared across the endless plain in the direction of Karas Berg. A vehicle of some kind was coming along the dirt track, leaving a small cloud of dust in its wake. Guardia cursed softly; even if it was only a truck full of Cubans, his siesta would be interrupted. As the lorry drew closer, he could make out its distinctive markings. He swore again, more expressively this time, for the lorry was the one used by the Russian commander. Reluctantly, Guardia lowered himself out of the hammock, and buttoned his shirt over his belly. Veslovsky was a stickler for smartness.

The lorry drew up in a cloud of dust, and Felipe Guardia waddled over to it, Veslovsky jumped down from the cab, choosing to ignore the Cuban's untidy attempt at a salute. 'Good afternoon, Captain,' he spoke briskly in Spanish. 'I would like you to prepare your men for a patrol.'

'What, now?' Guardia's face sagged with surprise.

'Yes, now. Tell them they're unlikely to be returning to this camp, so they should take all their essentials with them. While they're getting ready, I'd like a word with you. Can we meet in that tent?' And without waiting for a reply, Veslovsky turned on his heel and walked briskly away.

Once he had informed his men of the plans, Guardia returned to the tent, to find Veslovsky sitting at a table covered with maps. 'Now, Captain, listen carefully—there is not much time. What I have to tell you must remain secret for the next two days. As far as your men are concerned, they are going on an extensive patrol. Understood?'

'Understood.'

'But,' Veslovsky's eyes narrowed as he looked down at the maps, 'in fact, we are now preparing to cross the border into South Africa. Between now and next Thursday, all the troops stationed in the southern territory will engage in joint manoeuvres. These must be made to appear quite routine—we do not want to draw attention to ourselves, nor must the men know what is being planned until the last moment. But on Thursday our battalions will cross the border by the Aughrabies Falls; our immediate objective is the airport at Upington, eighty miles away. We will have air cover throughout; other battalions will be invading further to the west; of course we can rely on support from the local population. Any questions?'

Felipe Guardia had by now recovered from the shock of having his Sunday afternoon disturbed, but he could not digest all that Veslovsky was telling him. He smiled blankly and said, 'So there is to be fighting at last?'

'Yes—but the enemy will be overstretched, so it is possible you may not see much of it. You need not know the details, but there will be simultaneous offensives along the borders with Botswana, Zimbabwe and Mozambique. It will be a fine campaign . . .' For a moment the commander's attention was diverted by a noisy horse-fly which landed on the map in front of him. 'And as simple . . .' he took careful aim with a ruler, 'as this.' Veslovsky flicked his wrist, and the fly was silenced.

21

LONDON
November 2nd

The lights in Studio 4 had been on for an hour, and the room was becoming unbearably hot. Sitting in an aluminium and sling leather chair of the kind so beloved by television chatshows, Caroline Manning was trying to compose herself. Any minute now a tedious recorded film about changes in the EEC's Common Agricultural Policy would be finishing, and then she would be on, live. It was quite a coup, getting on to 'Weekend World'—after all, it was being watched this morning by more than a million people. This sort of thing was exactly what she needed to turn her expensive gamble of the last week into a financial success. The £150 fee she had been promised might even go towards another trip to South Africa, if things really were as promising as they looked.

She was pulled up by the producer's voice, which came crackling over from a loudspeaker. 'Thirty seconds, to go, Richard. Stand by, everyone.'

Richard Spencer, a pasty-faced thirty-three-year-old, straightened his tie for the last time and patted his hair. He was clearly very pleased with himself. He had got this plum job only six months ago, much to everyone's surprise. His interviewing technique was slick, fluent. But one of Caroline's friends had had the cruel idea of getting hold of a written transcript of his comments and questions. They revealed a complete lack of original thought, and hardly any understanding of his subject matter.

The light turned to red, and Richard Spencer smiled confidently into the camera. 'Well, that is doubtless something we shall be hearing more about in the future. But I'd like to turn now to a subject not so close to home, but, in its own way, of vital interest to us in Britain and the free world.' Richard Spencer was very keen on phrases like 'the free world', which rolled easily off his tongue. 'The position of white-dominated South Africa has for some years looked very exposed—surrounded as it is by independent black countries.'

Typical, thought Caroline: about sixty per cent of South Africa's borders are with the oceans, but mentioning that inconvenient fact wouldn't make what Richard Spencer called 'good television'. Spencer's voice was continuing, '. . . need to know exactly what is going on in Southern Africa. In the studio with me is a journalist who has just returned from an extensive visit to the region.'

Expensive would be more accurate, thought Caroline inconsequentially.

'I will also be talking to a former political detainee, and a member of the ruling Nationalist Party who is currently on a private visit to Britain. But first to you, Caroline Manning.'

Spencer's chair swivelled, and the red light lit up on the camera pointing at Caroline.

'Perhaps you could start by giving us your impressions of the political atmosphere in South Africa—the tensions between white and black, the growing black militancy as evidenced by the recent strikes, and so on.'

And Caroline, putting all thoughts of the beach at Durban and the Bar Four Stud firmly out of her mind, answered Spencer's questions with just the right blend of dispassionate accuracy and human commitment which made for 'good television'.

Eventually it was all over. The ex-detaince and the Nationalist MP had argued heatedly, and this had delighted Spencer. He pretended to be calming them down—'Now, gentlemen, I'm sure we all want to be civilised about this and let everyone have a fair hearing . . .' and then went on to ask another question calculated to have them at each other's throats. Caroline accepted the producer's invitation to lunch in the staff canteen, but the MP and the ex-detainee stalked off. She found herself sitting next to Spencer, who smelled of sweat and after-shave, and twice squeezed her knee. Caroline wasn't knowledgeable enough about television to decide whether it was the producer or the front man who should be chatted up. She didn't want to spoil the chance of another invitation to appear on 'Weekend World', so she laughed at Spencer's jokes, and even appeared to treat his political theories seriously. In fact they were pure colour-supplement stuff—pop sociology with a gloss. As soon as she could, she slipped away, taking care to sign her contract on the way out.

She was bound for a much more important appointment. She waited a couple of minutes before a taxi pulled up, and the driver wound down the window.

'11 Sheffield Terrace, please.'

'Certainly, love.'

She was going to be about twenty minutes early for an appointment with Sisekwe, arranged after some lengthy haggling over the telephone with an African whose name she didn't catch. He had sounded rather hostile, refused to put her through to Sisekwe, and eventually said she could come along and try her luck at three o'clock. Not for the first time, Caroline had thought how much Africa would benefit from a decent firm of P R advisers.

It was only last night she had decided to see Sisekwe. Even now, she was not quite sure in her own mind what she was expecting. As a journalist, her main interest lay in putting together the sort of copy which would be published. At the moment, she was certain no newspaper with a big circulation would carry her story. After all, she admitted to herself, she wasn't too clear what the story was anyway. The bits she knew about didn't seem to connect. There must be a link, or several links, and that was the challenge still facing her— as a journalist. But as a radical, she had lectured her reflection in the mirror last night, her responsibility was obvious. Glendinning was double-dealing: he was negotiating in some way with both the SARB and with ANC. The blacks must be told about this, must be made to realise they were perhaps being taken for a ride. What was the good of a liberation struggle if you ended up with the same smooth crooks who had been allied to your enemies?

The taxi pulled up in the quiet Kensington street, and Caroline paid off the driver. There was a light wind, which picked up the leaves and blew them along the pavement in front of her. She shivered slightly, and pulled her overcoat round her. For the next fifteen minutes she paced up and down, smoking a cigarette. Her mind was working quickly, but reaching no hard decision. She would have to play it by ear. Ostensibly, she was going to interview Sisekwe for what she hoped would form the body of a *New Statesman* article. Hopefully, he would ask her about her trip to South Africa —he might even have seen the television this morning. Then she'd choose the right moment to tell him about Glendinning.

She turned back into Sheffield Terrace, and rang the bell of Number 11. Presently the door was opened by a young African in dark glasses, jeans and a polo-necked sweater. She knew him as Sisekwe's assistant, but he gave no sign of recognising her. He nodded curtly, and led the way up the stairs to the room where last time she had sat for an hour before seeing Sisekwe. Her heart sank. 'I won't have long to wait, will I?' she said to the young man, trying to sound as bright as possible.

He shrugged. 'Dunno. Maybe not.' He walked out.

Caroline looked round the room. The walls were covered with posters depicting the long struggle: people behind bars, people marching with clenched fists, a young man holding a machine gun, proud and grim. The main wall was dominated by two photographs—one of the long-dead Albert Luthuli, in many ways father of the modern ANC; and another of a youthful-looking Nelson Mandela, who had been imprisoned on Robben Island since 1964. Angrily, Caroline wondered what he looked like now.

Her thoughts were interrupted by the young man returning. 'Mr Sisekwe will see you now,' he said, his manner still abrupt.

'Oh, thank you.' Caroline tried to be friendly, but it had no effect. She climbed more stairs and was shown into the room where she had met Sisekwe less than a fortnight ago. He came forward, smiling broadly. They had got on well last time, and Caroline found this welcome encouraging.

'I understand you have just returned from my country. Come and tell me how things are.' Sisekwe's voice was rich, excited.

She decided to mention 'Weekend World'.

'Yes, I saw a bit of it, but unfortunately I only caught the end of what you were saying. But I watched the other two— Viljoen and Ntuli—they had a good scrap all right.' He chuckled. 'Anyway, tell me what you saw.'

Caroline described her impressions, hurrying when she saw any hint of impatience, going into detail when Sisekwe's expression showed particular interest. She told him of the

ANC slogans she had seen daubed on the walls in Johannesburg, and he slapped his thigh with delight. Then his tone changed.

'And did you manage to get news of any detainees, or see any of the black leadership—Duma, Molambo, any of them?'

'No.' Caroline shrugged her shoulders apologetically. 'I was only there a few days, and went at short notice, so there was no time to arrange that kind of thing.' Her Durban excursion was better left out of this. 'My impression is that the struggle is going well, but of course the system is still efficient. Their lives are so carefully controlled . . .' Her voice trailed away as Sisekwe's eyes gleamed for a moment.

He said softly, 'But that means when the time comes, the regime won't know what's hit it. You control a people, and then find they can use that regimentation as a weapon against you.'

Caroline was on the verge of quoting the line from Marx about the bourgeoisie being their own grave-diggers, but thought better of it. The Marxism could wait; right now, these guys needed to get Whitey off their backs. Perhaps this was the right moment to bring up Glendinning.

'There's one other thing I learnt in South Africa which might interest you.' She tried to sound as casual as possible. Sisekwe's face was impassive, waiting. 'You may remember the last time I came to see you there were a couple of men from the BBC who interviewed you first.'

'Ah, yes, Mr Travers—an old friend of mine,' Sisekwe interjected.

'That's right. And there was another man with him—a Mr Glendinning.' Caroline paused, so as to give her revelation the maximum dramatic impact.

'Yes,' Sisekwe got in first, 'but he's not from the BBC.'

'You know that?' Caroline couldn't keep her voice from rising incredulously. She had been so sure she was on to a winner, and here was this man telling her in a conversational way what she had had to travel ten thousand miles to find out.

'Yes, indeed, he told me.' Sisekwe was smiling slightly at Caroline's bewilderment. 'A pleasant man, don't you think? As a matter of fact he was in here yesterday.'

'He's double-crossing you,' Caroline blurted out. She had been so stunned by Sisekwe's knowledge, and by the news that James had been here yesterday, that she had given up all her plans for breaking the news gradually.

'What do you mean?' Sisekwe asked, and Caroline thought she detected a hint of interest in his voice.

'Well, I saw him out in South Africa.' She was relieved to see some genuine surprise cloud Sisekwe's face for a moment. 'He spent a good deal of time at the South African Reserve Bank.' Sisekwe walked thoughtfully over to the window, and Caroline waited for him to speak first. Thank God, it looked as though she really did have something to tell him, after all.

There was silence for a few moments, and then Sisekwe turned round. 'Do you have any idea what he was doing at the Reserve Bank?'

'Not in detail. But I do know he spoke to a Dr le Roux, who, I discovered, is the Head of the Gold Department there.' Sisekwe's eyes narrowed, then he turned away again. Caroline decided to press on. 'I also know that after he left South Africa, Glendinning came back to London, and then went on to Washington, probably to the International Monetary Fund.'

This last remark appeared to make no impression on Sisekwe. Almost as though he had not heard it, he asked Caroline, 'As a journalist, Miss Manning, are you planning to publish anything of what you have told me?'

'Certainly I am, but not until I have a complete story. At the moment there are too many loose ends— no editor will take a chance with it.' She could have bitten her tongue off, realising too late that her next question would now get nowhere with Sisekwe. 'I wonder whether you would like to fill in some of the gaps?'

'Gaps?' Sisekwe's smile was so disarmingly innocent that Caroline could cheerfully have thrown her note pad at him.

'I'm afraid I know no more than you. I'm not even sure there is a story worth publishing.'

Caroline made one last attempt. 'Well, Glendinning didn't come here to talk about the weather, that's certain. If you could tell me what he was here for, perhaps I could tell you more of what he had to say to le Roux.' But the lie was transparent, and Sisekwe wasn't to be taken in.

'Oh, I can't think that what we spoke about was of any interest to you or your newspaper. But I can assure you, Miss Manning,' he walked towards the door, 'if I do come across anything interesting, I shall let you know at once. Thank you for calling.' And with a charming smile, he closed the door on Caroline.

While Sisekwe sat thoughtfully at his desk, his chin cupped in his hands, Caroline fumed down the stairs and out into the street. Damn and blast, you stupid bitch, she told herself. What made you do such a dumb thing? You come here as a radical journalist, and the radical in you plays all your trumps before the hand has begun, and the journalist comes away with nothing. Not for the first time, the virtuous glow which Caroline's radicalism provoked in her was swamped by the gut feeling that she had just lost a skiing holiday in St Moritz.

Her anger persisted all the way back to the Barbican. She hoped Charles would not be there—right now she felt she could scratch the face of anyone who spoke to her. Fortunately he had gone, leaving a crumpled bed and a note to say he would ring at six o'clock. This gave her time to ring Paul in Washington, and cool down. She got through to Paul at the first attempt.

'I reckon I ought to bill you for all this work,' he grumbled. 'Here I am behaving like some second-rate dick, while you swan it in London.'

'Stop moaning and tell me what you've found out.' Caroline was still in a foul mood, and not inclined to listen to Paul's complaints.

'Well, it's difficult to be very specific right now, like this, if you get me.' Paul's tone had her sitting up straight, her interest aroused.

'OK, but do what you can.'

'The front door was closed, completely closed. But I've spoken to some people, whose names I forget'—that meant he didn't want to mention names but they were reliable sources—'and there's certainly something going on. The Fifth has moved out and is heading south, very fast. This wasn't scheduled, but all the original plans have been cancelled. Others have been asked to stand by—no specific reason given—again unusual. Everyone is clamming up, but there're bound to be leaks before long.'

There was silence as Caroline tried to digest this news. The Fifth Fleet . . . moving towards South Africa . . . good God, there really was something in it after all. But surely someone in Washington would have picked up the story by now? Or was this really the scoop she'd half-joked about? Eventually she spoke again.

'Can you give me any more, details especially?'

'No. I couldn't get any more myself—was damn lucky to get this, I can promise you.' He sounded adamant, so there was no point in pushing it just now. But she still needed his help.

'Listen, are you interested enough to keep up the good work?'

He hesitated before replying. 'Well, I guess so. But I've got a hunch that we'll hear something, officially or via a leak, and fairly soon. You've probably got four, five days at most, and I doubt whether I'll find out much more in that time.'

'I guess you're right. But anything which you come across you'll relay on—right?'

'Right. Now, can I go back to bed?'

'Lazy sod. Do you realise I've got to cancel a dinner date, and get down to my typewriter?'

'Serve you right—it's about time you did some of the work. When are you coming home?'

'Never,' she said, and rang off.

While she made a cup of coffee, Caroline went over what she had heard. Reviewing all the options open to her, she had to admit she was still desperately short of concrete evidence. But there was no doubt in her mind that the Fifth Fleet heading towards South Africa was linked to the gold question. The real problem was to prove it. At length, she decided to do three things. First she rang Charles. 'Listen, honey.' She only called him honey to tease him. 'I'm tied up with my typewriter—do you mind if we forget tonight?' Charles moaned, and Caroline said cheerfully, 'It'll give you a chance to wash your socks. I'll call you before I go to sleep.'

She rang off before he had a chance to say anything. Then she took the receiver off the hook and sat down at her desk. She would write out all she knew about South Africa, building it into a major article, with some gaps which, hopefully, she would fill in tomorrow. Success with the gaps would depend on what followed from her third decision—to call on James Glendinning at the Bank of England first thing in the morning.

22

HERTFORDSHIRE

November 2nd

'What do you think this one is—28 across, six letters, beginning with C—"a distant rainbow beckons through the gloom"?' James Glendinning, absorbed in the *Observer*'s leading article on South Africa, grunted absentmindedly, and then sat up with a start as Sarah jabbed him in the ribs.

'You didn't hear a word I said,' she reproached him.

'Guilty, m'lord,' James conceded, kissing her on the nose.

It was nearly ten o'clock on Sunday morning, and they were sitting in bed, surrounded by the newspapers. James filled their cups with coffee from a percolator, and lay back on the pillows.

'What bliss this is. Just think, darling, a week ago I was on that farm, with a thick head and a sore stomach from too much beer and *boerwors*.'

'And what?' Sarah asked in surprise.

'*Boerwors*—it's a spicy kind of sausage. South Africans love it—at least the le Rouxs and their friends seemed to. And now I'm back home; it's cold outside and warm in here, so there's no need to make any difficult choices. In fact I might stay in bed all day. Does that appeal to you?' James reached over and kissed Sarah so enthusiastically that his glasses nearly fell off.

'Steady,' she whispered. 'Remember Mother's downstairs, and we've promised to help her in the garden.'

Reluctantly, James drew back. 'I'm very fond of your mother, as you know,' he said, 'but there are times...' His expression finished off the sentence.

'I know, darling. But she is going after lunch, so perhaps we could have a long afternoon nap.'

Consoled by that prospect, James swung his legs out of bed and walked over to the window. It was grey and damp outside, and the garden was looking at its worst. Last summer's magnificent flowers were all dead; the lawn was covered in leaves, and anyway needed one final mow; and the vegetables hadn't had any attention for several weeks. Sarah came across and put her arm round his waist. They both looked gloomily at the scene. According to their various gardening books, they had a good deal of work to do between now and mid-November.

'Yes, we shall definitely have an afternoon nap,' James said firmly, nuzzling her hair.

While he shaved, James listened to a Brahms concerto on Radio 3. He found his mind going back to what he had been reading in the *Observer*. Most of the leader had been quite predictable, but a few sentences had stuck in his mind. He picked up the paper and read them again. 'Attention in Washington must inevitably now be directed at the presence of the Cuban troops in Angola and Namibia. After being wrongfooted so badly in the 1970s, the United States has had no option but to accept these "guardians of the revolution", while constantly trying to play down their importance. This pretence has never been wholly convincing, but it is plainly inappropriate today. These latest disturbances may provide the Bennett administration with the opportunity it has been seeking to wrest the initiative in Southern Africa away from the Soviet Union.'

Of course, the last sentence could be simply journalistic kite-flying; but until then, James hadn't seen any reference to other countries becoming involved. Surely America and Russia had agreed they would keep out of South Africa? Wasn't that what 'the new era' was all about? The Governor had never mentioned anything about military involvement. But then, how much did the Governor really know?

The happy mood of a few minutes ago faded. When Sarah had met him at Bishop's Stortford station yesterday, James had felt all the cares of the previous week slip away. He was back home. On Monday, he would go into the Bank in the normal way, and things would click back into place. The negotiations preceding Stage 2 would not directly concern him, though he would still be involved within the Bank. But there'd be no more of this cloak and dagger stuff, no more long journeys to keep him away from home. He'd done his bit, and it had been a success. But now he was anxious to be out of it, particularly if—as the newspaper implied—the situation was about to get really complicated. He might then be caught up for weeks.

The thought unsettled him, and he cut himself twice before he had finished shaving. While he was repairing the damage, Wells came in and rubbed against his bare legs. Wells was a sleek black cat, with inscrutable green eyes and a seemingly unlimited appetite, and his arrival cheered James. He scratched Wells's head for him, and the cat made appreciative noises. Wells was one of the numerous progeny of their first cat, whom they had unimaginatively called Bath—because the friends who had given her to them lived in Bath. When the twins had persuaded their parents to keep one of Bath's kittens, James had wanted to call it Oliver, after the biscuit, and Sarah wanted Wells, after the Bishop. They tossed a coin, and Wells it was.

By the time Wells had tired of his attention James was dressed. He went downstairs and found Sarah and her mother at the breakfast table in the kitchen, talking brightly to one another.

'Good morning, Mama.' James went over and kissed his mother-in-law.

'Good morning, James. I hope you're feeling strong. There are some tricky roots in the big flower bed—I've been chipping away at them for a week, with no success. It really needs a man to get them out—and properly, mind you, otherwise they'll choke all your spring flowers.'

James groaned, but not audibly. Then he remembered something. 'Well, I suggest we get cracking. I want to pop in later and turn on the television, just to check if there's anything I ought to see on "Weekend World".'

'A fine excuse.' Sarah grinned knowingly at her mother.

'It's not an excuse at all,' said James indignantly. 'It's normally not worth watching, so I'll probably be out again in a couple of minutes. Anyhow, now it's you who's delaying us. Let's get out there.'

For the next hour and a half, they attacked the garden with vigour. A watery sun came out, highlighting the autumn colours.

'Season of mists and mellow fruitfulness, eh?' James smiled at Sarah as they took a breather.

'Don't remind me—it's something I've got to do at school next week, and I haven't prepared it at all.'

'I bet you could recite the whole thing straight off.'

'Thank you, darling. But I'm not going to risk proving you wrong. Well, let's get back to it—or are you about to sneak off?'

'Lord, look at the time—I nearly forgot. Yes, I'll just have a quick look to see what it's all about. Won't be long.'

'I've heard that before,' Sarah called after him, as James disappeared into the kitchen.

He turned the television on just in time for the familiar 'Weekend World' signature tune, and then Richard Spencer's face peered earnestly at him.

'Welcome to "Weekend World". We'll be taking a look at the latest row which has blown up in Brussels over the EEC's Agricultural Policy. And then we'll go further afield, to South Africa, to hear up-to-the-minute news and views on the situation there.'

That settles it, thought James. No more gardening for me this morning. While Spencer introduced the agricultural film, James went out into the garden.

'Darling, there's something on South Africa in a few minutes. It's frightfully important that I watch it. But I thought I'd first bring you and Mama a drink, by way of encouragement.'

'A peace offering, more likely,' Sarah snorted. 'I think we'd both like a large gin.'

James dutifully brought two glasses out, exhorted them to greater efforts, and sat back in front of the television, with Wells on his lap and a glass of beer by his side.

He was glancing idly at the sports pages of the *Observer* when the first part of the programme ended. He ignored the commercials, and actually missed the first few seconds of Richard Spencer. When he looked up at the television, there was Caroline Manning smiling knowingly at him. For a couple of seconds, James's brain refused to accept the message passed on by his eyes. Finally he calmed himself: after all, she knew nothing, certainly not about him. He had made up a perfectly good story to explain why he was in Johannesburg, and she had believed it. Reassured, he settled down to listen to what Caroline had to say.

She's very capable, he thought. No hesitations, her answers not too long and rambling. Just enough accent to make her voice different from the usual instant experts you heard on this kind of programme. But not too American either. And damn pretty, there was no getting away from it. Even prettier with a tan—wonder how she managed to find time for sunbathing? The thought of Caroline in a bikini was diverting. Pull yourself together, you're not listening to a word she's saying, he told himself. A loud tap at the window interrupted his thoughts. It was Sarah, making a face and holding up his spade. He grinned, shook his head and raised his glass at her.

A few moments later the cameras left Caroline, and Richard Spencer started a discussion with two men. James didn't catch their names, but he knew well enough that one was an Afrikaner and the other a black South African. On every point without exception, they were poles apart. At one stage, James thought they might even come to blows. He wondered whether le Roux and Sisekwe would behave like this if they were put in the same room.

'Who was that bird I saw you ogling on the television?' Sarah asked as they sat down to lunch. 'Now I can see why you wanted to watch that programme.'

'Oh, some journalist or other.' James hoped he sounded vague. 'It was all about South Africa—quite interesting, really.' The conversation moved on to other things— whether they should try planting courgettes this year, and what train Sarah's mother ought to catch. Eventually it was agreed the 5.35 would be the most convenient, which effectively put paid to James's idea of a long nap. They spent twenty minutes after lunch with the newspapers and then returned to the garden.

Digging, James had to admit, was quite therapeutic—at least, it was once you had developed a rhythm. It also gave you time to think, and James's thoughts were gradually swinging back to South Africa again. He still hadn't got used to the fact that nothing about his mission was to be committed to paper. No memos, no notes for the record; it seemed quite unnatural somehow. Still, he had recounted the main points to the Governor on the telephone last night, and he'd go into more detail tomorrow probably. There might even be another lunch with the Directors. The Governor beaming—happy to say the preliminary exploration is complete—both parties consulted—no difficulties foreseen— have reported to G10—very pleased—we can now begin to draft our joint proposals as soon as the political situation resolves itself.

And when, James thought, would that be? The disturbances in South Africa weren't getting any worse, but neither were they petering out. Perhaps the next stage would be delayed for some weeks. At any rate, he now had some time at home with Sarah. And to do this wretched garden, I suppose, he thought glumly, plunging his spade into the earth with surprising aggression.

23

PRETORIA

November 2nd

In the BOSS headquarters in Pretoria, Hendrik du Plessis was sitting at his desk and smoking a cigarette. It was unusual to find him there on a Sunday afternoon, for du Plessis was a man who spent as much time as possible with his family. This afternoon in particular he would like to have been at home. It was his youngest son's fourteenth birthday; he and his friends were going to play tennis, perhaps swim in the nearby public pool, and in the evening there would be a *braaivleis*. Hendrik du Plessis was in his element on such occasions, organising the *braaivleis* and joining in the games. He got on well with all his children, and their friends too. In the boys' eyes especially, he started with an advantage— they needed no reminding that he had captained the Eastern Transvaal rugby side from 1958–62.

Du Plessis dragged his thoughts away from home, and looked at his watch. Pieter le Roux was late, which was unlike him. When du Plessis had telephoned him on his farm last night, le Roux had said he would return early to Pretoria. The report sent to du Plessis from the Embassy in London had obviously aroused his interest. Not surprisingly either, thought du Plessis, as he searched through some papers on his desk and picked out a thin folder. Last Monday, when le Roux had asked him to keep an eye on a man called James Glendinning from the Bank of England, du Plessis had readily agreed. Strictly speaking, he should have got the agreement of BOSS's divisional head for external security; but he had decided to bypass him and ask the Embassy in London to put a man on to Glendinning for a day. Du Plessis hadn't questioned le Roux's interest: the two men had the kind of implicit faith in one another which made explanation unnecessary.

Now he could see why le Roux wanted Glendinning followed. The man had flown from Basle to London and gone straight to the ANC headquarters in London. Du Plessis was not as surprised by this as many whites in South Africa would have been. BOSS watched the comings and goings at Sheffield Terrace very closely, and the list of callers made interesting reading. Even people who were regular guests at the Ambassador's cocktail parties had been seen slipping into Sheffield Terrace, as furtively as a confirmed atheist going down on his knees in St Paul's. This man Glendinning had obviously been suspect in le Roux's eyes, and with good reason. Du Plessis sighed wearily. Eternal vigilance—that was what was needed. Which was where the Broederbond helped. If they hadn't been Broeders, le Roux might not have felt able to ask him a favour; Glendinning wouldn't have been followed; and none of this would have come out.

Ten minutes later, the door opened and Pieter le Roux came in. He was wearing an open-neck shirt and khaki trousers, and his complexion showed he had been out in the sun over the weekend. The two men shook hands.

'Sorry I'm late, Hennie.' Le Roux looked grim. 'I was held up by a road block just the other side of Middelburg. It seems there was an explosion this morning, and the army was called out. Christ, man, it makes you feel so helpless, just sitting in your car while all the young men are out there doing something.'

Du Plessis chuckled, trying to make light of it. 'You're not that old, Piet—your day will come.'

For a moment, le Roux seemed to take this remark seriously; then he smiled and said, 'Anyway, I'm here now. Have you got the report on Glendinning? I'd like to see that first.' He sat down in a chair, and read through the folder twice, his face set. Then he pushed his chair back and exclaimed '*Vragtag!*'

'Before you go any further,' du Plessis's voice was even, 'I also got out one of our files on this ANC building in London, so you could see what kind of company you're in.' He handed another folder to le Roux, who took it and read it through without comment. Then he put it down and swore again.

'Interesting, eh, Piet?' du Plessis smiled bleakly. 'Well, tell me who your friend is?'

Le Roux stared at him with narrowed eyes, as though trying to guess du Plessis's reaction. Then he laughed, a brief, barking laugh. 'OK, Hennie, I'll tell you. You ought to know anyway, and I think you might be able to help.'

For the next twenty minutes, le Roux described how Glendinning had approached him, their conversations on the farm and in the SARB, and how they had agreed to keep in touch. 'But somehow the man's story didn't ring true,' he concluded, as du Plessis sat hunched in his chair. 'I couldn't see why the Bank of England should suddenly be concerned about our gold policy. They kicked up a bit of fuss when we moved the market from London, but since then not a word.'

'So why was he interested?' Du Plessis felt the technical details were going over his head.

'I'm still not sure,' le Roux replied slowly. 'But this business with the ANC confirms my suspicion. Glendinning was out here because they,' he gestured with his arm, as though to embrace the entire outside world, 'they think there's real trouble here now. They've been quite happy to deal with us when the going was good—I bet no one from the Bank of England had seen anyone from the ANC before. But as soon as things get difficult, they begin to hedge.' A cynical smile played around the edges of le Roux's mouth as he spoke, and there was bitterness in his voice.

'The vultures are gathering, eh?' Du Plessis was thinking of all the people who had started to make contact with the ANC.

'It's always been the same with the British,' le Roux said, and for a moment his eyes blazed with anger. 'Well, what can BOSS do about it?' He was silent a long time, pondering his own question. Eventually he banged his fist on the table and said resignedly, 'It's not really the business for BOSS, is it, Hennie?'

'No, it's not,' du Plessis conceded. 'But that doesn't mean we just sit back. Look, Piet,' he was talking quickly now, wanting to change the dejected expression in le Roux's eyes, 'you just said how helpless you feel. But that's not true. Each of us has a part to play. This country's not going to disintegrate if we all do what we can. Being in the army or the police isn't the only thing. Anyway, I thought you intellectuals believed the pen was mightier than the sword.'

Le Roux grinned briefly at this. He'd never heard Hendrik du Plessis deliver himself of such a long speech, let alone one which ended with a literary allusion, however clichéd. 'So what do you suggest, Hennie?'

'That's for you to judge, Pieter.' Du Plessis was reverting to his usual taciturn self. 'All I'm saying is that you're being challenged now, on your own ground, just like the young men in the army. You have a duty to react, just like they do.'

Le Roux weighed up these words, the muscles in his jaws twitching. 'So, I try to outsmart Glendinning. But how can I do that if I don't know what he's up to?' He looked at du Plessis, seeking some assurance.

For lack of anything better to say, du Plessis joked: 'We could always use the security system.'

Le Roux smiled, glad to follow an easier path: 'You mean, lock the gold up?'

'Why not? If we wanted to, no one else—certainly not Glendinning—could do a thing about it.'

That was true. The SARB's security circuit was designed on the ratchet principle—it was easily triggered, but not so easily turned off. Once the alarms had been sounded, the doors locked and the vaults sealed, only a master switch could return things to normal. That switch was operated by a code, which could be dialled in le Roux's office or in the BOSS headquarters. The code was changed periodically—by le Roux and du Plessis.

The two men continued in light-hearted mood. Then le Roux said, 'It would be like a scorched earth policy, I suppose. You don't burn gold, you just lock it up.'

'Heh, that would fix the Brit!' Du Plessis was enjoying himself now, his son's birthday party temporarily forgotten. It was le Roux who first tired of their banter. His features hardened again.

'No, Hennie, I've obviously got more thinking to do. But listen to me. When I've found out what Glendinning's up to, I'll decide what happens. I know I can rely on you for help?'

Du Plessis nodded vigorously. 'Of course, Piet. And it all remains a secret between us.'

'Before I go, Hennie, I'd like to read those reports again.'

'Feel free. I'll leave you to it, if you don't mind. It's my boy's birthday—Johannes, you remember him?—and I'd like to get home. *Totsiens*.'

'*Totsiens*.' Le Roux was already opening a folder, and he didn't look up as du Plessis left the room. For an hour he sat absorbed in his reading. Occasionally he took a note, at other times he stared out of the window, eyes unseeing. When he finally left the BOSS headquarters, he was thinking of the young soldiers he had seen that afternoon. While he went back to his comfortable home in Waterkloof Ridge, they would be out on patrol. Tired, hungry, in danger. Making sacrifices for their country. Feeling curiously detached, as though watching himself from the outside, he wondered what kind of sacrifices Pieter le Roux, Chairman of the Broederbond, would have to make.

24

LONDON

November 3rd

The 8.20 from Bishop's Stortford pulled into Platform 6 promptly at 9.05. The doors opened and commuters spilled out. The week had only just begun, but already most of them were counting the hours till Friday. To James Glendinning however, the routine was welcome today, and he felt positively jaunty as he walked along Bishopsgate. Yesterday, he couldn't make up his mind what to think about his gold mission, but today he was in no doubt. It hadn't lasted long, and he had achieved everything that had been asked of him. The preliminary investigation was over: everyone now knew the views of the whites and the blacks. As for himself, he had come to the Governor's attention: and even if that wouldn't benefit his career directly, the Governor would undoubtedly make one or two complimentary remarks in passing to the Chief Cashier. He had also met people in the Fund and BIS, and this was certainly a plus. Central banking was a small world, even at the international level, and a lot of store was set by personal contacts. Altogether, a most satisfactory fortnight. Now, while there was a lull, he could get on with some real work.

The marbled floor in the main entrance, the messengers, the slightly gloomy atmosphere—all were as familiar and comforting as a favourite old jacket. As he reached the door leading to his office, James wondered whether Miss Higginson would be back yet: that would make his happiness complete. Alas, the inane smile on Miss Barker's face was there to greet him. 'Good morning, Miss Barker,' he declared breezily, hoping to infect her with his mood.

'Good morning, Mr Glendinning. I do hope you have had a good trip. Did you take any photographs?'

'Er, no . . . it wasn't really that sort of trip, you see.'

Miss Barker had a knack for throwing James off balance with a single remark. He made as if to go into his office, but was stopped by Miss Barker.

'Oh, Mr Glendinning, you have a visitor in the waiting room.'

'What, now—already? Did he make an appointment?'

'No, but she said it was very important to see you immediately.'

'She?' James's tone was sharp.

'Yes, a young lady. Now let me see, what did she say her name was . . . '

Without waiting for Miss Barker to shuffle through her papers, James walked into the waiting room and closed the door.

He didn't know whether to be angry or pleased to see Caroline. She was sitting in a chair reading a *Financial Times*, her legs demurely crossed. She gave him a fetching smile as he came in and said, 'I should have known central bankers have easy hours. Do you realise I've been trying to get in here since 8.30?'

James sat down, cleared his throat and tried to sound businesslike. 'I can't imagine how you knew I work here, still less what you've come for; but whatever it is, I have a busy day.'

Caroline smiled again, not in the least put off by this display.

'Well, I too have work to do, so I can't stay long either.' Then her tone changed, and she said abruptly, 'What would you say if I told you America was going to invade South Africa?' The question caught James completely by surprise. He blinked at her, aware that his mouth was open, but temporarily unable to close it. Then he recovered and tried to sound as casual as possible.

'I'd say you were rather silly. Really, Caroline, I've got two weeks' work to catch up on, a diary full of appointments, and no time to waste.'

'Well, it's true.' Her reply was quite categorical.

'How do you know it's true? I haven't seen any reports of it.' James mentally discounted the *Observer*'s leading article.

'That doesn't mean it isn't true. Remember, some journalist has got to be the first to pick up a story, and,' there was a look of quiet triumph on her face, 'on this occasion, it happens to be me.'

He stared at her, unsure what to say. Caroline continued, 'You're the only person I've told. To be frank, I thought you knew all about this, and I need you to fill in the gaps.'

'Well, I don't know all about it. In fact, it seems I know very little. Perhaps you'd care to fill in the gaps for me.'

Caroline found it difficult to size James up. Either he was genuinely ignorant of what she had told him, or he was an exceptionally good actor. After her experience with Sisekwe, she was determined not to reveal any more until she had got something back in return.

'Look, James, we could go on all morning protesting our ignorance. Let me put it to you straight. I am sitting on a great story. I know it's true—verifiable, anyway—but I'm not yet in a position to give it to a decent newspaper. I'd like to be able to say I have corroborative proof from a third party. You are that third party. Now hang on,' she held up her hand as James started to speak, 'I've got some information which directly affects you and all you've been doing in the past two weeks. I reckon you would do yourself some good by knowing about it, and probably a lot of harm if you tried to pretend it wasn't true.'

That point seemed to strike home, and suddenly it was clear to Caroline what her tactics should be. Until this morning, she had never seen James Glendinning in his natural habitat. Last week he had seemed, like her, to be something of a buccaneer—an individual engaged on a risky but exciting adventure. Now, in this cloistered atmosphere, she saw him as a career bureaucrat: an ambitious man certainly, but one who knew full well that his ambitions would be realised through cautious, solid achievement rather than flair. The last fortnight must have been alien to him, putting his career at risk, probably for the first time. She was tempted to feel sorry for him, but this was not the moment to go soft. Instead, while he continued to stare at her, she played a higher card. 'I've already got quite a good story, which I know could be published in tomorrow's papers. After all it's interesting enough that someone from the Bank of England should have seen an exiled black leader, and on two separate occasions, what's more. Even more interesting that he should also have gone to the South African Reserve Bank.'

As she was speaking, James Glendinning's face had dropped and then hardened. Now he could not keep the anger out of his voice. 'Look, Caroline, if you think you can come in here and blackmail me, you're bloody well mistaken. I have got . . .'

Caroline broke in, her tone suddenly conciliatory, 'Now, now, James, just relax. I'm not trying to blackmail you, and anyway I have too much respect for the Bank of England to believe you could be blackmailed. I'm simply saying we can help each other. It's not essential to my story to name you, or even the Bank. I could leave you out of it altogether. But I need at least some idea of what's going on, just as background. It's a journalistic ethic that we protect our sources, so you'd be quite anonymous, I promise you.'

Her words calmed James, though he could see she hadn't really changed anything—the threat to splash him and the Bank all over tomorrow's papers was still there. But it was equally clear he could prevent that only by collaborating with her, or at least appearing to. As for the American invasion, if that were true, even partly true . . . James made a conscious effort to steady himself.

'No, Caroline, I'm sure you aren't the blackmailing sort.' His voice sounded relaxed, and his assurance began to return. 'I'm sorry, I didn't mean to sound so angry. Actually I'm very grateful to you for coming to tell me all this. How can you be sure the Americans are going to invade South Africa?'

'Suppose I tell you that after you've helped me with my story. For instance, did you see Sisekwe and le Roux about the same thing? Was it about gold?'

'I don't know how you know about Sisekwe and le Roux. But listen—I do think you're making too much of this. It's really far less melodramatic than you are making it sound. It's only a minor part of the Bank's responsibility, but we are concerned because London is still the biggest of the secondary gold markets. A number of City firms are involved in the trade, the United Kingdom earns foreign currency from it. I was merely asked to check that nothing would be affected by any change of government in South Africa. That's all— simple contingency planning.' James had rehearsed this alibi so often in the past fortnight that it now sounded very convincing.

Caroline had to admit that his explanation seemed plausible. It helped to answer many of the questions she had puzzled over, but even so there was still something which didn't quite satisfy her . . . But before she had time to put her finger on it and ask anything more, he was speaking again.

'Well, that's my side of the bargain. Now I want to hear what you've got to say.'

For the next ten minutes, Caroline described what she knew and answered his questions. At first he was inclined to dismiss her story as hearsay, but gradually she overcame most of his doubts. She went further in her explanations than she had originally planned to, but decided this was a risk worth taking. She had a strong feeling James knew more than he had told her; and, anyway, he was the best contact she had at the moment.

Eventually he leant back in his chair. 'All right, let's take this at face value. There are still two things I'd like to know. One, when will this invasion take place? Two, when do you plan to start publishing your story in the press?'

'I'd guess the balloon will go up within three days, four at the outside. I'd like to break the story over the next couple of days. Right after seeing you, I'm off to persuade the *Guardian* they've got a world exclusive. With luck they may run it tomorrow. More likely, the editor will hum and ha, put a couple of others onto the story, build up some background, and so nothing will happen until Wednesday.'

While she was speaking, James decided to take a chance. 'Look, Caroline, I might be able to find out a bit more which would interest you. It might fill in some of the remaining gaps. But,' he pondered a moment, 'I don't suppose I would get anything very much today, though tomorrow could be possible. It's just a thought—let me know if it interests you.'

'Certainly it does,' Caroline replied immediately, 'but you'd have to tell me what kind of thing it might be.' When James made no reply. she said softly, 'Like why you went on to Washington to see the Fund.'

James's head swung round sharply. 'How do you know that?'

She smiled innocently at him. 'Oh, come on, James, you know I never disclose my sources.' She stood up, smoothed her skirt and said sweetly 'You can reach me at the *Guardian*. Otherwise, I'll call you this afternoon.' With another smile, she was gone.

For some time James sat motionless, frowning at the wall. He could not decide what to make of Caroline's story. It sounded far-fetched, but on the other hand she was a serious journalist. She wouldn't waste her time following a trail if she felt there wasn't enough in it to get published. Yet she seemed quite confident of getting it into the *Guardian* within the next couple of days. It would doubtless be hedged around—'usually reliable sources . . .' 'enquiries suggest . . .' 'it is understood . . .'—but the basic message would be clear, and would have been thoroughly checked out. He really couldn't ignore it— if it was true, then the gold plan would look very different. Even if the Americans didn't actually invade, their intentions could be enough to quieten things down in South Africa. The whites would be beholden to the West for saving the situation. The Reserve Bank would easily be persuaded to regulate the flow of gold. And the ANC wouldn't really matter any more—even if they got into power eventually, the important thing was to secure the West's monetary system from collapse in the next few years.

That thought stirred James into action. He buzzed the intercom. 'Miss Barker, could you put me through to GPS.

And would you also cancel all my appointments for today? Thank you.' He sat back and pressed his fingers together. The telephone rang. 'Reid, GPS.'

'Oh, David, it's James Glendinning here. I'd like to see the Governor immediately, if that's possible.'

'Hold on a minute, James, I'll ask him.' There was a pause, then Reid returned. 'Would you like to come along, James— he'll see you in two minutes or so.'

'Right, thank you.' He put down the receiver, relieved he would be sharing this with the Governor. The door opened and Miss Barker came in with a pile of red folders. 'I'm going to see the Governor, so I don't think I'll be bothering with those just at the moment,' he said. 'But I would like the *Financial Times*.'

'It was here this morning, Mr Glendinning,' ventured Miss Barker. With a sigh, James got up and walked towards the door. 'Did you happen to notice, Miss Barker, whether Miss Manning was carrying a *Financial Times* when she left here?'

'Oh yes, she was.' Miss Barker's tone was helpful. 'You ought to have asked if you could borrow hers.'

James regarded her wearily. 'Miss Barker, that *Financial Times* was not hers to lend.'

'Oh, really?' Miss Barker's brow furrowed. 'Do you mean she borrowed it from someone else?'

'Yes,' said James, opening the door, 'I suppose you could say that.'

Miss Barker returned to her office, thinking what a strange man Mr Glendinning was. To look at, he reminded her of a dear uncle, now dead—but the uncle had been a much kinder man. Miss Barker sighed, and her eyes misted over as she remembered playing in her uncle's garden near Sevenoaks. Her thoughts were cut short by the telephone ringing.

'Mr Glendinning's office.'

'Miss Barker?' The voice at the other end was friendly and familiar. 'It's Caroline Manning—I was in your office a few minutes ago, seeing Mr Glendinning. I'm a dreadful scatter-brain, I completely forgot to mention something. Could you put me through to him?'

'Oh dear, I do know what you mean, I'm always forgetting things myself,' Miss Barker tinkled. 'But I'm afraid you've just missed him—he's cancelled all his appointments, and isn't here now.'

'Oh, what a shame,' Caroline replied. 'Still, I suppose it's my fault. I'll try again later perhaps. Thank you, Miss Barker, and goodbye.'

Caroline Manning put down the receiver in the public call box in Moorgate. 'Very interesting,' she murmured thoughtfully. Then she picked up her purse and put it into her bag. 'Miss Barker, you're a honey,' she said in a loud voice, as she stepped off the pavement to intercept a taxi.

25

LONDON

November 3rd

David Reid was on the telephone when James walked into the outer office. He winked at James, and gestured to him to go straight in to see the Governor. James knocked and opened the door. Sir William was sitting at his desk, shuffling through a pile of pink folders. He looked up over the top of his spectacles.

'Come in, James. What's the problem?'

'I'm sorry to trouble you at such short notice, sir, but I felt there was something I ought to let you know immediately —about South Africa.'

Sir William sat forward, his shoulders hunched. 'Go ahead.'

'I've been told—by a journalist I met quite by chance in Johannesburg—that the Americans are planning some sort of military exercise in South Africa.'

He paused, feeling rather silly. Fifteen minutes ago, he had been convinced Caroline was telling him the truth. Now the story sounded hopelessly thin. Yet the Governor appeared to be taking him seriously.

'Who is this journalist? Is he planning to publish anything?'

'Well, it's a woman actually—Caroline Manning—you may have heard of her, she's freelance but quite a lot of her stuff is in the financial press. She has a good reputation for being accurate, so I very much doubt she would believe something unless her sources were reliable.'

Sir William snorted. 'Blasted journalists. They're all the same—snooping about. What are her plans?'

'Well, she's trying to get something into tomorrow's *Guardian*.'

'Tomorrow!' Sir William exploded.

James hastened to explain. 'But I think I've managed to delay her at least until Wednesday.'

'How've you done that?'

'Well, I had to improvise, really—pretend I might be able to help her with some background, but told her it would take me at least a day to get anything.'

'Do you think it'll work?'

'I suppose it could. She is still uncertain what to write and, apart from me, she seems to have no one else to give her a lead.'

The Governor pushed his chair back and looked down at the floor, while James ruefully reflected that this conversation had taken an unexpected course. Sir William hadn't asked him how he came to have met Caroline, nor what she knew of his mission; even more mysteriously, he had taken this news of the American invasion quite calmly, almost as though he accepted it as a fact. Surely he couldn't have known . . . But the Governor was speaking again.

'James, there are two things I want you to do. First, you must go back to South Africa immediately, see le Roux and sound him out on my idea of moving the market to London. Second, you must take this girl, this journalist, with you.

Persuade her the real news is out there, and say you will be able to help her with some contacts. At all costs, she must be prevented from writing about this American invasion for at least a week.' The Governor was speaking hurriedly, and the knuckles of his hands were white.

'But, Sir William,' James interrupted, 'how can you be sure the Americans are going to do something? And even if they are, can we be certain they'll succeed?'

The Governor frowned, got up and walked once round the room. Then he turned and said abruptly. 'Well, you seem to believe this girl. And, as a matter of fact, she's right.' He paused, enjoying the bewildered expression on James's face, then continued. 'You weren't supposed to know, but as you've found out, I daresay I can tell you. I received word from Dale Kendall that something like this was afoot. He swore me to absolute secrecy of course, and we agreed our original plans should carry on. After all,' Sir William was now in full stride, pleased to have someone to share his confidences, 'the blacks' view is still very important. Kendall assured me the United States was not partisan. They don't mind what colour the South African Government is, but they are concerned about Russian influence. They don't think the Russians and Cubans would intervene—Kendall says the State Department reckoned an American show of strength would scare them off, and for a time stabilise things internally—long enough for us to get the gold standard operating, at any rate. To my mind, that means it's the Reserve Bank people we should negotiate with, and Kendall agrees.

'I thought we'd be able to wait until the dust had settled. Beyond complaining, no one can do much about a *fait accompli*. But if the word got out *before* the Americans had moved, there'd be one hell of a row, and they might get scared off. Even worse, the Russians would have time to react. So you can see just how vital it is to prevent the news breaking. That's why you must get Caroline Manning out of the *Guardian* offices and on the way to South Africa as soon as possible. I think you ought to see to that right away. Come back when you've squared things with her.

'Meanwhile, I'll ring Kendall and Richter in Washington, tell them you're going out to South Africa again, and see whether they are happy for you to talk to the Reserve Bank—it's lucky their draft memorandum is here already.' He picked up a telephone and buzzed through to GPS. 'Could you cancel my next appointment and ask the Deputy to take Books for me.' He turned to James. 'Right. Let's get moving. I'll see you back here in fifteen minutes.'

After he left the parlours, James hurried back to his office. He still hadn't fully taken in all the Governor's words. But that could wait—for the moment, the important thing was to get hold of Caroline and take her away before she had time to do any damage. The stakes had obviously risen, but the Governor seemed very confident, and James found that infectious. The IMF memorandum on moving the market to London had arrived, and he could take this with him. But his main job would be to keep Caroline quiet.

That was a prospect which pleased him. For a few days they'd live in the same unreal world in which they'd got on so well last week. Of course, he would have to keep her busy, but there would be time to relax as well . . . These thoughts were interrupted when James reached the door to his office. 'Miss Barker,' he said, striding purposefully into her room, 'could you get me the travel office? Would you also telephone the *Guardian*, and try and get through to Miss Caroline Manning. I'll speak to her as soon as I've finished with the travel people.' In his office, he drummed his fingers impatiently until the telephone buzzed. It was the Travel Section.

'I want two tickets on the first Concorde to Johannesburg, today if possible. One is in my name, and the other,' he paused, not having given the matter much thought until then, 'is for Miss C. Manning. The Deputy Governor will authorise the expenditure, but I'm afraid you'll have to do that afterwards. Could you also book two single rooms with baths at the Carlton Hotel for three nights from the time we arrive there. Could you ring me back immediately—no, I'll hang on until you can confirm the flights.' Thank God

Concorde's so expensive, he thought. The aircraft was seldom more than half full on the South African run, which was reputedly losing British Airways about three million pounds a year. The girl's voice came back, quickly and efficiently. 'Yes, Mr Glendinning—two seats have been reserved for the flight this evening—it leaves Heathrow at five o'clock, and arrives in Johannesburg at midnight local time.'

'That's splendid—thank you very much. Would you ring my secretary with all the details, and arrange the hotel side of things with her as well.' James put down the telephone, which promptly rang again. Miss Barker's voice sounded puzzled. 'I have the *Guardian* offices on the line, but they don't seem to know where Miss Manning is—could you tell me which department she . . .'

'Don't worry, Miss Barker,' James cut in, 'just put me through.' He waited while the line clicked, and then a girl said wearily, '*Guardian*.'

'Ah, good morning, I'm sorry for the confusion. I urgently need to speak to Miss Caroline Manning. She's round in your offices at the moment, seeing either the Editor, or the News Editor, or the Features Editor.' James tried to sound as authoritative as possible, hoping he'd got the titles right.

'Just a moment, I'll put you through.'

The line went dead, then another girl's voice answered. For the next three minutes, James Glendinning was pushed from one extension to another, in a trail that seemed to get him no closer to Caroline.

'Damn and blast this!' he swore, his hand over the mouthpiece. 'This is exactly what secretaries are supposed to do.' Not for the first time, he wished Miss Barker in hell.

Suddenly a very cool voice spoke. 'This is Caroline Manning, can I help?'

'Caroline!' The relief in his voice was far too conspicuous. 'It's James Glendinning. You're very elusive. Look, I think there may be a few things which will interest you. I'm going off to Jo'burg this afternoon, and it would probably be easiest if you came along as well.'

'What, you mean, this afternoon?' She was clearly taken

aback, and James hoped she wasn't going to be put off by the suddenness of his proposal.

'Well, yes, if it's convenient.' He was trying to make it seem the most natural thing in the world. 'There's a seat reserved on flight BA 977—it's a Concorde, leaving Heathrow at five o'clock.'

'Listen, James,' Caroline was beginning to recover herself. 'I'm not in the habit of flying by Concorde, and I can't afford to start now.'

'Well, we can worry about that later. The Bank'll pay in the first instance—it's not overdrawn, at least I don't think it is.'

She laughed softly. 'OK, OK. I'm game—but the stories had better be good. Five o'clock you said? I reckon we should meet at the airport—I'll be in a tearing rush. No, even better, can you leave my ticket at the check-in and I'll see you on board?'

'Well, don't you . . .?'

'No, that's the safest thing to do. Don't worry, I'll get there.' Her confident tone reassured James.

'All right. I reckon we'll stay about three or four days. See you later.'

He put the telephone down, his mind already working out what other preparations he needed to make.

First he went back to the Governor. Sir William had spoken to Washington: Richter was apparently content for James to hand the memorandum over to the Reserve Bank, and a senior IMF official would be going to Pretoria in a few days. After a long talk with Sir William, James rang Sarah at school to tell her of the change of plans. She rearranged her classes, and came up to London on the train with a suitcase for him. By 3.30 he was sitting in the back of a Bank car being driven out to Heathrow.

At the airport, James killed time glancing through some paperbacks on the news stand. Then he rang Sarah to let her know all was well, and to thank her again for bringing his suitcase up to London. He promised to telephone from Johannesburg on Tuesday night, saying he ought to be home by Thursday at the latest. Would she be having her mother to stay again? She chuckled and told him to take care.

Fifteen minutes before the flight was due to be called, James went down to the British Airways desk and asked a bored-looking girl whether a Miss Manning had called to collect the ticket he had left for her. The girl scanned the passenger list: there was no sign of Miss Manning yet. James checked again that the two seats had been put next to each other, about half-way along the main cabin. Then he sat down beside the British Airways desk, so as to be sure of seeing Caroline when she arrived.

Rather earlier than he had expected, the disembodied loudspeaker voice announced the departure of BA 977 to Johannesburg, and told all passengers to proceed to the special Concorde departure lounge. James hurried over to the desk. 'There's still no sign of Miss Manning? Look, what is the very latest she could arrive and still get on this flight?'

'Oh, there's no need to worry, sir,' soothed the girl. 'She could still easily make it any time in the next twenty minutes. But we would prefer it if you took your ticket through into the departure lounge and waited for her there.'

'Oh, very well.' James picked up his briefcase and tried to smile at the girl. But he was irritated, and the look on her face told him that no smile had appeared.

Blast Caroline! he thought, joining a queue of people clutching their airline tickets. This of all times to be late! Still, to be fair, she had said she would have to cut it fine. He had a vision of her rushing across the tarmac just before the doors shut, her hair swept back from her face and eyes bright with excitement. For a moment his irritation passed and he looked forward to the next few days with undisguised pleasure. Then he thought of Sarah and all she had done to help him this morning, and he winced mentally.

He was still trying to sort out these conflicting emotions when the passengers were herded towards another door, which clearly led out to the aircraft itself. Caught in the press of bodies, James craned his neck round to see if there was any sign of Caroline. He glimpsed a dark, determined head at the back of the queue, and a great sense of relief swept over him. He looked round again, but the queue had moved round a corner and was shuffling into the mouth of the aircraft. He grinned cheerfully at the cabin crew, who were parroting their 'Good evenings' with relentless bonhomie. He moved slowly down the aisle, pushed his briefcase under his seat, and sat down to wait for Caroline.

As the line of passengers began to thin out, a dark-haired girl appeared at the entrance, her face turned towards the cabin staff. James put up his hand to catch her eye. The girl swung round, stared rather coldly at James's welcome, and walked past him. Damn it, I could have sworn that was her, James thought, his anger beginning to turn to uneasiness as he realised no one else was coming into the aircraft. He signalled a stewardess. 'I'm meeting another passenger booked on this flight, but she hasn't turned up yet. How much longer till we leave?'

'She'll have to hurry. We are scheduled to close the doors in two minutes, and we can't wait—it's a busy evening and we'd miss our place in the queue. Don't worry,' she added, seeing his expression, 'there's another flight tomorrow.'

James did not find that at all consoling. He debated whether to get off the aircraft and try to find out what had happened to Caroline. Perhaps she'd been held up in traffic? If he didn't go now, what would he tell the Governor? But what would he tell the Governor if he didn't get Caroline out of Fleet Street for a few days? He started down the aisle towards a stewardess when he heard the door slam shut.

Flight BA 977 left Heathrow punctually at five p.m., but the seat reserved for Miss Caroline Manning was empty.

26

LONDON

November 3rd

While James Glendinning was being driven out along the M4, Caroline Manning was sitting at a desk in the *Guardian* offices. She could not make up her mind what to do. If she was going to catch that flight to South Africa, she would have to leave in the next fifteen minutes. So far she had made precious little headway with the *Guardian*. Although her relations with the paper were close, she had always dealt with domestic matters before and so didn't know the foreign staff. She had only managed to see an Assistant Foreign Editor, who had fitted her in for five minutes at two o'clock. The man was rushed—he hadn't had any lunch, and the paper's principal US correspondent couldn't be traced to check out a new rumour about CIA involvement in British trade union elections. He listened half-heartedly to what Caroline was saying, scepticism written all over his face. She probably hadn't presented her arguments very well, so anxious was she to be believed.

Eventually he had agreed to arrange a meeting with the Foreign Editor.

'Some time this afternoon, I expect. As you'll appreciate, he's a busy man, but I think he will fit you in. Now, if you'll excuse me, Miss Manning . . . I'm sure you can find a desk and a typewriter down the corridor, if you'd care to draft your story.' A charming smile, and that was that. It was the old trick newspapermen always used with freelance contributors who claimed to have a scoop: hold things up until it was too late for them to sell their story to any other paper for tomorrow's edition. Then you could relax and study the story in detail.

Her first reaction had been to walk out and head for

Heathrow. She could be in South Africa tomorrow, following up the leads which James had promised her. She'd find the answers to all the riddles buzzing around in her brain, and come back with a real story. Then she'd have every editor in Fleet Street knocking at her door, their cheque books open. It was all most tempting. And yet . . . whichever way she looked at it, something didn't ring true. For all his blandness, James Glendinning was not being straight with her. Why, after she had seen him this morning, had he cancelled all his appointments? Why would he want to go back to South Africa at such short notice? And, above all, why had he booked her a seat on the Concorde, and tried to play down the question of payment? The return ticket must cost about £1,500, she reflected. She couldn't find that sort of money, and he surely didn't believe she could. But central banks weren't in the habit of handing out air tickets to journalists. Perhaps he thought she was on the *Guardian* staff, and the newspaper would pay? She couldn't decide what to make of it all, but she had nevertheless gone back to the Barbican to collect her passport and pack. Now, as she looked down at her suitcase by the side of the desk, the temptation to leave was almost overwhelming.

At that moment, the door opened and a young reporter came in. He crossed over to a desk where another man wearing glasses was sitting.

'Well, what a shower,' said the reporter.

'Oh, hello, how did you get on?' The older man looked up and smiled. They talked for a few minutes, and Caroline could not help overhearing their conversation. She gathered the reporter had just been to a press briefing at the Soviet Embassy, where the foreign policy implications of the recently announced Russian defence budget had been explained. Caroline was beginning to lose interest when something the older man said caught her attention.

'Did they talk at all about the South Atlantic—you, know South Africa, and so on?'

'It's funny you should mention that. Someone asked a question about the Cuban troops in Namibia and Angola—

were they going to be withdrawn, or would their numbers be increased? The man who was briefing us—the Foreign Attaché—had up till then been very smooth—answers to every question. But this one seemed to throw him right out. He went into a huddle with two other guys—who had just been sitting there, not saying a word . . .'

'Were you introduced to them?' the other man cut in.

'No, not at all.'

'Probably come in from Moscow specially. Anyway, carry on.'

'Eventually the Foreign Attaché read out a written statement they had concocted. Let me see, what did it say . . .?' He fumbled with a notebook, and then read, ' "The Soviet Union will continue to defend its sovereign interests, and the revolutionary peoples of Southern Africa, against aggression from any quarter. Any action threatened by the imperialists will be met with determined resistance." Then he sat tight, and refused to explain what it all meant.'

The older man looked thoughtful, and Caroline could contain herself no longer.

'Sorry to butt in,' she said pleasantly, 'but I heard what you were saying. I'm writing a piece on South Africa, so naturally I'm interested. Could I just ask—had anyone actually mentioned any possible threat to Soviet interests in Southern Africa?'

'No, that's just it,' replied the reporter, 'no one was even thinking of it, but it seems that was what the Russians had on their minds.'

'Do you think they were wanting to show this was some major change in policy?'

'Hard to say.' The reporter screwed his face up in thought. 'But if so, they certainly went about it in a strange way.'

'Did anyone take it like that—as being a big policy switch?' Caroline hoped her questioning didn't seem too persistent.

'No, not really. When it was clear they weren't going to say any more, people stopped asking about it.'

'Oh well,' Caroline's tone was matter of fact, 'perhaps

there's nothing in it anyway. Are you going to put it into your piece?'

'Doubt it,' said the young man, 'you can use it if it fits.'

'Thanks.' Caroline turned back to her desk.

Now her mind was made up. Her instincts told her this snippet was relevant. Several times already on this story she had had the same feeling, and she was prepared to back her instincts once more. With every new scrap of information she picked up, the jigsaw became bigger; it was no nearer solution, but it was certainly worth solving. She glanced at her watch, and kissed goodbye to her Concorde flight. And James Glendinning for that matter. She felt rather sad about that. He was so English, so straight in many ways, but very endearing. And rather attractive, in spite of himself. She pushed these thoughts away and slipped some paper into the typewriter.

For the next hour Caroline typed two versions of her story. The first was short, and talked in general terms—'Bank concern about South African gold policy . . . rumours of new initiative by Washington . . . possible change of Soviet policy.' The second was a feature-length piece, which went into the background. It described how 'a senior Bank of England official had met an exiled leader of the liberation movement to discuss gold sales . . . there is no doubt that the world's monetary authorities are taking these discussions seriously. The Bank official, who appears to be acting as a representative for Western central bankers, has reported to the IMF in Washington and the BIS in Basle . . . The connection is difficult to establish, but there are grounds for believing the gold question is tied up with renewed American interest in South Africa's future . . . naval exercises off the coast of South Africa by the US Navy's crack Fifth Fleet may be a prelude to a new American initiative in the area. Meanwhile Cuban troops under Soviet command are still stationed in Angola and Namibia.'

Caroline knew it read well. But she also knew how wary the newspapers were of this kind of story. She could already hear the denials being issued by official spokesmen: '. . .

unsubstantiated assertions . . . pyramid journalism of the kind that is now thoroughly discredited . . . the public would not expect us to take this report seriously . . .'

In the last five years, the press in Britain had been caught on the wrong foot far too often for its liking. The circulation battle in the middle and late 1970s had made newspapers greedy for all kinds of supposed scoops, which they had published without proper corroboration. Within days their jubilant headlines turned to embarrassed retractions. In 1980 the Prime Minister invited the Press Council to discuss with the Government a code of conduct for newspaper reporting. After six months, the Press Council came up with a new 'voluntary' code which involved heavy fines on those offending it. The word got round, none too subtly, that the Government would not hesitate to make the code statutory if it was broken.

This had changed the climate for what its defenders called 'investigative journalism' and its critics 'sensationalism'. It made the life of people like Caroline Manning more frustrating, and had blunted the enthusiasm of newspaper editors. Caroline reckoned her chances of getting either of her pieces onto the presses this evening were practically nil. Tomorrow she would be asked to run through her story half a dozen times, supplying sources and more hard proof than she at present possessed. The *Guardian*'s lawyers would be called in, cautious men in dark suits who would listen politely, look grave, and then proceed to hack her story to bits. With luck she might get a bowdlerised version into Wednesday's edition: if it was received calmly and no writs were threatened, a lengthier and more detailed piece might be risked on Thursday. Their confidence growing, the editorial board might then allow her to go all the way on Friday. And it would be the same with every other national, so there was little point in trying to go somewhere else.

Caroline's worst fears were confirmed that evening. She didn't get in to see the Foreign Editor until 6.30. He was charming, interested, but in the end quite adamant. A lot more work was needed: he'd get one of his staff to work with her tomorrow, double-checking every fact. The lawyers would have to go through it all. She would need to be more specific about the 'Bank official'—what interest did he have in South Africa's gold? The American invasion? Oh, yes, well, didn't that seem a bit far-fetched? He'd get a correspondent in Washington to dig into it later. Good night, Miss Manning, er Caroline, see you tomorrow.

Caroline went home feeling thoroughly depressed. She had run out of leads, ideas, inspiration. She lay a long time in a hot bath, drinking whisky from a tooth-mug. Then she rang Charles, and he came round with some bread, paté, cheese and a bottle of red wine. They talked and made love on the sofa for three hours, and in the morning she felt much better.

27

JOHANNESBURG

November 4th

The Carlton Hotel was familiar this time, and the tired receptionist seemed to recognise James when he arrived at two o'clock in the morning.

'Good morning, sir.' She managed a limp smile. 'Your room is ready for you—number 403. I've put the young lady into 404, just next door.'

James looked for the hint of a smirk, but the heavily powdered face was expressionless.

'I'm afraid Miss Manning missed the flight from London, actually. But she may be coming tomorrow, so I'd like the reservation kept, please.'

'Yes, certainly.' The receptionist handed him a key.

Upstairs in his room, James undressed and had a bath. He felt dispirited, not knowing what to make of Caroline's non-appearance, and uncertain what to do from now on. He'd have to ring the Governor first thing in the morning, to explain that Caroline must still be in London. Then he could go to Pretoria, and give le Roux the IMF memorandum. After that, there would be nothing else to keep him in South Africa, now Caroline had slipped through the net. He looked around the sanitised luxury of his hotel room and thought longingly of Little Hadham.

He was woken at 7.30 the next morning with a tray of tea. His head was muzzy, but a shave and a large breakfast helped to restore him. A call came through from the Reserve Bank to say a car would be meeting him at 9.15. James was in a quandary about ringing the Governor. London was two hours behind Johannesburg, but he had to get through to Sir William before seeing le Roux. If he waited until he reached Pretoria, the Governor might have left home. At this hour he could at least be sure the old boy was in bed. Anyway, he thought, people like Sir William secretly liked being woken up by intercontinental telephone calls—it fed their sense of importance.

Temporarily persuaded by this shaky logic, James gritted his teeth and dialled the Governor's home number.

The telephone rang twice, and then a sleepy voice answered.

'Sir William? Good morning, sir, it's James Glendinning. I'm sorry to disturb you at this unearthly hour.'

'Don't sound so hearty,' grumbled the Governor, 'but go ahead, I'm awake now and ready to listen.'

The line crackled and James had to shout. 'The point is that Miss Manning isn't here. She didn't catch the flight— I'm not sure of the reason.' He fancied the Governor swore roundly at this, but the interference made it difficult to hear anything.

'Sorry, sir, I didn't get that?'

'It doesn't matter. Have you any idea whether she's going to catch a later flight?'

'No, I haven't been able to get in touch at all. I'll try this morning if you like, but I don't know where she's likely to be.'

'Probably at the *Guardian*,' the Governor said testily, 'yes, get hold of her if you can.'

'Meanwhile I'm going ahead and seeing our friend this morning. I'll ring you later to tell you what's happened.'

'Yes, please do.'

The drive to Pretoria passed uneventfully, though the SARB's white Mercedes at one point passed a convoy of armoured trucks. In the back, beefy-looking white soldiers in khaki fatigues leant on rifles and machine guns. The driver made no comment, and James knew better than to ask questions.

At the Reserve Bank, he was escorted straight to le Roux's office on the third floor. The Afrikaner stood up to greet him.

'This is a surprise, James.' He smiled, but the brown eyes showed no warmth.

'Well, I warned you I might be back, Pieter.'

'Indeed, but so soon? Sit down and tell me what we can do for you.'

'Thank you.' The two men settled themselves into their chairs and James began. 'You remember I hinted that we at the Bank were considering whether any more should be done about the gold question—beyond establishing that your policies are not going to change, I mean. Well, the Governor and others have now decided the time is ripe to explore the chances of even closer collaboration.'

Le Roux's face showed no reaction, but he was listening closely as James continued. 'It occurred to us that even though you may want to continue with your regular sales, you may not always find it easy to do so. You may be considering whether it still makes sense to have the primary gold market in South Africa. If everyone is going to be watching your country, there might be advantages in taking gold away from the television cameras, so to speak.'

James paused, while le Roux digested what he had been saying. Then the Afrikaner spoke rather hesitantly.

'Yes, I can see what you're getting at . . . yes, it has certain attractions . . . of course, I couldn't give you a considered reply immediately . . .' He stopped, and then looked sharply at James. 'I take it you're suggesting London would be the best place to transfer to?'

'Yes, indeed, I don't think anyone would disagree with that. But I was going to suggest something more.' James measured his words cautiously. 'I believe there may be advantages in modifying the procedures for selling gold. The other Western central banks might play a more active role. I suppose it could make it more acceptable—internationally, I mean—if the SARB wasn't directly involved.'

Had he worked in the Foreign Office, James would have belonged to the school which rated diffidence as the key to diplomatic success. Now he felt he had judged le Roux very nicely. The Afrikaner was not offended, as he might so easily have been. It was time to be a little more specific.

'The IMF have been involved in these ideas, and a man called Richards—you may have heard of him—is going to come out and see you quite shortly. Some of the Fund proposals have been put down on paper—very much in draft form. But at least it will give you a chance to think about them, talk it over with your colleagues and so on.' From his briefcase James produced a thin manila folder, which he put on le Roux's desk. 'Let me give you a bit of time to read that. Perhaps I could go to another office—there's a bit of writing I need to do.'

'Certainly. There's one empty just down the corridor—one of our foreign exchange men has just gone off to Paris to watch the international. Lucky man.' For a moment James looked blank. Then he realised le Roux was talking about the rugger match between France and South Africa which was taking place tomorrow.

'Oh yes, of course. Is it just next door—the office, I mean?'

'Two doors down on the left—let me show you.'

'No, don't worry—I'll come back in about ten minutes.'

When James returned to le Roux's office, the Afrikaner was sitting at his desk writing on a pad. The IMF memorandum was open beside it. He looked up and motioned James to sit down.

'Very interesting, James, very interesting.' The accent seemed thicker than usual.

'Good, but no doubt it raises as many questions as it answers.'

'Yes, that is so. Perhaps we could discuss some of them now.' For the next hour, le Roux went through every detail in the memorandum, asking questions and making notes. By the time he had satisfied himself, it was past twelve o'clock. James hoped he would be asked to stay to lunch, and perhaps have a chance to meet the SARB Governor. Sir William had spoken with some affection of Dr Koornhof—they had met quite frequently at various international gatherings. Besides, James hoped he might take the opportunity to further his case directly with Koornhof. But le Roux was not thinking on the same lines.

'Well, I think I have got it straight. I will now put the proposal to the Governor himself, together with my recommendations. I think it would be best if you rang me again this afternoon—or leave me a number and I will ring you. You understand, it is unlikely we shall have a formal reaction for some time yet . . .'

'Of course, that's understood. All I want is some indication of your general thinking. Then I can go back to London and let Richards carry things further on that basis.'

'Good. Well, then, I will call you—at the Carlton Hotel, not so?'

'Yes, that's right, I'll be there all afternoon.' The two men shook hands, and James said he would find his own way out. As he walked down the silent corridor, he wondered idly which one of these offices belonged to the Governor. It would have been nice to meet someone in the SARB other than le Roux.

After James Glendinning had left, le Roux went quickly back to his desk. He picked up the telephone and asked for an outside line. His hands were trembling slightly as he slowly dialled a London number written down in his diary. He was on the telephone for nearly half an hour, most of which was spent waiting impatiently. When he finally got through to the person he wanted, he spoke urgently, at times almost pleadingly. At length he seemed satisfied, but when he put the telephone down, his face was drained of all its colour, and he had to rest his head in his hands for several minutes. Then he buzzed his secretary, and with only a slight tremor in his voice asked to be connected to the Prime Minister's office in Cape Town.

An hour later, the telephone rang in James Glendinning's room in the Carlton Hotel. James was sitting in a chair by the window, having tried unsuccessfully to contact Caroline Manning. Now he leapt up, glad of the diversion.

'Hello, Glendinning here.'

'Mr Glendinning?' A woman's monotone. 'I have Dr le Roux for you.'

'James?' Le Roux's voice was brisk. 'All is well. I have outlined your proposals to the Governor. He will study the draft memorandum, and talk to the IMF man about the details. He will also tell our government, of course.'

'That sounds splendid. You don't see any need for us to meet again?'

'Not immediately.'

'Right. Well, in that case, Pieter, I think I'll be going back. Many thanks for all you've done.'

'Very well. Goodbye.'

James put down the telephone feeling decidedly more cheerful. Everything was going smoothly, just as it did on good days in the Bank. Everything, that is, except Caroline Manning. He wanted to telephone the Governor—the old boy would be very chuffed—but first he'd better try once more to get hold of Caroline. The process was by now all too predictable; the same voices, the same excuses, the same result. Nothing. It was as though Caroline Manning had never been into the *Guardian* offices. He gave up and rang the Bank. He went straight through to the GPS; fortunately the Governor had just come out of a meeting, and had two minutes to spare before one of the clearing bank chairmen called on him. On an open line, James could not be specific, but Sir William was clearly delighted. He boomed his con-gratulations down the telephone; the best thing James could do was go straight to Washington and report to Richter at the IMF. Nothing more had been heard of Caroline, but the Bank's Press Officer was in touch with the *Guardian*.

The Governor's enthusiasm was infectious, and James spent the next five minutes savouring the days ahead. He had left the IMF in 1972 with his reputation secure—the sort of young man who would be prominent in central bank-ing circles in the 1990s. Now this unexpected twist had given him his chance much earlier than anyone would have ex-pected. Tomorrow he would be in Washington to report success. And on Thursday he would be back in London, perhaps to another of the Governor's lunches, his progress up the ladder assured. He'd be seeing Sarah, and this week-end they were going to Marlborough to take the twins out for the day. Preoccupied with such happy thoughts, James called the British Airways desk at Jan Smuts and booked a seat to Washington.

28

LONDON
November 5th

Remember, remember the Fifth of November—it was funny how that most British of lines now seemed familiar to her, Caroline Manning thought as she sat in a dressing gown and scanned the newspapers for any South African stories. Per-haps it would be a memorable day too. She had spent ten more frustrating hours yesterday at the *Guardian* offices, inch-ing her way through editorial caution towards the printing presses. But she still wasn't quite there, though a guarded inquiry from the Bank's Press Officer as to her whereabouts had sharpened the Foreign Editor's interest. Now she calcu-lated there were only two more days before her scoop would be the common property of every journalist in the world.

Before she left the Barbican, Caroline made a number of telephone calls. First she rang her brother in Washington, although it was only four in the morning there. Hoping he was too sleepy to lose his temper, she asked him immediately if there had been any developments. No, Paul mumbled, there was nothing new. Everyone had gone to ground, and there wasn't a leak in sight. She thanked him, apologised for the early call, and rang off. She smiled—by now Paul would be coming to his senses, sitting up in bed and cursing her. Always better to ask questions first and apologise later.

Her next call was to the ANC house in Sheffield Terrace. Could she speak to Robert Sisekwe, please—it was urgent. After a long delay she was told that Mr Sisekwe was not available to speak on the telephone. Well, Caroline persisted, would it be possible to meet him—it really was most important, and it wouldn't take much time. You could always try that—the voice on the other end was indifferent. Mr Sisekwe was in now, but would probably be going out at about twelve o'clock. 'Could you please leave a message,' Caroline said, 'that I will definitely be coming over within an hour.' She hurried out into the street, clutching an umbrella against a strong gust of rain. Maddeningly, there wasn't a taxi to be seen, so she ran down towards St Paul's and eventually found one pulled up at some traffic lights in Cheapside.

Inside, the taxi was warm and she had a chance to dry off and rearrange her hair. But the rain had its usual effect on London traffic, and it was twenty-five minutes' and nearly six pounds' of irritation before she was ringing the bell at 11 Sheffield Terrace. She was shown up to the drab waiting-room by an elderly, plump African, who complained jovially about the weather and again about the stairs. That cheered her up, but his friendliness did not extend to telling her when she might get to see Sisekwe. While she waited, drumming her fingers impatiently on a table, Caroline ran over what she was going to say. Before going to sleep last night, she had decided what to do; and now it still seemed the most sensible course of action. The last time she had come to see Sisekwe, she had failed in both her objectives. She hadn't got a story out of him, and nor had she helped the ANC cause by telling him something he didn't already know. This time it would be different. After her fruitless efforts at the *Guardian* she was ready to put her journalistic ambitions to one side. Today she was the radical. Today she really would tell Sisekwe something. And that, the journalist in her reasoned, might just provoke him into helping her.

These thoughts were interrupted by the appearance of a heavily built white man at the door. He was wearing a rumpled grey suit several sizes too small for him. He seemed lost, and looked around the room with a bemused expression on his moon-face. Caroline smiled at him and said pleasantly, 'Do you want the way out? It's down those stairs to the left. Keep going till you come to the bottom.'

The man muttered his thanks and walked out. Shortly afterwards, a young Indian came into the room and told Caroline that Sisekwe would see her now. 'But only for five minutes, you understand,' he said, with the air of someone who was continually running behind schedule.

'Of course,' Caroline replied with mock solemnity. She hurried up the by now familiar stairs and knocked on the door.

Robert Sisekwe was standing by the window looking down at the garden. The rain had fallen to a steady drizzle, and sodden leaves were covering the lawn. Sisekwe turned away, reluctantly it seemed, and greeted Caroline with his usual politeness. But he seemed preoccupied with something, and for a moment Caroline wondered whether he would really appreciate the significance of what she had to say. She decided to plunge in anyway.

'Mr Sisekwe, I'm grateful to you for sparing the time to see me.' Sisekwe waved his hand dismissively, but said nothing. 'As you know,' Caroline continued, 'I'm following events in your country very closely, and a number of newspapers have carried my material. I have now come across some information which I am confident is accurate, but I think it will be very difficult to get it published.' She leant forward, emphasising her words. 'It is vitally important for the future of your country, and it will affect your liberation struggle. The American Government is preparing to intervene in South Africa. The Fifth Fleet is at this moment sailing towards the Cape, and I understand additional support from the US Navy and Airforce is on its way.'

Caroline stopped speaking, and the room was silent. Sisekwe's eyes told her he was now paying full attention to what she had been saying. Chin cupped in his hands, he breathed slowly and stared down at his desk. At length he spoke. 'How am I to know that you are not speaking rubbish?' The bluntness of the question deflated Caroline, even though she had been prepared for some initial scepticism. She spread her hands expressively, unable to speak for a moment. Sisekwe was watching her closely, his brown eyes angry.

'I cannot *prove* anything—not to you, nor to any newspaper editor. If I could,' she smiled briefly, 'I wouldn't need to be sitting here now. You could be reading all about it in your newspaper. I still hope to persuade the *Guardian* to publish something tomorrow. But in the meantime, I thought you had a right to know. Obviously, there's nothing you can do about it. But there is one thing.' She paused, hoping for some encouragement, but Sisekwe continued to stare impassively at her. 'I'm quite sure Mr Glendinning is in some way connected with all this. Not personally, but his interest in your gold is the link. I'm not certain exactly how it all ties up, but . . .' Her voice trailed off. She felt helpless, just as she had done in the *Guardian* offices. At least this man wasn't so damned smooth: if he thought she was talking rubbish now, he'd say so.

'Miss Manning.' Sisekwe's voice was low. 'I'd be grateful if you could tell me everything you know—what your information is, how reliable your sources are—everything. I don't have much time, but it's very important that you are frank.' Caroline felt a stir of excitement. At least she wasn't going to be booted out immediately. She took a deep breath to compose herself, and began to describe to Sisekwe all the events of the past fortnight. He listened carefully, asking questions and taking the occasional note. His face was taut, motionless, but every now and then his eyes flashed angrily.

After she had spoken for about ten minutes, Caroline concluded apologetically, 'Well, that's it. As you can see, it's not hard proof. But for what it's worth, I thought it would interest you.'

In answer, Sisekwe picked up a telephone on his desk, and slowly dialled a number written on a pad in front of him. The call was answered immediately, and Sisekwe said, in English, 'Could I have Room 453, please?' A further short pause, and then he spoke again, this time in what Caroline took to be his native language. He was very brief, two sentences in all, and then he put the telephone down.

Turning to Caroline, he smiled slightly and said, 'Miss Manning, would you like to come to Paris with me? We will need to leave in three hours. I make only two conditions. First, you must bring a camera. Also, you must guarantee front-page space in one of tomorrow's newspapers. I expect to give you a story and a picture which will deserve the front page.' He laughed and then was serious. 'It is also very important for the future of my country. I suggest you go to the room directly below this one, and use the telephone. Come back when you have spoken to the *Guardian* and I will begin with some background.'

Ten minutes later, Caroline was back in Sisekwe's office. She knew she couldn't get a guarantee of front-page treatment from any newspaper, particularly when she didn't even know what the story would be about. But at least she had extracted a promise from the Foreign Editor to wait until he had heard from her before deciding on the lead story. She couldn't do any better than that; and the Foreign Editor seemed more enthusiastic than he had been yesterday. Apparently a Reuter's tape had just reported that the US Secretary of State, John Curzon, had at short notice cancelled a trip to South America. The State Department was playing the whole thing down, claiming 'pressure of work'. Did Caroline think there could be any connection? Of course, Caroline had replied with satisfaction, didn't she keep saying the whole thing was connected? She went back to Sisekwe's office feeling more optimistic than she had done for several days.

Sisekwe was standing by the window, talking to a young black man wearing dark glasses, whom Caroline had seen once before. He smiled enquiringly at her as she came in, and she answered as casually as she could.

'That's OK. The *Guardian* will hold their front page until I've filed my story. But tell me, Mr Sisekwe,' she changed the subject before he could probe too deeply, 'why are you doing this? Why don't you just call a press conference and tell the world all about it?'

'I have thought of that,' Sisekwe replied evenly. 'But in fact it is not that kind of story. I haven't got anything new—in a factual sense—to announce. It is very significant, but only against the kind of background you know about already. Besides,' he smiled broadly, 'I'd like to do the *Guardian* a favour. Over the years, they've been better supporters of my people than the other British newspapers. And there is a final point.' He was serious again. 'From what you tell me about the Americans, we don't have very much time to do anything. And what I will shortly tell you suggests there isn't very much we could do anyway. So I am looking for some symbolic form of resistance—something which just might scare the Americans off. It's only a chance, but I hope we will find that symbol in Paris.'

As he finished speaking, Sisekwe turned to stare out of the window, his face set. In the silence that followed, the young man shifted uneasily in his chair. Questions crowded into Caroline's mind, and she was grateful when Sisekwe spoke again. 'Are we ready?'

'Not quite—I must stop off at the *Guardian* and pick up a camera—remember?'

'Of course.' Sisekwe's face creased briefly into a smile.

'Edson,' he turned to the young man, 'can you drive us to the *Guardian* and then on to the airport? I hope we shall be back later this evening, but I will let you know.' He grinned encouragingly at Caroline's serious expression. 'Now to work.

You may want to write most of your story in advance, and I will try to tell you what I know.'

They left the room and walked down the stairs. 'Let me see,' Sisekwe said slowly, 'where shall I begin? Did you happen to notice a man, a middle-aged white man, leaving here as you arrived?' Caroline remembered the moon-faced man in his too-tight suit, and nodded.

'Right,' said Sisekwe, 'let's start with him.'

29

LONDON

November 5th

Although Sisekwe did not say so, the moon-faced man's name was Vladimir Mihalovnov. In the Diplomatic List he was described as a second secretary, cultural, on the staff of the Soviet Embassy in London. On the face of it, that was true: Mihalovnov was seen from time to time shuffling uneasily around a new exhibition of Russian art. He had even been known to deliver the occasional lecture on Soviet cultural trends to bodies like the Anglo–Russian Friendship Society. Some people remarked on the curious fact that he always read these lectures from a prepared text, and stoutly refused to answer questions afterwards. They would have found it even more curious had they seen inside Mihalovnov's bachelor flat in Bayswater, which had been acquired by the Embassy on a long lease in the early 1970s. The furniture was comfortable enough; but the walls were bare of pictures and ornaments, and the bookcase contained a dozen obligatory Marxist texts which were clearly consulted very infrequently. There was no record player and no records. In the corner stood a large, shiny television set permanently switched on to ITV 1: and Mihalovnov in fact spent most of his evenings slumped in front of it, smoking a chain of pungent cigarettes. Had anyone ever enquired about this apparent anomaly, Mihalovnov would have replied that he spent so much of his working day engaged in cultural affairs that at home he preferred to relax and do something completely different.

That would have been less than the truth, however. It was well known to British Intelligence that Mihalovnov's work was 'cultural' in only a very limited sense. He was in fact Russian liaison officer to all exiled revolutionary organisations with headquarters or representatives in London. In a typical working day, he might assist a man from the Palestine Liberation Organisation who wished to go to Moscow on a fraternal visit; meet the leader of the Argentinian People's Party who was passing through London en route from Moscow back to exile in Cuba; and, for the umpteenth time, request that 'solidarity scholarships' for the children of imprisoned Communists in Pakistan be made available (if only so the 'children', mostly in their early twenties and rather aggressive, would stop pestering him). Then he would laboriously write up reports on these and other meetings. Sometimes he would include his contacts' views on how the revolutionary struggle in, say, Northern Ireland or South Korea was developing. Then he would go home, feeling neither satisfied or dissatisfied. He had long since ceased to wonder what happened to his reports when they reached Moscow—which was just as well, as it was doubtful that anyone could have told him.

Today was different, however. During the night the telephone by his bed had jangled him out of a deep sleep. It was the duty officer at the Embassy to say that a cable had come in from Moscow, in code and marked 'Urgent and for the immediate attention of V. Mihalovnov.' Mihalovnov turned on the light and looked at his watch. It was 3.30 a.m.: he put his hand over the mouthpiece and swore roundly, then told the operator he would be there within twenty minutes. Taking a deep breath, he forced himself out of bed and into his clothes. He swallowed a cup of scalding coffee while running an electric razor over his face, and then went out into the street. It was raining steadily, and he pulled the collar of his raincoat up and cursed again.

He was very seldom called out at night. It must have something to do with those two from the Foreign Ministry, who had arrived on Monday. They were senior, but Mihalovnov didn't know them, so he wasn't sure just how senior. They had spent more than an hour asking him questions about South Africa, without telling him why they were interested. Then they had been present at the press briefing on the defence budget, and had apparently refused to answer any questions on Angola and Namibia. They had left London that evening, bound for the United Nations. Well, whatever they were up to, they'd certainly spoiled his sleep, Mihalovnov thought moodily, as he stumbled off the pavement and into a puddle.

By the time he reached his desk in the Embassy, the cable had been decoded. A young secretary with a neat bun and austere mouth put three pages of typed foolscap in front of him. Mihalovnov mumbled his thanks, yawned and began to read. After a few lines, he glanced at the top of the sheet and discovered the cable came from a senior official in the Foreign Ministry. The Foreign Minister would himself be sending a similar message to the Ambassador. Mihalovnov smiled inwardly at the thought of the Ambassador also being woken up at 3.30. The latter had been to dinner with the Bulgarian Ambassador that evening; he invariably drank too much on such occasions, which made him bad-tempered the next morning, even after a full night's sleep. It would be prudent to keep out of the Ambassador's way today.

Mihalovnov read the cable through several times, pausing only to light two cigarettes. His tiredness had left him, and his mind was separating the cable's contents into various strands. The main point was quite simple: the Politburo had decided the time was ripe to move against the racists in South Africa. Cuban troops stationed in Namibia would cross the border into South Africa within forty-eight hours. Reinforcements were being landed in Angola at this very moment, and logistical support for a full-scale military operation

was being built up. The news mildly excited Mihalovnov, but long years of training had taught him to concentrate
on the job in hand and leave the excitement to others. His
particular responsibility was clear: to inform the London
representatives of the liberation movements that salvation
was at hand. During the next few hours, in capital cities
across the world, exactly the same message would be delivered
by other cultural secretaries.

This was one of the services the Soviet Union had been
performing for exiled revolutionaries for many years. Dispersed around the world, their organisation rickety and their
finances weak, liberation movements found it very difficult
to keep all their leaders and supporters in touch with one
another. Without Russian assistance they would have had
to rely on telephones and the post, which were slow and
easily tapped. They were accordingly most grateful to the
Soviet Union for such valuable help—all, naturally, given
free. The help was not entirely disinterested, however. Moscow knew only too well that exiled politicians are very
prone to factionalism; it was no good supporting an entire
organisation—the in-fighting, the personalities, the twists and
turns were what really mattered. At the end of the day, one
faction would come out on top. By effectively controlling the
flow of information, Russian diplomats were in a strong
position to determine which faction it was. But even if that
proved impossible, it was always helpful to know in advance
which way the wind was blowing.

Mihalovnov got up from his desk and went into the next
room, where two secretaries were sitting and chatting. He
dictated a brief reply, saying that he would carry out his
instructions and report back as soon as possible. He poured
himself another cup of coffee and returned to his office. One
paragraph in the cable was still puzzling him. He read it
through again:

> 'Subsidiary purpose of intervention to secure access to
> gold reserves and production. Please raise with pro-
> visional governments question of bilateral gold contract.
> Early indication of attitude needed.'

The phrase 'provisional governments' amused Mihalovnov. Though Moscow was much closer to the African National Congress, it had never abandoned all links with the rival Pan Africanist Congress—on the well known principle that backing all the runners in a race will ensure you the winner. Even now, with South Africa on the brink of revolution, the question remained unresolved.

Mihalovnov couldn't quite see what the paragraph as a whole was driving at. Certainly, Russia's attitude towards South Africa had always been coloured by the massive mineral resources which it possessed. Only two years ago, Mihalovnov had attended a training session in Moscow which placed great emphasis on the West's exploitation of these resources. Lecturer after lecturer had explained how much more advantageous it would be for everyone when this imperialist relationship was replaced by trade between a liberated South Africa and progressive countries. At lunch one day a man who was stationed in Delhi had remarked irreverently to Mihalovnov that such a close study of capitalism's methods revealed surprising potential benefits for the Soviet Union. Pure coincidence, Mihalovnov had replied, and each time they had met after that, the two men had chuckled over their private joke. So it came as no surprise to Mihalovnov that his country should be interested in the prizes it could win for itself by helping to oust the white regime. But why the special mention of gold? Mihalovnov furrowed his brow and lit another cigarette. Obviously he would have to raise it with the ANC and PAC, but in a fairly oblique way.

Four hours later, he was standing outside 11 Sheffield Terrace, sheltering from the rain which gusted along the street. In the past, he had tried to see Robert Sisekwe or one of his lieutenants about once a month. But when things hotted up in Southern Africa, as they did quite frequently, Mihalovnov made it his business to keep in much closer contact. Sometimes they met at the Russian Embassy, which was convenient for recording their conversations. Otherwise they would have lunch at one of the numerous restaurants off the

Bayswater Road. Mihalovnov had only once been into this building before, to meet Sisekwe when he first arrived in London.

Their relations had always been cordial, but never very close. The exiled politician dares not bite the hand that feeds him, but equally he resents having to be fed at all. Mihalovnov understood that, and for the most part resisted the temptation to lord it over his contacts. Indeed, he regarded Sisekwe with considerable respect—chiefly because the man undoubtedly had a very strong power base in the ANC. This was confirmed by everyone who knew the ANC well. It was generally accepted that the men imprisoned on Robben Island were no longer in a fit state, physically or mentally, to lead a liberated South Africa. In which case, Robert Sisekwe would probably emerge as the principal national figure. Moreover, Mihalovnov knew that, despite its public rhetoric, the PAC leadership would be prepared to accept Sisekwe as President, while they would resist any of the other ANC candidates.

The door opened, and Mihalovnov was ushered upstairs to Sisekwe's office. The two men shook hands and exchanged greetings. But neither was given to small talk, and Mihalovnov immediately explained the purpose of his visit. Watching Sisekwe's face, he felt his bureaucrat's caution slipping away, as he talked of the proposed invasion. He concluded with what came as close to a flourish as he would ever get.

'So, comrade, at long last the liberation of your country is at hand. The Russian and Cuban troops and the oppressed masses will together drive the racialists and the exploiters into the sea. This is truly an historic occasion.'

Sisekwe nodded, his face wreathed in smiles. 'Truly historic. But, if you don't mind, there are a number of questions I should like to ask, Comrade Mihalovnov. First, why have you chosen this moment to intervene? Why not in 1976, or 1978, or last year?'

The Russian's answer came back smoothly, as though it had been well rehearsed. 'Objectively, a revolutionary situation did not exist then. But now the proletariat is roused to action, and needs only a defence against the oppressors' military strength. This we will provide—but the real victory will be won by the people's solidarity, and that we had to wait for.'

Sisekwe nodded, satisfied. 'Yes, in spite of all the suffering, the struggle was necessary, I agree. Now, some more questions, if you don't mind, comrade.'

'Of course,' Mihalovnov smiled, and Sisekwe proceeded to ask about the timing of the invasion, the number of troops involved, and whether neighbouring African states had been informed. To each, Mihalovnov had to admit ignorance, saying that no further information was yet available from Moscow. But he did assure Sisekwe that the exiled ANC leaders were all being simultaneously informed of the invasion.

'And the PAC?' Sisekwe asked sharply.

'And the PAC,' replied the Russian with a shrug.

Sisekwe smiled slightly at this, and crossed over to the window. Mihalovnov sensed this was the right moment to raise the gold question.

Sisekwe had turned back and was saying, 'Well, there is nothing more we can do for the present. I have preparations to make, and you will be busy, so let us waste no more time now. You will of course keep me informed throughout the day?'

'Indeed, comrade.' Mihalovnov smiled again, a little nervously. 'But can I make just one further point? When we have triumphed, and you are installed in your rightful place as a national leader, then our two countries can look forward to strengthening our revolutionary bond, eh? We will naturally be ready to provide you with any kind of technical and financial assistance you may need. I feel sure, too, that our trade will increase rapidly, to our mutual benefit.'

At this, Sisekwe nodded agreement and then said, 'But I'm not sure now is the right time to be discussing this kind of thing . . .'

'No, not in detail,' Mihalovnov interrupted hurriedly. 'But I have been asked by my government to give you an assurance of our long-term commitment to South Africa. In return,' he paused very slightly, 'we would be glad to know that you shared our desire to increase co-operation in all fields. And since this is bound to be one of the main considerations of the capitalists, I wonder if you could give me some indication of your plans for the country's mining industry once political power has been won?' Sisekwe seemed taken aback by this question, and Mihalovnov continued reassuringly, 'I'm only asking because mining is the sector most dominated by foreign capitalist interests. When these are expropriated, there is a danger that production may run into difficulties . . . of course, only temporary ones,' he added hastily, 'and my government might be in a position to offer advice and assistance. For example, the mining of gold and then its marketing . . . the Soviet Union has unrivalled experience in that field, and perhaps we could come to some arrangement over what was the best strategy for your country—a franchise, or something on these lines.'

While Mihalovnov had been speaking, Sisekwe had nodded his head slightly from time to time. Now he replied, his tone guarded, 'These are big questions, comrade, and you would not expect me to have a precise answer ready for you at once. I will consult with others here in London, but of course you will appreciate that ANC policy is determined by the Central Committee.' Then his voice became emotional. 'This is a crucial day for my country. The ANC will remember its friends, and, of course, should the need arise, we will turn to our friends for assistance. But,' he added slowly, 'we would consider any proposals put up to us from any quarter and judge them on their merits.'

Mihalovnov heard this last remark with relief. He was beginning to fear Sisekwe would be too overcome by the news to talk seriously about gold, or anything else for that matter. But, though the African was deeply moved, he had still kept his self-control and his presence. Mihalovnov mentally raised his respect for Sisekwe another couple of notches. Now he could go back to the Embassy with something solid to cable through to Moscow: 'Should you wish to pursue matter further, request detailed gold proposals which can be put to ANC, London.' For the moment, his task was over. If the PAC proved as co-operative, he might even be able to catch up on his lost sleep. The idea was attractive enough to raise him from his chair. Clasping Sisekwe's hand warmly, he said goodbye. 'An historic occasion, eh, comrade?'

'An historic occasion,' replied Sisekwe.

30

PARIS

November 5th

The South African Embassy is one of the many dignified buildings in the Avenue Hoche. It has an anonymous brown door; a discreet brass plaque is its only identification. The noise of the traffic roaring past towards the Etoile is never entirely silenced, not even inside the Embassy. But that afternoon the traffic had been diverted and the air was filled with chanting, police sirens and the acrid smell of tear gas.

In front of the Embassy stood a solid phalanx of CRS anti-riot police, their faces hidden by goggles and gas masks. They held enormous transparent shields in one hand, and truncheons in the other. Behind them were other figures, with tear gas launchers and guns loaded with rubber bullets. Across the street, a crowd of demonstrators, mostly in their early twenties, shouted slogans and raised their fists. Occasionally a bottle or a stone flew out from their ranks and bounced harmlessly off the CRS shields. Their eyes streaming from the single volley of tear gas, it was clear that the demonstrators were in no mood to clash directly with the police. Besides, they were only there as a token force. The real action, they knew, was taking place at the Parc des Princes, where the first rugger international between South Africa and France was now drawing to a close.

Two hundred yards away, in the Rue Balzac, Caroline

Manning could just hear the demonstration above the howl of the traffic. She had earlier been over to see what was happening outside the Embassy, a press card prominently displayed on her lapel. She had even taken the camera with her, in case there had been any real trouble which would have looked good on an inside page. But after twenty minutes she had decided she was wasting valuable time.

Now she was sitting in a *brasserie*, at a table covered with papers, and writing furiously. Occasionally she paused to sip some coffee and glance through the smoky glass at the scene outside. Paris was still just as glamorous as the first time she had been there as a student with a knapsack, staying in a singularly unglamorous youth hostel. She'd come a long way since then, and become blasé about many things—but not about Paris. She prided herself on having discarded most of her American traits during her years in London; but when she went abroad she was invariably treated as American. Much to her annoyance, she usually responded by behaving like an American as well. She had already, and quite unconsciously, called the elegant young Frenchman behind the bar 'waiter'. After that she could hardly expect to escape the kind of flirtatious attention perfected by waiters the world over for pretty American tourists.

The last four hours with Sisekwe had confirmed all her hunches. She was now quite certain she was sitting on one of the greatest journalistic scoops of all time. Everything Sisekwe had told her had fitted into place: there were still several large question marks, but they no longer mattered. By publishing what she knew, the missing pieces would be quickly flushed out into the open. She had telephoned the *Guardian* from a public call box outside the café—risky, but a risk worth taking. She had actually got through to the Editor, and explained what kind of story she would be filing later that evening. She had probably sounded garbled and breathless, but this time there was no mistaking the Editor's interest. He asked her to write a lead and a longer piece for an inside page. There would be more space kept on the front page for staff writers to tackle different aspects of the story. That was to keep the NUJ chapel sweet—it would never do to have the whole front page written by a freelance. Caroline understood this, and didn't mind: she had the lead, which was what really mattered. She'd claim an enormous fee; and the management, grateful for the first genuine scoop in six months, wouldn't argue. Then there'd be follow-up articles, television and radio appearances—the whole thing would net her at least five thousand pounds, possibly ten if she got on to the international circuit.

On top of all that, she reminded herself with satisfaction, she would be striking a blow for the radical left, and for the blacks in South Africa. For ten years she had stoutly been saying that Vietnam would happen again somewhere else in the world, because the American establishment and the military were, under the surface, as imperialistic as ever. Now she was being proved right. How she'd love to see the faces of some of her erstwhile comrades—the ones who had sold out, joined the government service in Washington and so shown themselves to be nothing more than soft liberals. No doubt they'd claim the Russians and Cubans were being just as imperialistic: in fact, she'd have to bow slightly in that direction for her *Guardian* readership. But she'd be able to emphasise that the Cuban invasion had the support of the liberation movements, who were the genuine representatives of the people. Anyway, the blacks were carrying out their own revolution: they just needed the military backing to prevent themselves being slaughtered wholesale.

What about Sisekwe himself? She stared thoughtfully out of the window at the hotel opposite. He was in there now, had been for nearly an hour. He had been very secretive about the purpose of this trip, merely saying he was going to meet some important people. But he'd insisted on her coming to Paris and then waiting until the meeting was over. This, he promised, would be the most newsworthy story of all. By now she was easily persuaded; besides, her curiosity was aroused. Perhaps the ANC leaders had been summoned from their various exiles to this central meeting. Or he might be talking to representatives of other African governments. But her favourite theory was that the two liberation movements, ANC and PAC, were at last going to bury their differences and agree on how to support the Cuban and Russian offensive.

Whatever it was, it was obviously going to be worth photographing, otherwise Sisekwe wouldn't have been so keen on her bringing a camera. She'd just have to wait for the answer, she decided, going back to her third cup of coffee and the jumble of paper. Outside the street lights were being switched on. The young waiter, seeing Caroline straining her eyes in the café's gloom, turned on some lights and fixed her with a dazzling smile.

Forty minutes later, the door opened and Robert Sisekwe walked in. He seemed agitated, and obviously in a hurry. 'Can you come over with me now?' he asked.

Caroline sensed his mood, and quickly gathered up her papers. She left twenty francs to cover her bill, and followed Sisekwe out into the street. They had to wait some time at a pedestrian crossing, but Sisekwe didn't speak at all. He looked straight ahead, the muscles in his jaw twitching slightly, his eyes narrowed. Caroline decided not to ask any questions. She followed him into the warmth of the hotel, and they took the lift to the fourth floor.

Two hours later, Caroline was in a taxi taking her to the Press Centre, a worried expression on her face. She would have plenty of time to cable her story and photographs to London, so that was no longer concerning her. Nor was she in any doubt that this was a real, twenty-four-carat scoop. She looked worried only because a large part of her Harvard-educated brain was still refusing to believe the evidence of her own eyes and ears.

31

LONDON
November 6th

Jet lag does curious things to the human body. At seven a.m. in the Concorde arrivals lounge at Heathrow Airport, James Glendinning's body told him that he should be lowering it into bed. In fact it was being bullied into the routine of a full day in London, expected to eat too much and sleep too little. James groaned involuntarily at the prospect.

Five minutes later, the passengers on the flight from Washington were told that a baggage handlers' dispute was causing some delay in the unloading of their luggage. British Airways apologised for any inconvenience which might be caused; passengers would be given a complimentary breakfast, and newspapers would be available within the next few minutes. On top of his tiredness, James began to feel very irritable. As an antidote, he decided to telephone Sarah. She would probably still be asleep, but undoubtedly this qualified as one of those 'worse' occasions referred to in her marriage vows.

Talking to Sarah—even a drowsy, mock-irate Sarah—always made him feel better, and when he came out of the telephone booth, James was looking forward to a cup of coffee. Another Concorde had arrived in, apparently from Africa, and its passengers were also milling around waiting for their luggage to appear. Across the room, a ground stewardess was standing by a table piled high with newspapers. James walked over and stood in a small queue. He was wondering whether he could ask for both *The Times* and the *Financial Times*, when he was suddenly riveted by the headlines in the *Guardian*. As in a dream, he thought inconsequentially that they seemed to be even bigger and blacker than the type in the *Daily Express*. 'US, RUSSIA, NEAR GOLD WAR IN SOUTH AFRICA'

James stumbled to the head of the queue and snatched up the *Guardian*. Now he could read the supporting headline, he felt his stomach knotting up, and a wave of dizziness threatened his balance.

BLACK AND WHITE JOIN HANDS AGAINST
'AGGRESSION AND INTERFERENCE'
By Caroline Manning

James was vaguely aware of the stewardess smiling and trying to say something to him. He stared blankly at her for a moment, and then fumbled in his pocket for some change. 'Oh no, sir, it's free—with the compliments of British Airways.' The stewardess showed a perfect set of white teeth. James walked away unsteadily, and then saw an empty seat to his left. Relieved, he sat down and for a moment closed his eyes to try and stop his head pounding. The two seats next to him were filled by two substantial American matrons with blue rinses and diamanté-studded glasses. They were complaining loudly about the 'goddam unions'. With mixed feelings, James stopped listening to them and forced himself to go back to the *Guardian*. Slowly, as though he found each word painful to digest, he read through Caroline Manning's exclusive.

The first paragraph was in bold type.

'The United States and the Soviet Union are on the verge of intervening in South Africa, according to top secret information made available to this newspaper. Both superpowers are apparently bent on securing South Africa's gold, which has prompted a remarkable display of national solidarity between an exiled black leader and a senior Afrikaner official in the South African Reserve Bank.'

James's hands were shaking so much that he had to put the newspaper down on his knees before he continued reading.

'The American Fifth Fleet is at this moment manoeuvring within thirty miles of Cape Town as the

United States prepares to intervene in the growing crisis in South Africa. At the same time, Russian-led Cuban troops have been moved up to the border between Namibia and South Africa, and the Soviet Union is understood to be preparing a full-scale military invasion of the last bastion of white supremacy in the African continent. But it is clear from material which the *Guardian* has been given that both the United States and the Soviet Union are there as much for economic as for ideological reasons. In particular, both countries appear to be interested in the gold stocks held by the South African Reserve Bank (SARB), and the output from the gold mines. This is made clear in a statement issued jointly by the Head of the Gold Department at the SARB, Dr Pieter le Roux, and the London-exiled leader of the African National Congress, Mr Robert Sisekwe (full text and photograph, see page 2).

In an extraordinary show of symbolic unity against what they described as 'unwarranted interference in South Africa's internal affairs', the two men last night warned that differences between whites and blacks in South Africa were transcended by the threats of invasion by 'superpowers with their own interests, and not those of the South African people, at heart'. This is a clear reference to the apparent desire of both Russia and America to obtain control over South Africa's gold wealth.'

James shifted uneasily in his chair.

"The precise reasons for the two great powers' interest in gold remain something of a mystery. But both Dr le Roux and Mr Sisekwe have in recent weeks received representations from the West about the future of gold, and Mr Sisekwe has also had similar overtures from the Soviet Union. Neither man is in any doubt that both countries are prepared to go to extreme lengths to secure South Africa's gold for their own purposes.'

James glanced down over the next paragraph, and now all his worst fears were confirmed.

'One man who has taken a leading part in the West's involvement in the gold question is a senior official in the Bank of England, Mr James Glendinning. He has held several clandestine meetings with Mr Sisekwe in London, and has visited Pretoria twice within the last fortnight for consultations with Dr le Roux. Ostensibly, the Bank of England wished to discover whether any change in Pretoria's gold policy, which would affect London's role as a gold centre, would follow as a result of the disturbances in South Africa. Last Tuesday however, Glendinning met le Roux at the SARB in Pretoria and presented him with proposals from the International Monetary Fund to return the primary gold market from Pretoria back to London. Glendinning claimed this would expand the market, since many potential buyers are at present deterred by the market's location in Pretoria.

In Washington, both the Defence and State Departments refused to confirm or deny that the Fifth Fleet was operating off the South African coast. The Soviet News Agency, Tass, dismissed the suggestion that Cuban troops were to be deployed in South Africa as 'desperate scaremongering'. There was no comment from the Bank of England about the involvement of Mr Glendinning; but a back-bench Labour MP, Mr Joe Roberts, who has been a persistent critic of the Bank and the City in general, said he would be asking the Chancellor of the Exchequer to make a statement in the Commons today.'

James closed his eyes and slumped back in his chair. Eventually, and with great reluctance, he lifted the paper again.

It seemed most of the front page was taken up with pieces related to Caroline's lead story. The Defence Correspondent described the estimated number of Cuban troops in Namibia, and the logistical problems of providing support for them; he then went on to write about the US Fifth Fleet. The piece had clearly been put together in a rush, as had another from the paper's Kremlinologist which rehearsed the long history of Russian involvement in Africa, and speculated on the possible reasons for an invasion at this time. There was even a paragraph on gold from the commodities correspondent, evidently ill at ease in the spotlight of the front page.

The loudspeaker was booming again, and James gratefully seized at an excuse to stop reading. The luggage was still delayed: the baggage handlers were apparently picketing the two Concordes, but British Airways hoped the matter would be resolved very shortly. In the meantime, they apologised for the inconvenience . . .

'Inconvenience, my ass,' snarled one of the American blue rinses. 'The trouble with this place is that everyone's too damn polite. The unions run this show, and the management step aside and say "After you, sir." Why, it makes me . . .'

But James Glendinning was very thankful for the inconvenience. He would have picketed the Concordes himself if that would have suspended time and reality a little longer. Outside this room, he could just imagine the kind of reality that would be building up. In the Bank, the first whiff of scandal would send the staff into discreet huddles, and by the end of the day the place would be stiff with rumours. But what about the parlours? The Governor would immediately call in the Directors and the Chief, no doubt of that. Probably he, James, would be asked in as well. Then there'd be a telephone call from the Chancellor, maybe even from the Prime Minister. How much did they know—how much had the Governor told them? Perhaps the Governor would be compelled to resign . . .

James shuddered at this ultimate horror, and tried a different tack. What would be going on in Washington? The

IMF, and Richter himself, would be seriously embarrassed. Did they know about the American intervention? The whole nightmare increasingly resembled an intricate web, but had it been spun by any one person? Or was it all a series of coincidences? 'Will you walk into my parlour . . .' Well, he'd been caught in the web, and would shortly be eaten alive. He'd have to leave the Bank, his career in ruins. And his life for that matter: the house was bought on a Bank mortgage, the twins were at Marlborough on a Bank loan. He might never get another job.

As these thoughts came crowding in on him, James valiantly tried not to panic. He focused on something else. What about Sisekwe and le Roux? That was the strangest thing of all. He remembered that he hadn't yet read what they had to say; picking up the *Guardian* again, he turned to the headline on page 2.

BLACK AND WHITE UNITE TO FIGHT
By Caroline Manning
Paris, November 5th

'In a Paris hotel just three hundred yards from the besieged South African embassy, a new and unexpected thread was added to the puzzling tapestry of South Africa. Dr Pieter le Roux is Head of the Gold Department in the South African Reserve Bank. It transpires that he is also Chairman of the Broederbond, a secret society of Afrikaners holding the most influential positions in South Africa. His father was leader of the Nationalist Party in the Transvaal, his grandfather and great grandfather fought against the British in the Boer War. As the leader of the Broederbond, le Roux embodies the spirit of Afrikanerdom, and its political philosophy, apartheid. Yet last night he met another South African who in all respects appears to be his exact opposite. Robert Sisekwe is black. He is a leading figure in the banned African National Congress. He has spent the last twelve years living in exile. Before that he was a prisoner on Robben Island, convicted of "plotting the overthrow of the state". Should the current unrest in South Africa lead to a revolution, Sisekwe would certainly play a leading role in the next government, possibly even as its President.

'Le Roux and Sisekwe have never had the opportunity to discuss politics, but they freely admitted to me last night that they would probably disagree on most things. On one point they are in complete agreement, however: that South Africa's political future must be worked out by South Africans of all races, free from outside interference. Both men are convinced that the United States and the Soviet Union are on the verge of intervening in South Africa, yet neither welcomes this. They are deeply suspicious of the superpowers' motives, but fear these will remain hidden under a thick coating of rhetoric. Having been approached by both Russia and the West on the gold question, Sisekwe and le Roux reckon that South Africa's economic attractions are a stronger magnet than any selfless regard for "liberty", as variously defined by the superpowers. Sisekwe is adamant the blacks are not going "to exchange one kind of servitude for another", even though its form may differ. For his part, le Roux points to the Afrikaners' long history of fighting for their independence against the British.

'Meeting in Paris last night, neither man was under any illusion that their action could by itself materially affect the course of events in South Africa. But it symbolised a widespread, if still latent, feeling on the part of many South Africans. They hoped their example would be followed by blacks and Boers in all walks of life. They appealed to Russia and America to think again before making any precipitate moves. The superpowers "would not be welcomed as saviours or liberators by the people of South Africa".'

James Glendinning put down the paper and sat very still
in his chair. After a few minutes—time no longer seemed
to mean very much—he became conscious of the American
women sitting next to him. They were still talking as loudly
as ever, but they had passed on from British trade unions to
their holiday in Africa.

'Why, you know,' said the older and more aggressive of the
two, 'in one place we went to—I suppose it was Kenya, but
the names were so confusing, I left all that sort of thing to
Harry—we saw some native dancing. Real primitive it was,
with drums, the lot. And do you know what our guide said?'
She paused long enough for some dramatic effect, but not
so long as to give her companion a chance to speak. 'He
said this was some sort of spell, to cast out evil spirits. In
the 1980s, still believing that baloney—would you credit it?'
The two women shook with silent mirth, and James wondered
if he had the energy to move to another chair. The younger
one recovered first, and putting a bejewelled hand on her
companion's arm, she confided, 'Yeah, Africa sure is a funny
place. I guess I'll never really understand it.'

32

NEW YORK

November 6th

Air Force Two touched down shortly before eight a.m. in a
light flurry of rain. Once it had taxied to a halt in a distant
corner of the McGuire Air Force Base, the teleprinter on board
went silent. Simultaneously, another teleprinter started chattering in a large black Lincoln which was parked on the
tarmac. Cables were coming in from the State Department,
the Pentagon, the White House, and from American embassies around the world. The Secretary of State was being
kept in touch.

As he hurried down the aircraft steps and into the Lincoln,

John Curzon was sorry that security prevented photographers from recording his arrival. Still, they'd be there in force at the UN, no question of that. When the telephone by his bed had shrilled him awake six hours ago, Curzon had been, in his own words, 'poleaxed'. But within an hour, he was sitting in his office with the Defence Secretary and a dozen advisers reading the full text of the *Guardian* report. The American newspapers were changing their front pages, and the Press Office was being inundated with enquiries. He had telephoned the White House and spoken to the President for ten minutes. First they had agreed Curzon should go to New York to address an emergency meeting of the UN. Secondly, they had decided to stick to their original plans for the moment. These they would review every hour, and leave themselves time to change course if that proved sensible. Curzon reminded the President of the 1962 Cuban missile crisis: resolute action had called the Russians' bluff then, and it was still too early to judge who was bluffing this time.

The Secretary of State had talked to the President four times since then. As the cables piled up, so their confidence began to return. Who, the President had asked, was this guy le Roux anyway? They were assured by the Defence Secretary that the Russian and Cuban presence in Namibia hadn't been increased in the last forty-eight hours; the element of surprise had been lost, but then if the Russians were really thinking of intervening, they must have been counting on surprise as well. On the whole, they thought, the balance hadn't changed: the Russian bluff would still be called.

Helped by a motorcycle escort, the Lincoln was now picking its way through the Manhattan traffic. Inside, the Secretary of State was handed another cable. He read it hurriedly, and then turned to the man sitting next to him.

'Take a look at that, Richard. The Russians have denounced this fellow Sisekwe—say he doesn't represent revolutionary opinion amongst the blacks. Damn it, that's the most transparent hedge I've ever seen.'

Richard Rourke, the State Department's senior Africa

specialist, replied, 'Yes, it's possible they've been caught out. It's a trick they've tried before, to make out they have the support of the real leaders. They may be so shaken up by what Sisekwe has done that they're ready to pull back.' There was silence for a moment, then Rourke added, 'Of course, it works the other way round, too. They may figure we'll back down because we don't have the support of the whites . . . it's a classic problem in games theory.'

The Secretary of State nodded impatiently. Rourke could sometimes be a bore with his theorising—he was too much like all those earnest academics at the Curzon Center.

'Well, which is it? Is Sisekwe the real leader or an Uncle Tom? How much weight does le Roux carry with the white government?'

Rourke was about to answer the Secretary of State's questions with measured agnosticism, but the Lincoln was gliding to a halt in front of the United Nations Building. John Curzon was suddenly more concerned to smooth his hair and prepare for the photographers. Then, surrounded by bodyguards, the Secretary of State's party moved towards the hall of the General Assembly. An aide handed Curzon two cables. The first was from the State Department: Robert Sisekwe was on his way to New York, intending to address the General Assembly. The second was from the White House. It read: 'DEPLORE SOVIET AGGRESSION. EMPHASISE PEACEFUL INTENTIONS OF US. NAVAL ACTION WILL PROCEED AS PLANNED UNLESS YOU ADVISE DELAY BEFORE 09.30 EASTERN TIME.' John Curzon read this through twice, winked at Rourke, and walked determinedly into the hall.

Seasoned diplomats and UN observers are normally immune to the atmosphere in the General Assembly. But there are moments of high drama which even their blasé adrenalin finds irresistible. Today was one of them. Despite the unusually early hour, the chamber was packed as the Secretary of State took his seat amongst the American delegation. Shortly afterwards, Igor Tushin, the Soviet Ambassador to the UN, strode in—a stern-looking man with glasses and a heavy jowl. Several Soviet delegates hurried over, and he listened intently as they recounted their soundings among the Afro–Asian bloc.

If he was worried by what he heard, Tushin showed no signs of it. He had spent much of yesterday in the company of two senior officials from the Foreign Ministry, who had arrived unexpectedly from Moscow. From them he had learnt just how fully his country was committed to a successful South African intervention and why. His task was plain: to convince every country except the United States that Russia was, in the circumstances, incapable of aggression. Squaring such a circle was the supreme diplomatic challenge, and Tushin was a past master. Over the years he had also perfected the theatrical side of his job. Now, knowing how many eyes were watching him, his movements were slow and deliberate. He put on his headphones, fiddled with a switch on the desk in front of him, and a light glowed green. He was ready.

It was exactly nine o'clock, the time the session was scheduled to begin. With one conspicuous exception, every desk was crammed with expectant delegates: the South African representation was restricted to a single young man, who sat nervously fiddling with his headphones. The President of the General Assembly, a Bolivian who had only taken on the office the previous week, seemed uncertain what to do. He glanced several times at the clock, muttered to a UN official sitting next to him, and then announced the session was to begin. He stressed the extraordinary circumstances of the emergency session, and called for the Assembly 'to talk and act in the interests of world peace and justice'. He then invited the American and Russian representatives to address the Assembly, and sat down with evident relief.

John Curzon rose to speak at 9.06. He knew he had to be brief, as he must hear Tushin out before 9.30. The best thing he could do would be to lower the temperature. The more America showed itself disinterested and reasonable, the more bellicose would the Russians be made to appear. Aware that his words would be transmitted round the world and examined in minute detail, he read from a prepared text which Richard Rourke had handed to him. First he spoke firmly against apartheid: America would never defend a system 'fundamentally at odds with the great landmarks in our history—the Declaration of Independence, the Gettysburg Address, the Constitution itself'. On the other hand, John Curzon went on, there was nothing in these or in the UN Charter which sanctioned the kind of intervention now being threatened by Cuba and the Soviet Union in South Africa. John Curzon glanced at his watch. It was 9.11, and he had managed to sound unequivocal without revealing anything. As he sat down, no one in the General Assembly felt sure of what the Americans' real intentions were.

Not even Igor Tushin. When he rose to reply, his brain was working furiously. He decided to restrict himself to a simple persuasive point: Cuban troops had been in Africa for more than seven years without precipitating an emergency UN session, still less being considered a threat to world peace. The one new factor was the American presence in the area; that was responsible for the change. He would later propose a resolution condemning United States aggression and calling for the immediate withdrawal of the Fifth Fleet. They could hardly remain there, surely, in the face of world disapproval?

The clock on the wall showed 9.16, and at this point Tushin lost the Assembly's attention. The door to the chamber opened, and the South African Ambassador walked in to take his seat. He spoke briefly to the young man who had been listening to the debate, and then indicated to the President that he wished to intervene. Tushin decided it was sensible to stop. He replaced his headphones, the green light went on, and he waited attentively as the South African Ambassador got slowly to his feet. For Johannes Coetzee, this was a unique experience. In the six years he had held this post, he had grown used to speaking without being heard. But today no one was walking out. He shuffled some papers in front of him, and began.

'Mr President, I am addressing the General Assembly at

a crucial moment in my country's history. The Ambassador of the USSR and the American Secretary of State have already spoken. I understand both chose to ignore the report in today's edition of the *Guardian* newspaper which has prompted this meeting. Both apparently overlooked the joint statement, issued yesterday in Paris, from an influential Afrikaner and a leading African politician. Mr President,' Coetzee glanced towards the American and Russian delegations, 'many people will be surprised at this omission, and will wonder why the two great powers are apparently intent on intervening in a country whose people neither need nor want interference from outside. I think it may be necessary to underline this point. Accordingly, I have this morning spoken with my Government, and am authorised to do two things. First, to express agreement with the action and words of Dr Pieter le Roux, who, you will now know, is the Chairman of the Broederbond. Secondly, to invite Mr Robert Sisekwe of the African National Congress to address the Assembly as a member of the South African delegation.'

Coetzee raised his hand towards the door. After a slight pause, the tall, bearded figure of Sisekwe came into the hall. There was an excited buzz of conversation: very few of the delegates were expecting this. Then some started clapping, and by the time he reached his seat every delegate had joined in. But, Tushin and Curzon noted with approval, the welcome was muted and hesitant. For many years, official minds of all political persuasions had been accustomed to thinking of South Africa solely in terms of good guys and bad guys. Suddenly the familiar stereotypes had been whisked away, and no one was quite sure what to think. John Curzon looked at his watch: it was 9.27.

Sisekwe was on his feet now, and the massive hall was silent.

'Mr President, I am honoured to be here this morning to address the General Assembly. I am grateful for the invitation, and proud to take my place in the South African delegation. Yesterday, as you will know, I expressed my views in a somewhat unconventional way. Today, these same views can be heard where they belong—in the forum of the United Nations, where threats to world peace are always debated. Yesterday, the time was short. Today, it is shorter still, but even at this late hour, I hope the Soviet Union and the United States will turn back from intervening in my country. South Africa's message is a simple one . . .'

As Robert Sisekwe's voice rose and his hands clawed the air, two green lights in the chamber went off, rejecting his simple message. Tushin and Curzon turned and stared steadily at one another.

The clock on the wall told the delegates it was 9.30.